MW01701132

CROSSING THE TRACKS

As history unfolds from Greensboro to Selma to Memphis, one man takes his own stand for justice.

DREW HILL

CROSSING THE TRACKS

FIRST EDITION SOFTCOVER
ISBN-13: 979-8-89025-023-0

Editor: Lane Diamond
Cover Artist: Kabir Shah
Interior Designer: Lane Diamond

EVOLVED PUBLISHING™
www.EvolvedPub.com
Evolved Publishing LLC
Butler, Wisconsin, USA

Printed in Book Antiqua font.

BOOKS BY DREW HILL

Crossing the Tracks

It Came Even To Me

DEDICATION

For Grandpa,
Save me a spot near you on heaven's front porch.

FOREWORD

How do you write a novel about a real person in your own family, part biography and part history, pieced together, and all wrapped up in fiction? With due respect, the names of characters outside of the family have been fictionalized, but the family names are real. We are who we are. Historic places and events are accurate to the best of my research. In this case, fiction is a wonderful gift, granting me a chance to tell a true story that deserves to be told.

CROSSING
THE
TRACKS

INTRODUCTION

"The ultimate measure of a man is not where he stands in moments of comfort and convenience, but where he stands at times of challenge and controversy."
~ ***Martin Luther King, Jr.***

Prologue

The best stories are told, not written, better suited for the front porch than the library. Great stories are lived, not just imagined. They play out in real time, the drama of life. Such sagas are populated with living, breathing people, not with stuffed and stilted characters from an alternative world. These stories become family heirlooms, faithfully recited, priceless in the hearing.

So, it falls to me to tell Pap's story as only his eldest son can tell it. I may miss a detail or two, and when memory fails me, I'll fill in the gaps the best I can. Pap never told a story without dressing it up a bit, so I'm sure he wouldn't mind a little license on my part. A man's life takes shape on the canvas of a larger story, and my father painted his portrait against the dark hues of bigotry, depression, and war.

That such a man lived and died, you may at times have your doubts—hard and skeptical as our world has become—but the witnesses persist, though they be fewer with the passing of time. I am one. Let me testify, and then decide for yourself.

Chapter 1 – Genesis

"What we remember from childhood
we remember forever—permanent ghosts,
stamped, inked, imprinted, eternally seen."
~ *Cynthia Ozick*

Keep in mind from the start, my pap was a white man. An odd reminder, I know, but it would be easy to lose track. Things were plain enough in the beginning, when three generations of Hills pulled up stakes in St. Clair County, Illinois, crossed the Mississippi at St. Louis, and trekked southwest across Missouri to settle in Springfield, the seat of Greene County. Oscar, my pap, was just a boy then, stuck between his brother, Arthur, and his kid sister, Ellen, born into a railroad family in the summer of 1908, his family tree ripe with coachmen and brakemen, conductors and engineers.

Nothing saturated a bloodline quite like the railroad. Steam-driven power churning those massive wheels, unending rails merging at the horizon, the hopeful howl of a whistle in the distance—life on the railroad created its own lore and legend. Melvin Hill, Pap's father and my namesake, worked his way up to brakeman on the Missouri Pacific. He made a good living, better than most working men in those days. With his promotion, the family moved north and west to Nevada, Missouri, and rented a more spacious house as they welcomed their fourth child, little Margaret.

And then he was gone. The year was 1919.

When the railroad superintendent and the pastor walked up toward her door, Oscar's mother, Mae, reached for her sweater and pocketbook. Twice before, when employees had been killed in railroad accidents, she had been asked to accompany these men to help break the news and provide support to grieving women suddenly widowed. She pushed open the screen door to join them, but Rev. Harms caught the door in his hand and slowly shook his head.

She knew in that moment, even as her face flushed, and the pastor caught her as she collapsed in tears. Melvin, her husband, her everything, was gone, dead at forty-four.

The gruesome details of his death made her loss more agonizing. Her husband had been working on the coupling of a freight car, the huge metal clasp that held the cars together. The disconnected cars began to silently creep along the track, moving up behind the men as they worked. Someone had neglected to set the brake. Melvin had been caught between the couplings, cut in half at the waist, his pocket watch crushed, frozen in time. They'd laid his body in pieces beside the tracks, covered with a bloody blanket until the coroner arrived. No need to bother with an ambulance. The newspaper carried the story in grisly detail.

Oscar, just eleven years old, took the news in stunned disbelief. All that was strong and secure in his world was shaken, suddenly at risk. As he stood bravely beside his mother in a rainy, windy cemetery, he shed no tears for his father, bracing himself for an uncertain future.

Whatever remained of his childhood vanished on that bloody day at the railyard.

***

Mae Hill received a settlement from the Missouri Pacific Railroad—five hundred dollars for the life of her husband, not a lot of money even in 1919.

The baby turned one on the day of her father's funeral. Little Margaret had suffered a severe case of meningitis as an infant, leaving her with epilepsy and a permanent mental disability, requiring medications and treatment.

In fairness to the railroad, had they known the full extent of the baby's needs, they might have been more generous, but they didn't, so they weren't. In those days before Social Security or any kind of public assistance, a thirty-four-year-old widow now stood alone, determined to find a way to survive, to feed and clothe her four children.

Using her meager settlement, Mae moved the family back to Springfield and opened a restaurant in a vacant storefront. Oscar fried burgers, washed dishes, and whatever else needed doing—his mother's only help. School began in the fall without him, as he dropped out after the seventh grade, while his brother Arthur stayed in class. Mae planned for Oscar to work only until his brother graduated. Then, Art would work while his little brother went back to school.

That never happened—Oscar being too far behind and too far down the road. Life would have its own lessons to teach, and Oscar learned most of them the hard way.

After a year of struggle and loss, Mae closed the restaurant and started taking in boarders and doing laundry and ironing at her home on north Pacific. She doubled-up the boys, and brought Ellen in with her and the baby, leaving two rooms she could let out. The endless cooking and cleaning wore her down and drove her to exhaustion. Her hands grew chapped and pink from scrubbing sheets in hot, soapy water, and lugging laundry bundles on her tiny frame, not quite five feet tall, pushed her physical limits, but she never wavered or complained.

"Oscar," she said. "Where have you been? I need you to sweep off the porch and fix that dining room chair that keeps coming apart."

Her son shook his head and shrugged. "Mom, that chair is just kindling. There's no way to tack it or nail it again, and the glue won't hold. It's shot." He must have caught the glint in her eye, and certainly knew better than to press the argument. "I'll try, but don't let that salesman from Fort Smith sit on it. It'll never hold up his big backside. Come to think of it, just don't rent to anyone over a hundred pounds and we'll be fine."

Mae turned with a smile. "Just fix the chair, son. Do the best you can." His wry wit kept her going many weary mornings.

***

In the dog days of summer, the little Baptist church on Pacific hosted an annual revival meeting—two weeks of evangelistic services, bringing in a hot-blooded preacher to denounce all worldliness, rouse the faithful, and call sinners to salvation. Oscar's mother determined to be there, with her children in tow, each evening, but after three nights, a rebellion broke out.

Not again. It's the same show every night." Art spoke for the three of them. "Give us a break. Let us stay home tonight. Enough's enough."

They could read the disappointment on their mother's face. Since her husband's sudden passing, Mae had grown fearful, troubled by the fragility of life, and worried about the souls of her children, especially her fatherless sons.

"You boys wash up," she said, "and put on a clean shirt. Ellen, help me with your baby sister. Let's get a move on. The service begins at seven."

Some much for the uprising. No discussion or debate, just get moving.

Two nights later, on Friday night, it happened. Art and Oscar never saw it coming—the answer to their mother's prayers. As they sat restlessly in the hard, straight-backed oak pews, anxious for the sermon to end, the boys finally fell under the preacher's spell.

The evangelist, Brother Asa Singleton, a broad, balding man with a friendly round face, focused his message that night on these words from Psalm 68: "A father to the fatherless, and a judge of the widows, is God in his holy habitation."

Oscar wondered: *How does he know? Did someone tell him about us?*

On and on the preacher spoke, painting a picture with his words, drawing in two boys—vulnerable, defenseless.

"Like as a father pitieth his children, so the Lord pitieth them that fear him," he said. "If ye then, being evil know how to give good gifts unto your children, how much more shall your Father which is in heaven give good things to them that ask him."

Somehow his words gripped their imaginations, stirring up grief and desires never expressed.

Just before the altar call, Brother Singleton told the story of two brothers, one that ran off and made a mess of his life before finally heading back home to beg for forgiveness. The boys had heard the story a hundred times, but this time was different. The words struck deep, describing the kind of father they had lost, the kind of father they longed to find. And when the preacher read those words, "But when he was still a great way off, his father saw him and had compassion, and ran to him, and fell on his neck, and kissed him," Oscar felt the embrace of a heavenly Father, the warmth of God's love swirling around him.

Before the first chorus of "Just As I Am," Oscar found himself on his knees at the altar, the pastor's big arm around his shoulder. He lifted his head to look for Art and found him kneeling close by—two young brothers, reluctant converts, captured by Gospel love.

Sunday afternoon, Mae Hill stood on the banks of Wilson's Creek, just south of Springfield, gathered with a throng of the faithful and the newly converted to witness her boys' baptisms. The August heat beat down and boiled up at the same time, and Sunday hats and bonnets provided little defense against the glaring sun. People dipped handkerchiefs in the cool water to mop their brows.

But one mother seemed immune to the heat or any discomfort that day. With little Margaret in her arms and Ellen by her side, Mae watched as Oscar took his turn.

He waded out into the waist-deep water, and stood still as the pastor raised his hand to God and said in a loud voice, "In obedience to our Lord and Savior Jesus Christ, and upon your profession of faith in Him, I baptize you, Oscar Hill, in the name of the Father, the

Son, and the Holy Ghost. Amen." Oscar came up with a wet smile, waved to his mother, and turned to watch Art take his turn.

Then, together, arm in arm, two brothers climbed the creek bank and toweled off as their mother blessed God for this answer to her most fervent prayer.

***

"Boy, you ever seen the like of this?" The stocky man from Neosho held up a small chain with a piece of bone, maybe an inch long, attached.

Oscar finished clearing the breakfast dishes from the dining room table, took the chain in his hand, and rubbed the smooth, white surface of the bone. "What's it from? A squirrel? A dog?"

"Hell, no," the man responded, snatching the chain from Oscar's hand. "You ever hear tell of that hanging back in '06?"

"No, sir, we're not from around here, at least not back then."

The man smiled, amused, anxious to tell his story. "Well, I was there when them three niggers were hung and burned right there on the courthouse yard." He dangled the piece of bone for the rest of the guests at the table to see. "Not sure which nigger it's from, of course. They was selling off the fingers and toes, a nice little souvenir. A finger bone, I reckon. I drilled that little hole for the chain. You ever see anything like that?"

"No, I never," Oscar replied. "What did they do?"

The man shook his head as he tucked his chain away in his vest pocket. "Don't recall, really. Rape maybe, I think it was. Some white man, the boss of them niggers, said they was at work when the lady said she was attacked, but it don't matter. It was a good lesson for all them niggers. Steer clear and stay in your place. In fact, a whole slew of 'em moved out of Greene County that very same summer, so it got the point across." He leaned back in his chair and lit a cigarette. "Surprised you never heard about it, son. Where are you folks from anyway?"

Oscar explained, "We come from Illinois, just across the river, St. Clair County."

The man smiled in surprise and shook his head. "St. Clair County, that's East Saint Louis. Hell, boy, your people know how to deal with niggers. Just a while back, in '17, I think it was, why they plum went to war, burned down that whole side of town, killed a couple hundred of 'em. Dug a big whole in the ground for the whole mess. No more nigger problem, I'm telling you. And that's where you come from?"

"We don't have any family back there now, just some of our kin buried there. I guess we were long gone before that happened."

The man nodded as he flicked his ashes in his empty coffee cup. "Better know your roots, boy. That's how you learn what's what in this world."

Later that evening, after chores, Oscar and Art sat on the back steps talking about the man's story. Oscar summed up his thoughts. "Hanging them guys just to keep niggers in their place? That's not right. Nobody deserves that. If they did wrong, they should have a trial like anybody else. Sounds like they might not have done it."

Arthur shrugged it off. "You think a trial would've made any difference? They still would've hung 'em. You know the way things go around here, Oscar. Heck, if Mom ever rented a room to a black man, it'd be our house burning down. Niggers at the back door, that's the law around here."

"That may be the law," Oscar said, "but that bone made my skin crawl. Some souvenir."

Art nodded. "Yeah, no cause for that."

***

Back and forth it went. When they rented the rooms and caught up on the washing and ironing, Mae could make a go of it. But the calendar never quite filled up, and money was short.

Oscar decided over his mother's protest to go to work, though he was barely fourteen years old. Whatever he could find—cleaning up construction sites, sweeping out stores, unloading trucks—Oscar roamed the streets of Springfield doing whatever might earn himself a dime or a dollar. Nothing permanent for a boy his age, but rarely did he come home without a few coins to put in his mother's tired hands.

Oscar learned quickly to exaggerate his age when asking for work. Sometimes he would swear, "I'm Art Hill and I'm seventeen," but even mimicking his big brother didn't help much. Of course, if they didn't ask, he didn't tell.

Then the word spread that they were going to build a new highway across Missouri from St. Louis to Joplin, what would become Route 66. Oscar showed up to go to work, standing in line with dozens of men, many old enough to be his father. The highway department didn't seem too worried about age with so many jobs to fill.

"I need some drovers who can handle a team of mules," the foreman said, looking up from his clipboard.

Oscar didn't hesitate. "I can handle a team," he said, raising his hand as he stepped forward.

"What's your name, son? You sure about that?"

"Oscar Hill. I learned to work a team on my grandpa's farm. I can do it."

Three days later, Oscar went to work driving a team of mules pulling an earthmover along the new roadbed. He was fifteen years old.

The job lasted seven months, and Oscar walked away callused and confident, less a boy and more a man.

At sixteen, he managed to get a job on the Frisco railroad, fetching tools, pushing a broom, and cleaning up after the workmen, until one day his mother brought his lunch pail, which he had forgotten. The foreman quizzed Mae about Oscar's age. Unable to lie even on her son's behalf, she answered truthfully. Oscar's boss sent him home with his mother, but only after a stern lecture about all the trouble he would have caused if he had been injured on the job.

Those few weeks on the Frisco convinced Oscar of an obvious truth. The railroad looked like a good job to have in hard times when jobs were scarce. No luck this time, but he would try again.

***

After a day's work, Oscar never missed a party at a friend's house or a dance at the YMCA downtown. He ran with a girl named Lucille in those days, though he danced with whoever was handy. One week, Lucille said she would have to meet him at the Y since she had to bring her cousin with her. Oscar imagined a little boy or girl tagging along, but his heart skipped a beat as Lucille came through the door with a smiling girl of sixteen. That image immediately etched itself forever into his memory: her brown curls ringing her round face, her green eyes that matched her sweater, her kind smile.

He didn't wait for an introduction, just stepped forward and extended his hand. "I'm Oscar. You must be the cousin."

Lucille, annoyed to be so obviously ignored, did the honors. "This is Verna Campbell. Verna, this chump is Oscar Hill."

Verna shook his hand and nodded with a smile. "Nice to meet you, Oscar."

Maybe it was chemistry or fate or some kind of romantic hunch, but something moved in that moment, capturing a young man's heart. He summoned whatever charm he possessed, and they danced the night away, much to Lucille's consternation. They danced the Shimmy and the Foxtrot to popular tunes like "Everywhere You Go" and "Kiss Your Baby Tonight." As they slow-danced to "Looking at the World Through Rose-Colored Glasses," Oscar noticed how perfectly they fit together while gently rocking her in his arms.

Verna apologized for her clumsy dance steps. "I'm sorry I'm not a good dancer. I haven't had a lot of practice."

Oscar reassured her. "You do just fine. I never had a better partner, but if you want to practice, I'll dance with you anytime. How about next Saturday?" He smiled.

Verna blushed and said, "That would be fine with me, but I'll have to ask my parents."

"Well, ask real nice," Oscar replied, "cause I hope they say yes."

After the dance, Oscar rode the streetcar with Lucille and Verna back to Lucille's house. Walking two girls to the door was a new experience for him, and more than a little awkward. He knew what he wanted to do, but he didn't want to hurt anyone's feelings.

Lucille took matters into her own hands, grabbing Oscar by the shoulders and kissing him squarely on the lips. "Goodnight, Oscar. Next time, dance with me a time or two." She turned to open the door.

Oscar saw his chance, and leaned forward to kiss Verna on her cheek. "Goodnight, Verna. I hope you had fun tonight. I sure did."

Verna blushed and smiled back as she stepped through the doorway. "I had a wonderful time, Oscar. Thank you."

And so it began.

Unfortunately, Verna's parents were not so impressed with her new boyfriend. A year older than Verna, without prospects, Oscar had more freedom than they were willing to allow their daughter. Earnest Campbell worked as a streetcar motorman in Springfield. Crisscrossing the city each day gave him a window into the ways of aimless young men carousing about town, and without cause, he put Oscar in that same category. Verna was forbidden to see him, in hopes that he would move along and forget about her.

The first time Oscar showed up at the Campbell house, May Campbell, Verna's mother, met him at the front door. She was a small woman, straight and stern. Oscar held his cap in his hands and gave her a friendly smile, but her expression didn't change.

"Hello, Mrs. Campbell. I'm Oscar Hill, a friend of Verna's, and I wonder if I could see her and talk for a little while, or go for a walk? I won't stay long."

She began shaking her head even before he could finish his request, and her grip on the screen door handle tightened as she replied. "No, Verna is busy, and besides, she doesn't want to talk to you. You may as well go on about your business. No need for you to be coming around here."

Oscar knew better than to believe her. "Please, I won't make any trouble. I just want to talk to Verna for a few minutes, that's all. Please, Mrs. Campbell."

"I know who you are and what you want, but the answer is no and that's final. You'd best be on your way, and don't be coming around here anymore, you hear me?" She stepped back and closed the front door, leaving Oscar to stare at the carved wooden plaque hanging from a nail: *Welcome*.

If May Campbell thought that was the end of it, she soon learned better. Oscar still believed that if he could speak to Verna's father man to man, he could make his case and come to an agreement, so he kept coming by the house.

When he finally did catch Mr. Campbell at home, Verna's father was angry that Oscar had ignored his wife's words and come back yet again. "Look here, you've been told time and again: you are not to come here. You are not welcome here. Now get off my property."

Oscar stepped off the porch and then turned back. "Mr. Campbell, I'm not here to see Verna. I came back to talk to you. Can I just explain?"

Too late for reason or conversation, Verna's dad picked up a brick from the base of the porch steps. "I've got nothing to say to you except get on your way. Go on. Get off my property."

Risking one more plea, Oscar stopped at the street and faced Mr. Campbell across the yard. "Please, Mr. Campbell, I don't mean any disrespect. I just--"

A brick came hurling toward him. Oscar jumped aside and the brick fell in the street. No sense sticking around while the man found another brick, so Oscar hurried down the street, disappointed but still determined.

Verna worked part-time at F. W. Woolworth's on the square. It was on her father's streetcar route, so he could keep an eye on her and take her back and forth to her job, but Oscar had ample opportunity to slip in and out of the store to see Verna, who usually worked at the lunch counter. He would come in for a grilled cheese and tomato soup, or maybe a BLT, and Verna would bring him his lunch. Not much chance to talk, with other customers around and Verna's manager keeping her busy, but they could see each other and exchange notes.

Oscar soon learned Mr. Campbell's work schedule, and Verna mentioned that her father's early hours meant they went to bed at 8:30 most evenings.

Oscar would steal over to the Campbell house late in the evening, and treat Verna to ice cream sodas hoisted to her upstairs window on a rope of belts and stockings. She sat in her windowsill, enjoyed her ice cream, and talked quietly with Oscar, careful not to wake her folks.

"Oscar," Verna asked one evening from her window ledge. "What was it like growing up without your daddy? That must've been hard."

Oscar leaned back under the stars, sitting in Mr. Campbell's wheelbarrow. "My pap was a good man, good to us kids. He taught me how to garden, how to grow things. He used to take me and Art on the train when he had to make short runs. My pap was a big man, a head taller than me, and people respected him. I never recall anyone giving him trouble. And then one day, he didn't come home."

Verna let those words linger a moment. "I'm sorry, Oscar. You were just a little boy."

"Yeah, it was a sad time. Mom managed the best she could, and I tried to help. We got by, we made it, though I'm not sure how. I thought about it a lot. My pap never got to raise his family, to finish the job, to see it through, and I don't want that to happen to me. I think that would be the greatest thing, to raise a family, kids and grandkids, to give them my best and make a way for them. I'd work mighty hard for that, whatever it took—finish what my pap started."

"That's beautiful, Oscar. Family is the sweetest thing."

Oscar shook his head and laughed. "Well, it'd be fine with me if your sweet family would quit throwing bricks at me."

***

Before spring turned to summer, the subject came up again. Oscar skipped out of Sunday evening youth meeting at church, and he and Verna met at Washington Park, a rare opportunity to take a stroll together. As the sun sank behind the old maples, they sat down for a while in the garden gazebo.

Oscar's frustration and impatience had reached a breaking point. "I've about had it with all this sneaking around, Verna. I haven't seen you in almost a month. Enough of this. Let's get married. Let's just do it."

Verna provided the pragmatism to balance the romance. "Momma and Daddy aren't going to let me marry you, at least not now. I'll be eighteen next month, but they have to sign for me until I'm twenty-one. Daddy won't do it."

"Well, I'm not waiting on them. Do you want to get married or not?"

Verna leaned closer and kissed him on the cheek. "Of course, I'll marry you, Oscar, but where would we live? How will we make it? Maybe we should wait until we can make a go of it."

He pulled her close and tried to reassure her. "We'll make it just fine. I'm back on the Frisco. I've been just bucking the board, taking whatever temporary jobs come up, but I'm done with that. I made apprentice, just this week, and you know what that means? Four years of steady work. We won't get rich, but we can make it. That will satisfy your father, won't it?"

"That's wonderful, Oscar. I'm so proud of you. But I don't know if anything will change Daddy's mind. He won't listen to me."

This conversation echoed back and forth, week after week, until one day, the day after Verna turned eighteen, Oscar hatched a plot. At his request, a friend telephoned Verna's house and pretended to call her in to work at Woolworth's. Mrs. Campbell took the call, since Verna was helping with Vacation Bible School at the church. Then she called the church, and Verna started walking towards the square to go to work, but she never arrived.

On her way, Oscar pulled up to the curb in a borrowed Model A coupe and opened the door.

Verna got in, and soon realized they were not headed to the store. "I'm supposed to be at work."

Oscar shook his head without taking his eyes from the road ahead. "No, that was Norma that called your mother. You don't work today."

"Then where are we going?" she said, more curious than concerned.

This time he looked her in the eye. "We're going to Arkansas to get married."

She absorbed his words without shock or surprise as they headed south to the state line.

Oscar had learned that the legal age for marriage in Arkansas was eighteen. Two hours later, they arrived in Berryville, Arkansas, and stopped at the courthouse for a marriage license. They walked from there just down the street to the Baptist church, and found the pastor at the parsonage next door. There, in the pastor's living room, with his wife and the church caretaker as witnesses, Oscar and Verna became husband and wife. It was done and legally attested.

Then, with nowhere to go and no money to go there, the newlyweds drove back to Springfield in a driving rain, a baptism of blessing on their marriage.

Their first little tiff began just as they crossed the city limits. "Where are we going?" Verna asked.

Oscar had not planned much beyond the ceremony. "We'll go to Mom's house."

"Does she know about us? Did you tell her?"

"It'll be fine, Verna. She'll be fine with it."

Verna's anxiety rose as she considered the possibilities. "You didn't tell her, did you? We're just going to show up and surprise her? What were you thinking? And what about my folks? They must be worried sick when I didn't come home."

Oscar pondered her questions as the rain pounded the roof of the car. "Mom will be fine, happy to see you. You can call your folks from Mom's. It'll be all right." He was not nearly as confident as he sounded.

The downpour persisted as they pulled up to the little white frame house on Pacific Street. With no raincoats or umbrellas, they made a run for it across the yard, and jumped up on the front porch soaked to the skin.

Oscar's mother hurried out with a blanket, and wrapped her new daughter in a warm embrace. "Come in, Verna. Let's get you dried off and a cup of hot tea for you."

Oscar followed behind, still sopping wet, but happy to see his mother's friendly welcome. Somehow, she seemed to know before they told her about their marriage. Through the eight years since her husband's tragic death, Mae Hill had leaned so heavily on her second son that she trusted his judgment as well as her own. If it was time for him and Verna to marry, then it was time.

A pot of vegetable soup with roast beef was simmering on the stove, and Oscar's mom ladled steaming bowls for everyone.

Before she came to the table, Verna made a private telephone call to her parents. She returned wiping her eyes as she sat down. "It's fine, really. They're just upset, but it will be all right."

Oscar put his handkerchief in her hand.

After dinner, the newlyweds retired to Oscar's room upstairs for their wedding night. Verna borrowed a flannel gown from his mom, having brought nothing from home. When she left home for Vacation Bible School that morning, June 20, 1927, she never dreamed it would be her wedding day.

The next day, after dinner, Verna's parents came by the house. Mr. Campbell met his new son-in-law in the yard and stuck out his hand. "We had a rough start, you and me, but that's behind us now as far as I'm concerned. What's done is done. You're family now."

Oscar shook his hand and nodded. "Yes, sir, I appreciate that, and I will take good care of Verna. I'll be good to her."

Mr. Campbell put his hand on his shoulder and smiled with moist eyes. "I know you will. Verna told us about your apprenticeship on the railroad. That's good news. I may have misjudged you, Oscar, and I certainly underestimated you. I apologize for that."

Oscar nodded. "Like you said, let's just forget about all of that and start over. That's fine with me."

As they turned toward the house, Mr. Campbell spoke softly. "Don't mind Verna's mother. It may take her a little longer to warm up to you, but she'll come along."

Together they stepped to the porch and inside the house.

***

I was born in the front bedroom of Grandma Mae's house in Springfield, the firstborn child of Oscar and Verna. As Grandma remembered it, my birth was more traumatic for my dad than my mother, who endured her labor and delivery with a colored midwife at her side. Oscar was beside himself with fear, not so much for Verna as for the prospect of being a father. Having lost his dad when he was just a boy, he had no idea how to be a father to a child. When Grandma brought me out on the porch and put me in my father's arms, he was overwhelmed with joy and anxiety.

"Hello, little fella. I'm your Pappy," he said, tears tracking his cheeks. "I'm your Pappy, and I don't know a thing about it." Shaking his head as he rocked me in his arms, he said, "I'm no Pappy, but I'm your Pappy. I'm all you've got, little fella."

My name was a forgone conclusion: Melvin Marion, after my grandfather and my great, great grandfather.

My first year, we lived with Grandma Mae until Pap could build a two-room, white frame house on the west edge of town. Working on the house after his long shifts on the railroad wore him thin, and the weekends brought more of the same. The bitter winds of that first winter couldn't keep him from picking up his toolbox and hiking the fourteen blocks to frame up the little cottage, night after night, week after week, determined to provide a home for his little family. Money was tight as Pap tried to pay upfront for materials, sometimes salvaging secondhand lumber and fixtures from a local contractor. When the Frisco updated the Springfield depot, Pap bid for an old woodstove that was being replaced. It needed some repair, so he got it cheap and fixed it himself.

Easter weekend was moving day, though there was hardly anything to move. Grandma loaned them a few sticks of furniture, and Pap found a table and chairs at a used furniture store. The porch still needed to be painted and the gutters put on, but it was home—our home.

As they sat in church on that Easter morning, Mom beside him and holding me in her arms, Pap's heart swelled with pride and gratitude in equal measure. He might just make a real pappy after all.

Chapter 2 – Dues to Pay

"We are not rich by what we possess,
but by what we can do without."
~ *Immanuel Kant*

When the stock market crashed in October 1929, our family fared better than most, at least for a while. Pap's apprenticeship on the Frisco kept him steadily employed as he mastered the skills of a sheet metal worker and pipefitter. He had no debts to speak of, having built their modest home without taking out a mortgage. Pap's only regret about the house was wishing he had added a third room or maybe an upstairs. By the spring of 1930, Mom was pregnant with their second child, my little sister, Joyce. Money was tight and the two-room house was full, but we managed. Whatever cash might be left at the end of the month went to Grandma Mae to help with Margaret's needs.

As the Depression deepened, even the railroad began to shrink its workforce—no new hires or apprentices, and they didn't replace those who retired or quit. By then, Pap had entered his fourth and final year of his apprenticeship, and hoped to move to full status as a sheet metal worker and pipefitter, but the job was not available, not even for a well-trained apprentice. The prospect of being laid off after four years as an apprentice unnerved him, and he decided to make an offer. He would be willing to work one more year as an apprentice for the Frisco, drawing the wages of an apprentice. The railroad would have the benefit of a skilled mechanic without having to pay higher wages. This was just the kind of bargain that management liked, all to their advantage, but Pap didn't mind. He needed work and knew he and Mom could make it on an apprentice's wages. Hopefully, when his extra year ended, a regular job would be waiting for him.

By the summer of 1932, with the economy in freefall, nearly a fourth of all workmen were unemployed. Pap's fifth year as an apprentice ended with a layoff—no jobs available. His foreman had nothing but praise for his work and promised to let him know when a job came open. Still, the bottom line was no job, no income, and hardly any savings.

Unable to find any work in his trade or experience, Pap tried his hand at a new venture—selling W. T. Rawleigh products door to door. The company sold medicinal and household products directly to customers. Best known for their antiseptic salve, medicated ointment, and arnica balm, they provided each salesman with a canary yellow suitcase of various products. They sold every item with a satisfaction guaranteed, "time and trial" system. Customers could take the product, try it out, and only pay later if and when they were happy with the product. People liked the Rawleigh products, even swore by their healing properties, but the problem was obvious: nobody had any money. As Pap walked house to house across Springfield, most folks politely declined to purchase anything. A few would buy his wares on the "time and trial" agreement, and when Pap returned to collect, they had no money to pay him, so they claimed to be dissatisfied with the product. The pitifully small number of paying customers didn't provide enough to keep a family fed and clothed.

Citizens who voted in the election of 1932 did so in deadly earnest. Desperation sent droves of people to the polls, grasping for hope wherever it could be found. In this case, hope came in the person of Franklin Delano Roosevelt. Pap cast his ballot for change, for jobs, for the working man.

Every Tuesday and Friday, Pap dropped by the Frisco yard to check the job board. Disappointment dogged his steps as he trudged home, bringing only bad news. In the fall, he spent two months on a road crew, clearing brush and re-digging ditches for twenty-five cents an hour. Then, as winter set in, his road crew began taking out an old roadbed, breaking up concrete with sledgehammers, back-breaking work for that same twenty-five cents an hour. Swinging a sledge for ten hours in the bitter cold pushed Pap and his two-dozen fellow crewman to the edge of collapse. When he felt like he couldn't lift his hammer for another blow, he glanced up on the bluff at the long line of equally desperate men waiting for a man to quit so that they could take his place and his job. Some men did give up and walk away, unable to stand such grueling work. Exhaustion made even walking home after work a test of endurance.

Mom always had something hot on the stove when he got home, so that Pap could eat before he fell into bed.

Pap kept going, day after day, whatever the weather, for seven weeks, until the job was finished and he was laid off once more. He always remembered those weeks on the road crew as the hardest work he ever did, the coldest he ever was, and the most tired, but he always told the story with the satisfaction of a man who provided when providing was hard, a man who stood firm when others faltered.

***

In the early spring of 1933, a sheet metal/pipefitting job opened up on the Frisco line in Monett, Missouri, about an hour south and west of Springfield. Pap bid the job and got it, and moved his family into a rented farmhouse with a small acreage. After work on the Frisco, Pap planted a few acres with peanuts and corn and added a mule, a milk cow, and a brood of chickens to the family. Mom made the house a home, planted a vegetable garden, and welcomed a new baby, my brother, LaClede, who Pap immediately nicknamed Buster. I started to school, first grade, in September.

Our little farm felt like paradise to me and Joyce—room to run, so many places to hide, animals to pet and chase, and my favorite place of all, the loft of Pap's little barn. When I perched at the door of the loft swinging my feet above the ground below, I could see the green Ozark hills in the distance, which slowly brightened to golden yellows and deep reds as the breezes turned cool and autumn came on. Joyce, barely three years old, was determined to climb the steep ladder to my hideaway, but again and again, I shewed her away.

"You can't come up here," I scolded. "You're too little. You'll break your neck and I'll be in trouble."

Nothing I said could dissuade her, though.

Late one afternoon, while watching from my perch as Pap worked in the peanut field below, Joyce cried out—more of a scream, really. I hurried to the top of the ladder and looked down into her desperate eyes. She had managed to pull herself up to the third wrung, but didn't know how to go up or down from there. Caught between her curiosity and her fear, she just hung there, stuck and terrified, but not for long.

Pap had heard her scream and came running. He swept her off the ladder and into his arms, and Joyce's expression changed instantly, smiling at her rescuer with tears still on her cheeks.

Then, to my dismay, Pap carried Joyce up the ladder to the loft... *my* loft.

"But she's too little to be up here," I argued. "What if she falls?"

He waved aside my protest, and he and I sat in my favorite place dangling our feet, Joyce safe on Pap's lap, and together we watched the sun go down over the hills, the clouds catching the last gleams of orange and purple. Even little Joyce sat mesmerized. Only Mom's call to wash up for supper could break the mood.

Those days in Monett, our family enjoyed our first taste of prosperity, or so it felt after such lean times. Still, good times never lasted for long during the Depression. Just seven months into Pap's new job, he got bumped by a cutter/fitter with more seniority. Just like that, Pap again had to buck the board, looking for whatever temporary work might be available until a permanent job opened up.

***

Earl Simpson, foreman at the west Frisco yard in Springfield, called on an autumn Saturday. "Oscar, I got a call yesterday from the yard super at the Great

Western in St Joe, said they're real shorthanded, need a couple of sheet metal men for maybe three or four weeks. They have three engines down, two J-class and a big six. If you're interested, they need you Monday. What do you say?"

Pap glanced at the unpaid bills on the table and replied with not a second's hesitation, "Sure, I'll go. Thanks. I'll catch the train Sunday afternoon."

"Just get yourself back down here when you're done. Don't go moving to St. Joe. One of these days we're gonna find you a spot on the Frisco."

The soft maple, ash, and oak were in full color as Pap rode the northbound train three hours north to St. Joseph, a bustling, rowdy town settled by fur traders and wagoneers headed west. The town sat at the eastern end of the Pony Express, and still had a free range, frontier spirit.

Each day, Pap walked from his boarding house downtown to the Chicago Great Western yard on the north end of town. One Tuesday evening in late November, he noticed more people than usual on the streets. The closer he came to the center of town, the greater the swell of people, hundreds moving towards the Buchanan County courthouse.

He noticed a lanky man in work clothes like himself just coming from his job, so he inquired. "Excuse me, I'm not from around here. Can you tell me where everybody is going on a Tuesday evening?"

The man stopped and stuck out his hand. "Delbert Chaney's my name."

"Good to meet you, Delbert. I'm Oscar Hill." Pap shook his hand, and they continued walking at a brisk pace.

Delbert began to explain. "It's that boy, that nigger in the jail. Warner's his name. They say he attacked a white woman last night. She's still in the hospital. I heard the sheriff got a confession out of him late last night, but now he says he didn't do it, lyin' to save his hide, but it ain't gonna work. Somebody's got to pay."

Pap couldn't quite grasp what was happening. "So what's going on? Is there a hearing or something?"

Delbert shook his head in surprise. "Hell no! We don't need no damn hearing. Around here, we just take care of it ourselves. The sheriff's been holding out, trying to send people home, but nobody's goin'. I heard the deputies even used tear gas on the crowd this afternoon, but they done run out of it. No stopping us now."

As they came down Fifth Street, Pap gazed at what looked like thousands of people—men and women, young and old, boys and girls—an all-white ocean of people. Most of the folks seemed calm and content, as if going to a picture show or a picnic. Only those closest to the courthouse seemed agitated, venting their wrath, bent on violence.

Pap and Delbert kept moving forward through the crowd, until standing perhaps fifty feet from the entrance of the Buchanan County Jail. An ugly confrontation raged between the angry vigilantes and the determined deputies, and the crowd continued to push forward, closer and closer to the door.

About 5:30, as the late November sky faded to black, the sheriff came out of the jail and spoke to the crowd. "Well, boys, it took 20,000 to lick a Dutchman. You can have him."

As quick as the words left his mouth, a dozen men pushed past the sheriff, and within a few minutes emerged with the prisoner, nineteen-year-old Lloyd Warner. They practically ran, dragging him to a large ash tree on the opposite corner of Fifth and Jules. Without hesitation, they prepared a rope and placed the noose around the boy's neck, but whoever tied the knot bungled the job. When they yanked the boy into the air, his neck didn't break, and he struggled to breathe and get his hands free.

Pap watched in horror as some of the men brought cans of gasoline or kerosene and doused the boy's pants and socks and shoes. While the boy still desperately tried to free his hands, one of the men held a match to his feet and the flames engulfed his body. The cheers of the crowd almost drowned out his screams. Almost. Pap was close enough to hear and near enough to catch the stench of burning flesh. When the fire went out the first time, someone applied another dousing of gasoline to finish the job. Soon the rope burned, and Warner's charred body fell to the ground still smoldering. This time, they piled wood over and around the body, and the burning resumed.

The crowd slowly dispersed, but hundreds filed by to see the burning body up close. Dozens posed for pictures.

Delbert didn't seem at all troubled by the lynching, or even surprised. "Nice to meet you, Oscar. How long are you in town? We'd be happy to offer you a homecooked meal. My Dottie is a fine cook."

Pap kept looking over his shoulder at the ghastly scene behind them. "I appreciate the offer. Does this kind of thing happen around here a lot?"

"Not too often, but from time to time. You see, this kind of thing helps keep the peace. All the niggers know better than to get into any mischief, if they know what's good for them."

Pap walked to his boarding house that evening in a fog of disbelief. He'd heard about lynching since his boyhood, but never witnessed such a scene for himself. Try as he did to clear his mind, those dreadful images seared into his memory forever—the shouts, the screams, the smell of that evening in St. Joseph.

Days later, Pap noticed the local papers reported that the young woman, the alleged victim of the attack, expressed her concern they may have killed the wrong man.

***

The Frisco called early that next spring with a job in Oklahoma City, and Pap jumped at the chance, desperate for work. But, with the garden planted, me in school, and Mom pregnant with their fourth child, moving didn't make much sense, especially when the job came with no guarantee that Pap wouldn't be bumped again. So, Pap ventured to Oklahoma City alone, and came home on the train when he had time off, while Mom managed things in Monett.

Pap's brief visits were hardly restful, with crops to tend and his little farm to manage. I was only six, barely old enough to handle daily chores, but Pap taught me to feed and water the animals and gather the eggs each morning. Mom milked the cow every day and taught me to gather the vegetables ripe enough to harvest.

Every time Pap left to go back to Oklahoma, Mom packed a shoebox of little coffeecakes that he could take along on the train. A cafe near the yard in Oklahoma City advertised a "Nickel Beer Buffet." For the price of a five-cent beer you could also eat your dinner, not really a buffet but your choice of chicken or meatloaf. Pap survived on one meal a day and a handful of stale coffeecake as the weeks went by.

As he walked back to his boarding house after work one rainy afternoon, Pap spotted a little red toy tractor in the hardware store window, and remembered my seventh birthday coming up. It cost nearly all the coins in his pocket, meant to last all week, but Pap's heart was always bigger than his stomach. He could skip a meal or two. After all, he still had plenty of coffeecake.

Later that week, as he crossed the alley behind his usual supper stop, he noticed two colored men escaping the rain under the wide limbs of a big maple, eating their dinner spread out between them. Coming off a twelve-hour shift with no lunch, Pap's stomach churned and ached with hunger. He recognized the older man as the custodian at the railyard, so he took shelter under the same tree.

"Just wonderin'," he said. "Could you boys tell me... is the price the same at the back door as it is inside?"

The older man smiled and shook his head. "Damn right it is. It cost as much but the food ain't the same, no sir. Pay for fried chicken, and get a tomato sandwich, just scraps and leftovers, but they'll take your money. Be sure about that. We bring our food from home."

Pap just nodded.

The old man sized him up and said, "You runnin' a little short this evening? No shame in that, hard times for everybody."

The smell of fresh bread and hot food wafted from the café as Pap's gut growled. "Yeah, something came up I didn't plan for, I guess."

The two men glanced at each other, no doubt guessing it was booze or shooting craps or the company of a friendly woman. Pap didn't feel like explaining himself to strangers and was ready to move on when the old man spoke again.

"I got half a sandwich here. Tuna fish. It's still in the wax paper. I ain't touched it. Welcome to it." He held up the sandwich.

Pap protested. "No, thank you. I don't want to take your dinner. No thanks."

The old man wasn't turned aside. "You're hungry, ain't cha? You too good to eat with colored folks? Just take it with you then."

Pap hesitated, then took the sandwich from his hand. "No, it's not that. I appreciate it. Thank you."

The old man smiled as Pap made short work of the sandwich. As the men were finishing up, he handed Pap his paper sack. "Not much left here," he said. "Just some of my wife's sweet pickles and a couple of shortbread cookies. Take it along with you."

Pap took the sack and extended his hand.

The men stood to their feet and shook his hand.

Pap stammered out, "Appreciate it. Real kind of you."

The old man replied with a smile. "I was hungry and you fed me. That's what the Lord says we supposed to do."

Pap nodded and tucked the sack under his arm. "Thanks again."

Days later, when I opened my birthday gift, Mom stared in surprise and shook her head in wonder as Pap beamed a proud smile.

Small wonder he never cared much for coffeecake after his stint in Oklahoma.

Pap had to believe that going wherever he was sent, bucking the board for the railroad, would someday land him permanent work, a job where he could put his feet under his own table each night.

***

The job in Oklahoma City lasted just six months, and Pap got bumped once more.

When Mom met him at the door and heard the news, she said, "I'm glad you're home. I've missed you so much."

She tried to hide her anxious thoughts, but Pap could read her clouded expression. He shared her worries and with good cause. He'd checked across the Frisco line, from St. Louis to San Antonio—no jobs for cutters or fitters. Hard times everywhere he looked.

The fall of 1935 was the worst of times for my family. I was seven, Joyce was five, and Buster was not quite two years old. Their fourth child would be arriving in January. We had to move back to Springfield, unable to keep up the rent on our little farm in Monett. Pap loaned his mule and milk cow to a nearby farmer in the hopes of getting another little acreage, but with no work, the only choice was to move in with Grandma Mae in her house on Pacific. At least they'd all be under one roof, and hopefully, Pap could scrape together enough cash to keep everyone fed and clothed. Grandma had always depended on those few extra dollars from Pap each month, her circumstances no less desperate than our own. Now, in the worst of times, the burden of providing for three generations weighed heavy on Pap's shoulders.

As we squeezed our meager possessions into Grandma's house, we took some comfort in being together. Aunt Margaret's childlike mind was immune to stress or worry. For her, our arrival felt like an extended holiday, Christmas come early, and we kids celebrated with her, playing checkers and hide and seek.

Pap and Mom considered their options, with nothing on the railroad and no jobs around Springfield. It seemed like half the town was out of work. Programs like the Civilian Conservation Corps were only open to younger unmarried men. He had the skills to do furnace work or metal fabrication, but no one was hiring. He could do car repair or paint houses or do plumbing or carpentry, but no one had the money to have work done. Dimes were scarce, let alone dollars. It was too late in the year to put in a garden in Grandma's tiny yard. Fortunately, we had all the fruit and vegetables that Mom had put up in Monett, several boxes of Mason jars that would help keep us fed.

Day after day, Pap walked the city looking for work, however menial—loading docks, salvage work, trash crews, anything he could find to make a buck—but most days he came up empty. One weekend the furnace broke down in Grandma's little Baptist church down the street from her house. Pap repaired the furnace, getting it up and running before services. The pastor tried to pay Pap for his work, but he refused.

"Pastor, if you don't mind, just let that be my offering. I haven't been able to put anything in the plate for quite a while. Still looking for work, you know."

The pastor shook Pap's hand and nodded. "Thank you, Mr. Hill. That would be a big help to us. You're very kind. God bless you for your generosity."

"Yes, Pastor, and hopefully sooner rather than later."

One December afternoon, I noticed Pap sorting through his tools, laying them out on the front porch in two piles. On the right was a small collection of necessities: his framing hammer, a crescent wrench, his good plyers, a few assorted screw drivers and wrenches, and his leather tool belt. Everything else went into the larger pile, all kinds of tools that Pap had collected and used through the years. I noticed his ratchet set, chisels, his metal shears, and his welding equipment, all tools that I had seen him use, and I knew even as boy how he prized them. He found a wooden crate and loaded everything from the larger pile inside.

"Son, I want you to put these back in my old toolbox," he said, pointing to the smaller collection still laying on the porch.

I nodded but had to ask. "Okay, but what are you going to do with this whole box of tools?"

Pap hesitated before he spoke. "Well, sometimes you just have to get rid of a few things. I have so many tools, maybe too many, so I reckon I better let some go." He couldn't hide the regret in his tone.

I understood. "If you say so, Pap." I watched him carry that crate down the block to catch the streetcar.

He returned in time for dinner emptyhanded.

I had no idea as a boy of seven that Pap was selling his tools to provide Christmas gifts for his wife and children. Nor did I understand the deep connection between a mechanic and his tools.

That night, Pap went to bed feeling at least some relief, mingled with his grief and frustration. He had promised himself he would not disappoint his family. He couldn't bear the thought of sad faces on Christmas morning. Nothing could be worse than that.

***

On Christmas Eve, our family crowded into a pew at church next to Grandma Mae and Margaret. Two-year-old Buster squirmed in the seat between Mom and Pap. Joyce and I were mesmerized by the candlelight that cast a mysterious glow around the usually drab sanctuary.

Mom struggled to get comfortable in the hard, narrow seat, now in the eighth month of her pregnancy. She turned to Pap and whispered, "What's wrong, Oscar. Are you all right?"

Pap nodded and patted her hand. "I'm fine, Verna. Just a lot on my mind. I'm okay." He told her the truth but not the whole truth. What troubled him on that Christmas Eve ran deeper than the holiday blues or his lack of a job or a place for his family to live.

It's one thing to be disappointed with God, frustrated by unanswered prayers, angry at the hand you've been dealt, but to find yourself at the end of your rope, when every door is slammed in your face and the road you're on leads nowhere, you're tempted to give up—give up on yourself, give up on God.

Pap couldn't bring himself to mouth the words, "Joy to the World! The Lord is come." Try as he might, he didn't have the heart for it on that Christmas Eve. His world felt dark and foreboding, hard and unfeeling, and he couldn't bring himself to pretend otherwise.

Our pastor, Brother Miles, read the words of the prophet Isaiah: "Therefore, the Lord himself shall give you a sign, behold a virgin shall conceive, and bear a son, and shall call his name Immanuel. It means 'God with us,'" he said. "God with us in this world, in all our worries, in all our struggles, like Jesus said. 'I am with you always, even to the end of the world.'"

After the sermon, communion was served, first the bread, then the cup. Joyce and I were curious onlookers, too little to participate. After the bread was passed, Brother Miles said, "Take, eat, and know that you are not alone. Immanuel has come. God is with us."

Pap ate the tiny morsel of bread and breathed a silent prayer. "Lord, I can't find you. Please, come find me. I need you. I need your help. I don't know what else I can do. Help me, Lord." Tears rolled from his eyes.

When we all stood to light our candles and pass the light, the darkness no longer clouded Pap's face, the burden lifted, the gloom dispelled. While we sang, "Silent night, holy night, all is calm, all is bright," Pap no longer felt alone, unheard. Immanuel had shown up after all.

After the service, we hurried home for bath time. Before bed, we huddled around Pap as he recited with delight one of the many story poems he had memorized, "Twas the Night Before Christmas." We sat captivated, our imaginations running wild with anticipation.

I'm not sure how we ever got to sleep that night.

On Christmas morning, 1935, I opened toy cowboys and Indians and a western-style cap gun, and Joyce got a toy sewing machine and a doll.

I don't recall what little Buster got for Christmas, but I do remember my mother's smiling tears when she opened the perfume and lotion from my father. I also remember the smile on Pap's face that morning as his children played around his feet; it was pure joy.

***

On a Friday evening in late January, 1936, as Pap finished up a three-week project in Kansas City, the shop foreman for the Frisco took him aside and made an offer.

"Thanks for your help, Mr. Hill. You do good work. We're needing another sheet metal man around here. How would you feel about moving to Kansas City?"

Pap had already rehearsed his reply. "Yes, sir, I'm interested. I'll bid any job opening you have. Are you talking about a full-time, permanent job? There's no way I could move my family up here for temporary work."

The foreman nodded and smiled. "Sure, that's what I'm talking about. We'll keep you plenty busy right here. We'll start you out as a regular cutter and fitter. What do you say?" He extended his hand.

Pap didn't hesitate. He took the foreman's hand and said, "That sounds good to me. When do I start? Monday?"

The foreman laughed and shook his head. "No, not so fast, young man. Go home, pack up, and take care of your business. Be back here ready to work the first of the month. That work for you?"

"Thank you, that's sounds fine. I appreciate it." He left the shop with a spring in his step, and headed south towards Union Station hoping to catch the last train to Springfield.

Pap knew then what I only learned looking back in later years: for a man trying to raise a family in the Midwest in 1936, the railroad offered just about the best of jobs. As he rode the streetcar down Grand Avenue, the city seemed to come alive before his eyes. The office buildings and department stores stood taller, grander. The lights of early evening burned brighter, holding off the darkness. The bustling crowds hurrying home for the weekend didn't seem so much like strangers. Kansas City would soon become his home, his town. Though he loved the soil and seasons of life on the farm, he would learn to love a different way of life.

As Pap walked along Pershing Road, he stopped to take in the majestic view of Union Station, a towering edifice of gray limestone and granite with a façade of three huge archways separated by massive columns. As he entered the main hall, the rose brown marble floor reflected the glittering chandeliers suspended from the ceiling nearly a hundred feet above. Locals and visitors alike marveled at this masterpiece of Beaux-Art architecture. An ornate four-sided clock, six feet across, hung from above, keeping travelers on schedule.

As he stood in line for a ticket, it struck him that all of this beauty and grandeur was built by the railroads. Here he stood in the beating heart of the city, the hub of the whole region, and it made him proud to be a railroader, if only just beginning.

This would be his life. This would be his city. Like his father, Pap was finally a railroad man.

***

"Well, it's a nice neighborhood," Mom said as she stood at the curb. "And I like the dead-end street, not a lot of traffic."

Pap had found the house on 54th Street Terrace just off Swope Parkway on the south side of Kansas City, and this was Mom's first glimpse. From the outside it looked tolerable, two stories with green siding and red brick, and a broad porch across the front. But inside was a filthy mess, stale and musty after being unoccupied for nearly three years. Most of the lath and plaster walls needed to be redone, the plumbing was clogged, and the foundation leaked. The previous owner, a bootlegger, had run off, leaving a still in the basement.

Mom stood in the moldy kitchen with her hands on her hips. "Oscar, this won't do. It's a such a mess. Let's find something that doesn't need quite so much work."

Pap couldn't bring himself to tell her that he had already paid down on the house. So, he focused on the positives, like the fifteen-hundred-dollar price. Plus it had four and a half acres of land that extended a hundred yards back to the alley, and down to the tracks and an abandoned limestone quarry—plenty of room to garden and keep a few animals around, even in the city.

"It's not so bad, Verna. We'll get it cleaned up. We've never had so much room for the kids, and we don't have to get rid of Rosey or Moonshine. Plenty of room, and there's a little barn on the north end."

Rosie was our milk cow and Moonshine was Pap's mule.

Mom smiled a half smile. "Better change that mule's name before the law finds that still in the basement. Let's call him Oscar. He's as stubborn as they come."

So began the transformation of an old, dilapidated house into a warm and inviting home.

It would be Pap's address for the rest of his life.

***

That first spring in Kansas City, the farming began. Hard to imagine a more unlikely spot, on a dead-end street in the city, sandwiched between the neighbor's backyards and the old quarry, but Pap was determined to raise a crop on his tiny urban acreage. Imagine the typical backyard vegetable garden, and then multiply by ten. He planted long rows of tomatoes, sweet corn, green beans, potatoes, lettuce, turnips, beets, radishes, carrots, bell peppers, and onions. He added mounds of squash and pumpkins, cantaloupes, and watermelon. Grapevines ran along near the property line. Cherry, plum, and peach trees grew to give shade to what little yard was not under cultivation.

Closest to the house was Pap's pride and joy, his flower garden, about a quarter acre of rose bushes and assorted flowers. His love affair with roses lasted a lifetime. The simple act of bringing a fresh cut bouquet into the kitchen for Mom never lost its romance for Pap. Giving flowers meant giving love.

None of us kids shared Pap's passion for fresh flowers and farming, though we all grew up on the food he provided. As soon as we could hold a hoe in our hands, he assigned us to work details in the garden. He worked long shifts at work, so he mobilized his homegrown source of free labor to keep the weeds from overtaking his little farm.

In the heat of summer afternoons, I wondered why we planted so much—more than we could ever use ourselves. Mom canned and preserved all the produce that would keep, and the basement shelves were lined with dozens of labeled Mason jars. She worked so hard, determined not to waste anything, but why did we grow such a surplus?

As I grew older, I solved the mystery, which was no mystery at all. Pap and Mom weren't just feeding their family. They farmed for the whole neighborhood and for anyone in need. As the Great Depression lingered through the late 1930s, jobs remained scarce, and money was tight for everyone.

I was nine years old the first time I carried a sack of potatoes and a loaf of Mom's bread down the street with Pap, who toted a box of canned vegetables and homemade jam. I didn't know the details about the Henderson's situation; Pap just called it "a hard time," and knocked on the door.

Mr. Henderson came to the door, and when he saw the food, he looked sheepish, embarrassed.

Pap put him at ease, saying, "Verna wanted me to drop off these vegetables. She put up way more than we can use, and I'd hate for it to go bad. Could you do us a favor and use this up? If you would, I'd be obliged. You might bring us back these jars so we can use them again next year."

Mr. Henderson nodded and smiled. "Sure, Mr. Hill, we can do that. That's kind of you. I appreciate it, and we'll get these jars back to you right away."

I handed the potatoes and bread to Mrs. Henderson, who took them and patted me on the head.

"No hurry on that," Pap said. "Have a good evening."

As we walked home, Pap explained why we would do such a thing. "Son, being a neighbor is a lot more than just living next door or down the street. Always take care of your neighbors. Always be a good neighbor, son. Love God, love your neighbor... that's what the Bible says."

***

Pap was not an imposing figure at just five-nine, about one-sixty-five, wiry but strong, with dark hair pushed to one side and clear blue eyes. Cutting sheet metal and fitting pipes all day developed his forearms to massive proportions. When he rolled up the sleeves of his blue chambray work shirts, he looked a little like Popeye, and the kids in the neighborhood caught the resemblance. His grip could bring his sons to their knees in an instant. Pap could bend a six-inch, ten-penny nail, connecting the two ends in his hands. Arm wrestling him was downright dangerous. Our sandlot football games took on a different goal when Pap joined the game. Tackling him required a team effort... sometimes both teams.

Always a smoker, at least as long as anyone could remember, Pap started out on no filter Camels as a young man, and somewhere along the line he began smoking cigars, and then almost exclusively a pipe. The pungent aroma of his Granger Rough Cut tobacco hung in the air around his chair, his personal aura.

On Sundays, when he wasn't working, Pap shaved and put on a suit for church, being one of few men who could shave once a week and not look unkept. He smiled broadly and friendly, and when Pap laughed, he tilted his head to one side and his eyes seemed to spark with joy. When angered or annoyed or threatened, his blue eyes turned to steel. Gentle and yet fierce, humble and yet fearless, stubborn and yet forgiving, Pap never wavered from his faith, his family, or his convictions.

Chapter 3 – Eyes to See

"I cannot be awake,
for nothing looks to me as it did before,
or else I am awake for the first time,
and all before has been a mean sleep."
~ ***Walt Whitman***

"Somebody's cow's loose in the garden. Been there all afternoon." One of my jobs as a third-grader was keeping animals from grazing on our vegetables, so I anxiously announced my news as Pap walked through the door.

"Go shew her out of the garden," he said. "Must belong to somebody."

I did as I was told, but within an hour the cow came back for more. This time Pap took a different approach. As I tagged along, he led the cow out of the garden and tied her up by the back porch.

The next morning, Mom milked the cow before I left for school.

A few days later, my friend Roy came over after school and saw the cow beside the porch. "Hey, you stole our cow!" he said.

I set him straight right away. "No, we didn't steal your cow. That cow wouldn't stay out of our garden. We tried to shew her off, but she came back."

Roy wasn't hearing any of it. "I'm telling my dad. You stole our cow." And off he went to tattle on us.

After dinner, Roy's dad came for his cow. He was a tall man, barrel-chested and boisterous. The two men had never met, and it didn't begin well.

"What do you think you're doing keeping my cow? You've had her for nearly a week. You owe me for the milk you used."

The big man frightened me, but Pap was not easily intimidated.

"Maybe you should keep track of your animals, not leave them to stray onto other people's property. The truth is, you owe me for the damage to my garden and everything your cow ate."

Harsh words continued with no agreement or satisfaction until Roy's dad and his cow finally went home.

Later that evening, as the sunset faded and I was getting ready for bed, a knock came at the front door.

Mom answered, surprised to see Roy's dad standing there, his hat in his hand.

"Excuse me, ma'am. I'm Roy Hopkins, little Roy's father. Is your husband home?"

Pap came to the door and stepped out on the porch, not sure what to expect.

The big man offered his hand. "I didn't even tell you my name. I'm Roy Hopkins and I want to apologize for the things I said before. I was in the wrong."

Pap took his hand firmly. "I'm Oscar Hill. I was short with you, I know. Let's just forget about it. You've got your cow."

Roy wasn't finished. "Thank you, but I'm embarrassed to tell you, I'm a Christian and I know I shouldn't behave that way. Truth is, I'm a deacon over at Parkway Baptist Church."

"Is that right?"

Roy shuffled his feet and continued. "Yes, and if you folks don't have a church, I'd like to invite you to visit Parkway. I hope you won't let my misbehavior keep you away."

This time, Pap offered his hand. "I appreciate that. I think the kids have come for Sunday School. Maybe Verna and I will see you there."

"I hope so," Roy replied. "Goodnight."

When Pap came back in the house shaking his head, Mom looked up from her chair and asked what had happened.

Pap said, "Just when I thought I might get punched in the mouth, he invited us to church. How about that? A bigger man than I thought he was."

***

I never knew who gave Pap the tickets. I only know my parents hardly ever spent their hard-earned money for such an outing. I was nearly nine years old, just getting up from the breakfast table, when Pap picked up his lunch pail and paused in the kitchen doorway.

"Mel," he said, "I'm going downtown tonight to see a fight, a boxing match. Want to go with me?"

I didn't hesitate. "Sure, I'll go with you. Just me and you?" Pap already knew I would go anywhere with him, especially when we left my brothers and sister at home.

He nodded. "Just us. I only have two tickets and thought you might like to come along. We'll have to hurry our dinner and catch the streetcar. You be ready."

All day at school, I stared at the clock, so excited about the evening to come. Pap listened to boxing on the radio sometimes, and I liked to imagine the fight in my mind. Stories that Pap told about Jack Dempsey and Gene Tunney were my favorites. Now, to see a real live fight with my father made me feel like a grown-up man. I couldn't help bragging to my friends at school, though I didn't even know who was fighting that night. It didn't matter to me.

I sat on the porch step waiting for Pap to make it home. It was past his time and nearly dark on that February evening when he came ambling down the street, and I wanted to turn him around and head back to the streetcar, but he knew better than to skip the dinner Mom had prepared.

By the time Pap quickly changed his clothes, Mom had wrapped up our roast beef on bread and sent us on our way.

Pap and I squeezed into a crowded streetcar on Swope Parkway. I held tight to his sleeve and steadied myself as the streetcar jolted forward. We stepped off on Main at Thirteenth Street and walked west toward a massive stone building I'd never seen before, Municipal Auditorium, just a little over a year old, a stunning display of Art Deco style and design. The sheer size overwhelmed me, reaching in every dimension beyond what I could see or grasp. I stood there with my mouth open as Pap gave the man our tickets, and we shuffled inside with hundreds of eager fans.

By the time we found our way to the upper level, the fight had already begun. Our seats were in the fifth row from the top, about as far away from the ring as we could get. Most of the crowd was standing, only sitting down between rounds. Pap stood me up in my seat so I could see the ring far below, and cheers and jeers rose from the fourteen thousand people riveted on the fighters in the ring. That's when it struck me, something

I'd never seen before—a white man fighting a black man.

Actually, it was a first for everyone in the building. Natie Brown, a Jewish American fighter, was matched against a young Negro heavyweight named Joe Louis. It would prove to be the first interracial sporting event ever held in the state of Missouri, and not everyone was happy about it. The mostly white crowd around us made their loyalties known in unmistakable terms.

"Put the nigger down, Jew boy. Send that black bastard back to the cotton field."

"Knock him out! Get that darkie outta here. Bust his thick skull."

The third round came to an end, and we sat down to catch our breath.

Pap had something to say, pulling me close to him. "Son, I'm sorry you heard what those men said. I want you to know, I don't talk like that, not ever. Every man has a right to stand up for himself, no matter what color his skin. Don't you forget that, you hear?"

I nodded. "I won't forget."

Pap stood up and I climbed back on my seat, my hand on his shoulder as the fourth round began. As if on cue, the Negro fighter decided the time had come to decide the matter. His white opponent slumped against the ropes under a barrage of hooks and uppercuts, and then it ended, Natie Brown pummeled to the mat, counted out as Joe Louis retreated to his corner. Most of the crowd booed and jeered the young, victorious fighter.

On the way out, I saw a flyer on the floor and scooped it up—pictured there, Brown and Louis, a white man and a black man, ready to do battle. I folded it and stuck it in my pocket, a souvenir of a night I would not soon forget. Thousands came to see a black man beaten and put in his place, a kind of lynching in the ring. Instead, we watched a quiet gentleman display his strength and skills and the heart of a champion.

On the streetcar headed home, I tugged on Pap's coat. "Can you teach me to box? If I saved some money, could I get some boxing gloves?"

Pap smiled and jostled my hair. "I'll bet we could do that, might even get you some lessons when you get a little older. You sure you want to try that?"

I bobbed my head up and down with my almost nine-year-old enthusiasm. "Sure, I do, that would be great. Thanks."

As we walked home from the streetcar, I shadow boxed in the moonlight.

***

For a few months, Mom had been sending Joyce and I to church on Sunday mornings. In those early years on the Frisco, Pap worked twelve- and sixteen-hour shifts, only occasionally allowing him to attend services, but Mom insisted that we go while she stayed home with little Buster and Danny, our baby brother. It was just a few blocks, so I held Joyce's hand and we wandered down 54th Street Terrace on our way to Sunday School each week.

When we came home no one asked for any details.

"Did you have a good time? Did you behave yourself?" That was the extent of our questioning.

So, imagine Mom's and Pap's surprise at what they discovered when they decided to take the whole family to Parkway Baptist Church on a Sunday morning.

We all walked together, Mom carrying Danny and Buster in a stroller, and when we turned left at the corner on Jackson, I was puzzled.

"Where are we going?" I asked.

Mom said, "We're going to church, just like you go every week."

Little Joyce shook her head, and I spoke for both of us. "That's not the way to church. Our church is that way." I pointed back down Jackson in the opposite direction.

Mom wrinkled her brow and asked, "What church have you been going to?"

We did our best to explain. Apparently, we should have turned left on Jackson, but we had been turning right and found another church just down the street, the Assembly of God church near Chick Elementary.

Mom was flabbergasted and embarrassed, but Pap doubled over with laughter. Neither one had thought to show us the way or walk us to church at least a time or two.

Mom said, "Didn't I tell you kids to go to Parkway Baptist Church? We go right past it almost every day."

Joyce and I just shrugged and looked at each other.

"We walk past that church on the way to school," I said, pointing back down Jackson. "The people were really nice."

Mom began to calm down, but Pap couldn't quit laughing.

Mom said, "I guess it's not your fault. We should have walked you to the church, at least showed you the way. Besides, there was no harm in it."

"I don't know," Pap laughed. "They might start speaking in tongues any minute, Verna, Then, what'll we do? Kids, did you learn any new languages at church?" Mom failed to see the humor of the situation, but Pap savored the moment.

When we finally arrived at Parkway Baptist that morning, it was new to all of us. The modest red brick building, plain and simple inside and out, had room for perhaps a hundred and fifty people. Two stories of classrooms attached to the sanctuary and a basement fellowship hall provided space for dinners and receptions.

The Parkway folks welcomed our family with kindness. Mr. Hopkins shook hands with Pap and introduced him to the pastor, James Herald, a tall, thin, older man with a wisp of gray hair and a friendly smile. Some of the ladies asked if they could hold Danny, just a few months old. One lady said she thought Danny looked like his father, while the rest of us looked like Mom.

The kids earned a peppermint for learning a Bible verse in Sunday School, and Mom quizzed us to find out where we got the candy. Joyce and I decided that this new church suited us just fine, and we were no longer tempted to turn right on Jackson. Parkway became our church.

***

Pap walked to work about eight blocks up to Swope Parkway at 55th Street to catch the streetcar each day, switched at 31st Street, then west to Main, north to 12th, then hiked just over a mile through downtown and over the viaduct to the West Bottoms and the Frisco railyard.

The streetcars exposed the city from one end to the other, the glory and the grime—the well-groomed businessman picking up the morning papers from a friendly corner vendor, a truck pulled to the curb, the weary driver unloading his freight as the impatient shopkeeper checks off the merchandise on his clipboard, a sleepy wino rousted from his alley hideaway, squinting at the morning sun, people in a rush and people with no place to go, prosperity and poverty, industry and indigence... on display block by block.

One evening on his way home, riding the streetcar and worn out from a long shift at work, he sat across from an old black man. The man's denim coveralls were filthy, stained with grease and soot, and hard-packed mud clung to his boots. A grimy cap covered what was left of his gray hair. The old man's weariness shown through the sweat and dust of the day. Pap shook his head and turned away in disgust. The railroad provided the men with a place to wash up after work and a locker to keep some clean clothes, so Pap never traveled in his grimy overalls. He always cleaned up before heading home—no excuse for riding the streetcar such a dirty mess. Even a ditch digger, even a garbage man, could wash his hands and face.

In that moment, Pap had an epiphany of sorts. The sounds of the city faded away as something stirred deep inside him. As he looked over the hapless stranger once more, a voice spoke to him with unmistakable clarity: *'I died for him just like I died for you.'*

Pap shuddered at those words, a voice he'd never heard, a truth he'd never considered. He sat there with no answer, no reply, as the words seeped into his soul.

The streetcar came to a stop along 31st Street at Troost, and Pap glanced from the window at a Negro boy, perhaps fifteen years old, begging on the corner. His awkward gate and dazed look reminded him of his sister, Margaret.

The boy held out his hat as people hurried by, ignoring his eager request. "Please, sir, can you spare a nickel or a dime?"

A tall man in a pinstriped suit dropped in a few coins.

The boy dug in his hat and counted the change, delighted and yet pitiful.

As the streetcar lurched ahead, the voice whispered again: *'I died for him just like I died for you.'* Moved and troubled, Pap bowed his head and tried to answer in his own muffled prayer. "I hear you, Lord. I'm listening."

When he switched lines, people crowded aboard, pressing in shoulder-to-shoulder. Pap could hardly squeeze his way inside. Standing before him was a black woman in a blue wool coat and a paisley scarf over her graying hair.

She gave him a tired smile and stepped back to make room for him.

Pap nodded his thanks, and a third time it echoed through his mind: *'I died for her just like I died for you.'*

As Pap walked home those last few blocks, he could still see them—the old man's grimy face, the boy's silly grin, the woman's tired smile—black folks not so unlike himself or Margaret or Verna, just people doing their best with what they had, finding their way.

How does one explain such an epiphany? Do such things happen?

For Pap, it was unmistakably real, nothing less than the voice of Christ—his own Damascus Road, etched in his memory, replayed through the years, a lifelong reminder. No one is worthless. No one is excluded. No one is less than a child of God.

***

In the darkest days of the Depression, men road the rails into the city looking for work. No two men told the same story. Some of them left families back home desperately awaiting whatever earnings they might muster and send. Others deserted their families out of despair and sheer hopelessness.

Whatever their story, all who jumped from the freight trains and came up the alley behind our house hoped to quiet their growling stomachs. Mom and Pap never turned away a hungry soul. They shared whatever food or provision they possessed, little or much, never anticipating how such hard times might stretch their hospitality.

The first time a man knocked at the back door, it startled and frightened Mom such that she nearly dropped a bowl she was drying. Her heart skipped a beat, but then she sensed the stranger meant no harm.

"Sorry, ma'am, didn't mean to scare you. Just wondered if you might have a little something to eat for a hungry traveler," the weary stranger said while holding his hat in his hands.

Mom opened the door regaining her composure. "You surprised me, is all. Sit right down on that top step and let me pour you some lemonade and see what I can find for your lunch."

The man, maybe forty years old, ragged and thin, in a blue chambray shirt and overalls just like Pap wore to work, gave Mom a tired smile and a nod of thanks.

This being her first such guest, Mom found little in her kitchen to offer. She fried some bacon with some leftover creamed potatoes on toast, and sliced him some cheese and an apple to take with him.

He cleaned his plate and tucked the apple and cheese in his pocket. "Much obliged, ma'am. Sure appreciate it."

Mom stood at the door watching the stranger disappear down the back lane, and breathed a prayer of thanks that her husband *repaired* trains rather than riding them aimlessly across the country.

After that, and for several years, Mom kept a big pot of vegetable or potato soup, or ham and beans, on the stove and plenty of homemade bread. Word got around the network of drifters that a man could get hot food at the green house at the top of the lane. Pap set down some rules, welcoming our guests to eat at the kitchen table when he was around. If Pap was gone to work, the men stayed outside and ate on the back porch, which was not large. Before long, Pap picked up some secondhand lumber and built a picnic table so the men could sit and eat in the shade.

In the summer and fall, Pap saved up feed and seed sacks and grocery bags for the guys to use. "Use this sack and pick yourself some fruit and vegetables, whatever's ripe that you can use. You can wash 'em off at the pump and take them with you."

The men were obliged to Pap for his generosity, though a few had already swiped and stashed a few tomatoes on the way in.

There was no way to track how many wanderers made their way to Mom and Pap's back door, or how many pitchers of lemonade Mom poured, but no one walked away hungry or thirsty.

When the war came, Mom's feeding station closed for good. No more customers.

***

I was nine years old the first time our family ventured downtown for the American Royal Parade and Horse Show. Joyce and Buster tagged along with Pap and me, while Mom stayed home with the little one, Danny. Pap determined that his children would not grow up as "city kids," with no knowledge or appreciation of animals and farm life. I confess I was more interested in the parade than I was in the livestock shows, which had every imaginable species and breed on display. The horse show captured our attention, with the majestic stallions performing with amazing precision and beauty. Loula Long Combs headlined the horse show every year, entering the arena in her phaeton with her two Boston bulldogs. Her horses behaved better than her bulldogs, but it was great fun to watch.

I stood on the Grand Avenue sidewalk as the parade began with riders on horseback carrying flags and banners followed by colorful floats, marching bands, more than a few politicians waving from wagons and cars, and all kinds of horses and saddle clubs. Plenty of folks in cowboy hats paid tribute to the Old West.

Joyce squealed with excitement to see the American Royal Queen, a young blonde who waved from her float. Then, a drumline from Paseo High School kept everyone in step, and finally more riders on horseback—all kinds of horses.

Even as a kid, I could figure it out, just why all those riders were at the end of the parade. The manure dropped freely on the pavement all along the way, from sidewalk to sidewalk.

After all the horses, four black men followed, each with a shovel and a wheelbarrow, scooping up manure from curb to curb. I hadn't noticed until then a colored family just down the walk from us, keeping to themselves, but close enough to enjoy the parade. In fact, I hadn't seen any other black people at the Royal that day, visitors or participants. As the scoopers passed by, a tall white man in Western clothes spotted the colored family and walked towards them as he pointed at the men in the street.

Almost shouting, he said, "There's your parade, right there. That's the nigger parade, picking up horse shit off the street. Hope you like it."

I never forgot the horrified look on the mother's face as she covered her little girl's ears and turned her away.

Her husband put himself between the tall man and his family. "Mister, we don't mean no harm. Let us alone. We don't need no trouble."

But his antagonist was just getting started. "Well, you got trouble. What do you expect coming down here among decent white folks? This ain't for your kind. Get your little black asses on out of here."

That's when Pap stepped between the men and held up his hands, trying to calm the situation. "There's no call for that kind of talk, not here in front of the children. Let's just calm down."

The white man looked at Pap in disbelief. "Standing up for a nigger? What kind of man are you?"

Pap looked him square in the eye. "The kind you need to listen to. Now get going."

Something in Pap's expression must have got his point across, because the tall man walked away in a huff.

The black man calmed his family and turned to Pap. "Thanks for your help. We weren't trying to start nothing. My kids just wanted to see the parade."

Pap agreed. "Mine, too. If parades aren't for our children, I reckon they're not for anyone."

***

Mom had two cousins about her age, Hershel and Roy, who lived across the city northeast, her only extended family this side of Springfield. Every two or three months, we would get together for what always became an extended card game, whether at our house or theirs. Pap enjoyed playing cards while Mom caught up with Dottie, Hershel's lady friend, while keeping an eye on her brood of children. The guys never played for money, so gambling wasn't an issue for Mom's sensitive conscience. Nobody had a dime to spare anyway. Matches or toothpicks worked just fine. Sometimes friends of Hershel or Roy would show up for the game. Mom would bring along a puzzle or a board game for us kids, not anxious for us to become card players ourselves, but after dinner, we would soon lose interest in the puzzle and scramble around the table to watch and listen to the stories.

More than once, Mom had to remind Hershel that there were children in the room. He usually watched his language but didn't give much thought to his subject matter.

Roy had married young, by all accounts a miserable marriage followed by a bitter divorce. He never remarried or had kids of his own, so he talked to children like little grownups.

"Mel," Roy said, "pull up a chair and I'll deal you in. Did you bring any money with you?"

I never knew when he was serious, but I did know that Mom had no interest in her nine-year-old son learning the ins and outs of poker, even with no cash on the table. But before long, even little Joyce learned that a full house beats two pair.

I learned pretty quickly that the card games supplied a handy excuse to get together and drink. Hershel and Roy guzzled beer all evening, which made for some lively conversation. Pap was never much of a drinker, maybe a cold brew after a long, hot shift, or a beer on the weekend. A six pack might last a month at our house. At Hershel's or Roy's, the rules were different. The beer flowed freely, by the pitcher, and every empty glass around the table was topped off again and again.

On one unforgettable Saturday night, the game ran later than usual, and each time Pap finished his beer, Roy refilled his glass. Mom fretted about the late hour, anxious to get her little ones home, but the men played on—always one more hand.

"Oscar, it's time to go. We need to get the kids to bed," Mom said, steamed by the poor example Pap was setting, but that was just the beginning of what set Mom off.

When the card game finally came to a merciful end, Pap couldn't get out of his chair.

"Whoa there, buddy. Easy does it." Roy offered a hand as Pap struggled to get to his feet.

Unaccustomed to large amounts of alcohol, Pap was thoroughly hammered. Hershel and Roy managed to get him to the bathroom, and Mom had to drive us home with Pap nearly passed out in the front seat.

I couldn't remember my mother ever being angrier than that night.

"What were you thinking, drinking like that, in front of your own children? You should be ashamed of yourself!"

Pap had no defense to offer and knew better than to try.

When we got home, Mom hurried into the house.

I helped Pap up the steps before he lunged to the side of the porch and vomited.

Little Joyce was horrified and ran inside to tell. "Momma, Daddy's getting sick on the porch. He threw up," she said sympathetically.

Mom's reply was classic. "Let him be sick then."

I didn't know if Pap slept in his chair on the porch or if he made it upstairs to his bed that night. What I did know was that he made it to church with us the next morning, and when he swore never to drink more than one beer in a day for the rest of his life, I believed him.

***

From his first day working in the Kansas City yard, Pap had been forced to choose sides. The movement to unionize the Frisco had been brewing for over a year and the tension between the organizers and management was obvious and threatening.

Sarge, the shop foreman, began to press Pap, trying to gauge his intentions. "Oscar, you just keep your head down and get the work done and you'll be fine. You won't have any problems on this railroad."

Pap had a hunch where this was leading. "I'll do my job," he answered. "A day's work every day. I'll earn my pay."

Sarge agreed. "I know you will. Hell of a worker, I can see that. On the other hand, some people around here are never satisfied, always bitching and complaining, can't leave well enough alone. They want to turn the Frisco into a God-damned union shop. That ain't gonna happen."

Pap thought about keeping still, but the words escaped him. "You sure about that, Sarge. If the boys upstairs take a hard line, there'll be trouble, throwing gas on a fire. They might want to hear them out. Got to be something they could all agree on."

Sarge shook his head and took the measure of his young pipefitter. "Didn't figure you to be taking up for the union. Not a wise move for a man like you just starting out."

Pap thought a minute and chose his words carefully. "I reckon things can be better for everybody around here if we all listen and do right by the Frisco and the men that work this railroad. I imagine we could get along."

Sarge leaned against Pap's workbench and looked across the yard toward the supervisor's offices. "I'm not so sure about that, Oscar. I'm thinking there might be trouble, and you'd be wise to steer clear of it." He then turned and left.

Pap pondered the warning for days, but knew from the beginning he would stand with the working man, come what may.

What made Pap a union man from the beginning? Plenty of reasons in his brief life: his father's death on the railroad and the pitiful settlement his mother had received; being bumped from job after job with no notice or recourse; no job after four years as an apprentice; and finally hocking his tools to get some Christmas for his children. His work on the railroad had always been tenuous and unreliable. He figured men like him ought to be able to work hard and provide for their families with some measure of security.

Railroad men learned quickly that management would treat labor no better than required or demanded.

Pap would be a union man.

***

Trouble came sooner than expected, in the fall of 1938, and Pap was the instigator, and nearly the casualty. For the one and only time in his railroad employment, Pap called in sick when he wasn't ill at all. In those days, an employee would likely be terminated for such behavior, and Pap had less than three years under his belt in the Kansas City shop.

What could tempt Pap to take such a gamble? We had seen the advertisement in the newspaper, growing larger each week, until a full-page ad in the Star carried the banner, "The Greatest Show on Earth." Pap couldn't resist the chance to take his kids to the P. T. Barnum and Bailey Circus. Joyce, Buster, Dan, and I rode the streetcar downtown with Pap leaving Jack, the little one, at home with Mom.

What an incredible spectacle, with the Municipal Auditorium somehow transformed into a giant three-ring circus tent. I remember the high-flying trapeze artists soaring above us, the enormous elephants marching by in single file, trunks to tails, and the big cats answering the whip and call of their tamer. Mom had packed some sandwiches for us, but Pap bought peanuts and cotton candy for us to share. I would have been hard pressed to say who had the most fun—us kids seeing the circus for the first time, or Pap, who delighted to point out every detail so we wouldn't miss a thing.

What Pap did miss was the photographer who snapped a picture of Oscar Hill and his little brood at the circus, and ran it the next morning on the front page of the Kansas City Star. Not having seen the paper, Pap stood stunned the next morning when he punched the time clock and saw the clipped picture taped above the clock.

Before his shift started, Sarge called him upstairs to the railyard supervisor's office. Pap had never been called on the carpet before.

"Nice picture in the paper, son. I must say, you looked pretty damn healthy to me, well enough to spend the day at the circus." Mr. Stevens, the supervisor came right to the point.

"Yes, sir," Pap replied. "About that... it won't happen again." Pap was the only one standing, but no one offered a chair. His pulse raced as he stood there sweating, expecting the worst.

"Did you have to get your damn picture taken? Now every person in the railyard knows what you did, and if I keep you on, everyone will start calling in sick for every damn ballgame and floor show in town. I can't have that."

Mr. Stevens turned to Pap's foreman, and his interrogation continued. "Sarge, what's the status of this man? Can we do without him?"

"It's just his third year in the yard, but he's already the best cutter and fitter we've got. I'd hate to lose him. We do have some extra work on 1630 that he could do, require some overtime."

Mr. Stevens shook his head in disgust. "Hell, that's no punishment. He wants the hours. He's always bidding the extra work, still bucking the board."

Sarge stated the obvious. "Do we really want to lose a man like that? He wants to work. He's a railroad man."

Mr. Stevens was at the end of his patience. "All right, Mr. Hill, for today you keep your job, but I'm making note. You're on thin ice with me, you understand? You give me the slightest excuse, one more reason, and I'll throw your ass off this railroad. You're not indispensable. You're not the only mechanic in the world. Just the luckiest one today. Go on, get back to work."

"Thank you, sir. You won't get any more trouble from me." Pap had survived his first clash with railroad management.

It would not be his last.

***

Christmas at Parkway Baptist Church never had amounted to much. The folks gathered a few meager gifts and extra food for a needy family or two in the neighborhood, and if the cold and snow held off, we might do some Christmas caroling around the block or at the old folks home over on Cleveland. A painted plaster nativity scene on a white cloth graced the communion table, a modest but meaningful approach to the birth of the Savior.

Then, in 1938, Mom suggested to some of the parents that we put together a little Christmas pageant with the kids. The idea spread quickly to Pastor Herald, who immediately enlisted Mom to oversee the project.

Sunday night before Christmas would be Parkway's first pageant celebrating Christ's birth. Mom put Pap and the dads to work building a stable of sorts, while Mom and the ladies worked on costumes. Mom also sat down at the kitchen table with her Bible and some paper and scratched out the script.

Next came the casting. Most every kid in Sunday School raised their hand eagerly seeking a part in the play. Joyce begged to be Mary, the leading female role, and squealed when she got the part. I didn't care so much, as long as I didn't have to be an animal, like a camel, a sheep, or a donkey—not for me. Though I never raised my hand, Mom pointed to me and made me the final Wise Man of the three. Buster joined the band of shepherds in oversized bathrobes with towels on their heads. Everybody else became an angel, at least figuratively, with tinsel wings and pipe cleaner halos.

The big question still loomed before us. Who would play the lead, Baby Jesus? The Millers had a baby girl, Sarah, just three months old, but some of the folks objected to a female Jesus. My brother Danny, a two-year-old toddler, seemed a little big for the newborn king, more than Mary could hold on her lap. Mrs. Miller offered a life-sized doll that seemed to do the trick, but somehow that didn't seem quite right either—a plastic Savior. Catholics went for that sort of thing, I was told, but we wanted the real McCoy, an actual baby. That just left one option—my new baby brother, Arthur, whom Pap had already nicknamed Jack. Barely four months old, Baby Jack just fit in the timber manger that Pap had put together.

Mom felt a little uneasy about her Jack playing Jesus—a lot to live up to—but she took some comfort knowing that his sister Joyce would be there to keep an eye on him. During pageant rehearsal, Jack fell asleep in the church nursery, so he didn't have to practice his part. Joyce held the doll in her arms, and the shepherds gathered with their flocks until us wise men finally showed up with our gifts.

The ladies had outdone themselves on the costumes, with bright-colored tunics and robes and sashes. My wise man suit had fancy gold thread and a braided chain around my waist. Buster was pretty jealous, standing there in Pap's robe while I had a shiny crown on my head.

Pap had located a couple of refrigerator boxes to open up and paint with a Bethlehem skyline under the looming star. Propped up from behind, it made an impressive background for the story to unfold.

When the big night arrived, the church filled quickly, everyone anxious to see the children present the Christmas story. The kids beamed with excitement as they gathered in their classroom to put on their costumes, while Mom nervously reminded each child of their part in the play. Soon everyone found their place, Mary and Joseph approaching Bethlehem with the shepherds to stage left, the wise men off stage to the right, while the angelic chorus waited behind the cardboard background.

Pap, drafted to be the narrator, begin with the nativity store from Luke.

"And it came to pass in those days, that there went out a decree from Caesar Augustus that all the world should be taxed... And Joseph went up from Galilee, out of the city of Nazareth, unto Judea, unto the city of David, which is called Bethlehem, to be taxed with Mary, his espoused wife, Mary, being great with child."

Pap paused as Joseph and Mary made their way down the center aisle, a pillow tucked under Joyce's costume.

That's when the trouble started. The innkeeper, the only real villain in the story, was played by Joey Sutherland, the same age as me, but Joey didn't have the heart to be the bad guy. When Joseph explained his situation and pleaded for a room, Joey choked up and stepped back.

"Sure," he said. "Come on in."

Everyone was stunned, and Joseph most of all.

"Come in?" he replied. "Are you kidding me?"

Laughter rippled across the sanctuary.

Mom, seated on the front pew, frantically whispered their lines, trying to get them back on script.

"Okay," Joey said dejectedly, nodding to Mom. "No room, but you can use my stable."

Joseph took his rejection well, breathing a sigh of relief, and he and Mary crossed the crowded little platform to the stable and made themselves at home.

Pap kept the story moving.

"And she brought forth her firstborn son, and wrapped him in swaddling clothes, and laid him in a manger; because there was no room for them in the inn."

As the lights came back on, Mary had lost her pillow and Baby Jack lay in the manger while Joseph stood watch.

The shepherds soon arrived, with their sheep and goats on all fours hamming up their animal sound effects. Maybe that's what bothered Baby Jesus, because he began to fuss like he was working up a good cry. Mary tried to shush him, but Jesus was getting restless.

Mom whispered, "Pick him up, Joyce. Be careful."

Joyce reached in the manger and scooped up her baby brother like a real momma, and rocked him back forth, but try as she did, Jesus grew progressively unhappy.

Before Mom could come to her aid, Baby Jesus spit up on Mary, who looked with horror at the gooey white mess running down from her shoulder.

Joseph jumped back as if he had seen a snake.

Joyce was close to tears when her brother stepped in. Buster, a lowly shepherd, pulled the towel from his head and leaned down to hand it to his sister, but as he reached down, a little nervous energy escaped him in the form of gas, a resounding fart. At this point, the choir of angels broke into uproarious laughter, along with most of the cast. Buster just smiled and returned to his place minus his towel headdress.

Pap tried to keep reading, but by now his words bore little resemblance to the story unfolding onstage.

By the time we all stood to sing "Silent Night," Baby Jesus had disappeared, replaced by Plastic Jesus, Mary was wearing a sweatshirt over her costume, and Mom was thoroughly mortified.

Pap thought it was wonderful, better than he'd imagined—a Christmas to remember.

***

We had just sat down for supper at the kitchen table when we heard a commotion erupt in the backyard. Pap went out the back door while I ran to the window to see what was happening.

Four men, our hobo guests, were sitting at the picnic table, having jumped off the 4:00 freight train. Mom had served them ham sandwiches and potato soup and set a big platter of fresh fruit on the table. The problem was a fifth man, a colored man, who had just walked up from the alley and tried to take a seat. That's when the uproar ignited.

"What do ya think your doin', boy?" one of white men said. "You can't sit here. I ain't eatin' with no nigger." He stormed to his feet, grabbed the black man by his collar, and yanked him backward to the ground.

Two of the other white men kicked and stomped while the fourth man hurled the black man's bundle across the yard.

"Get your black ass outta here," the first one said, the one who'd instigated the trouble.

That's when Pap arrived. "That's enough! Get your hands off him. What's the matter with you? You sit at my table eating free food and you want to run another man off? You," he said, pointing to the white man doing all the talking. "Pick up your bag and clear out. Go on, move!"

Two others left with him, and the fourth went his own way, but not before they all grabbed another sandwich for the road.

Pap helped the black man get to his feet and gather his things. "C'mon inside, we're just getting started."

Reluctantly, the black man climbed the stairs while explaining, "I'll be fine sitting outside. Don't mean no trouble."

Pap just opened the back door and waved him inside. "Our hospitality is usually a far sight better than what you got so far. Come in and have a seat."

I scooted over closer to Buster, and the stranger sat next to me.

Mom set a place for him as Pap made the introductions, pointing around the table. "I'm Oscar Hill, my wife Verna, our kids, Mel next to you, then Buster, and Joyce. Over here, Dan, and the little man is Jack. What's your name?"

"My name is Avery, Mose Avery. Nice to meet you all. Mind if I wash up? Didn't get a chance to use the pump."

Mom reached for a hand towel and said, "Here, just use the sink. Help yourself."

When our guest settled back into his seat, it was time for the blessing. As always, we joined hands around the table. Without a thought, Pap and I took Mr. Avery by the hand as Pap prayed.

"Father, for these thy gifts we give thanks, and for all our blessings. Forgive us our sins. Bless our guest this evening, Mr. Avery. In Jesus name, I pray. Amen."

When I let go of his big hand, our guest brushed a tear from his eye.

Joyce passed the sandwiches to our guest while Mom ladled the potato soup.

"Where you from, Mr. Avery? Where's home?" Pap asked as he filled his plate.

"I was born in Henderson, Kentucky, but I doubt I ever see that place again. I left my wife and kids in St. Louis with her kin. Heard there was more work around here, but I ain't had no luck so far. No decent jobs for a colored man. The unions got no use for men like me."

Pap asked, "What kind of work can you do?"

"I'm a lumberman, do some carpentry, roofing, field hand if I have to."

Pap nodded and tried to be encouraging. "I reckon with those skills you'll find something around here. Schutte Lumber up on Southwest Boulevard might be your best bet. I know a man there, Albert Jameson, goes to our church. He's not a super or anything, just a lumberman like you. Might be able to put in a word for you. I'll let Albert know you might be coming by."

Moses gave a tired smile as Mom refilled his soup bowl. "That's real kind, Mr. Hill. That's the best word I've heard since I left St. Louis. Sure appreciate it."

As we were finishing supper, and Mr. Avery headed to the back door, Mom handed him a bag with two more ham sandwiches inside.

"Thank you, Mrs. Hill. That's nice of you. Appreciate it."

That was the first time a colored person ate with us in our home. I wondered what all the fuss was about.

Chapter 4 – Wartime

"The true soldier fights not because
he hates what is in front of him,
but because he loves what is behind him."
~ G. K. Chesterton

Sunday afternoons in December were meant for football in the vacant lot up the street, or on frigid days, naps in front of the fireplace. This Sunday, the 7th of December, 1941, was different—just a sandwich for lunch instead of the usual roast beef or chicken, and Mom's reminder not to change out of our church clothes.

"And be careful not to spill anything," she said. "I want to get a picture of Joyce with Brother Herald and one of our whole family, a day to remember."

Joyce beamed with excitement. Today she would be baptized, taking her place as a full member of the church, and finally qualified to take the tiny flatbread and grape juice of the Lord's Supper, as Baptists observe it.

It took a good-size tank to baptize by immersion, even an eleven-year-old girl like Joyce, and our church, Parkway, was too small to have its own baptistry. So whenever someone requested baptism, Brother Herald scheduled an afternoon service in one of the larger churches around the city. On this day, we'd be at Forest Avenue Baptist Church, just off Troost at 43rd Street.

The seven of us piled into Pap's '35 Chevy sedan and headed north on Troost. The streets seemed strangely deserted, even for a Sunday, with hardly anyone around. It struck Pap as odd enough that he turned on the radio to catch the news. No music played, as the news broadcasted from every station.

"This is WDAF radio, 610 AM, with this special news bulletin. Early this morning, the U.S. naval base at Pearl Harbor, Hawaii, was attacked by Japanese forces. Here is the live report recorded earlier today from our NBC affiliate in Hawaii."

> 'Hello, NBC. Hello, NBC. This is KGU in Honolulu, Hawaii.... We have witnessed this morning a distant view of... a severe bombing of Pearl Harbor by enemy planes, undoubtedly Japanese.... This battle has been going on for nearly three hours.... It is no joke. It is real war.'

"Pentagon sources indicate that our losses have been heavy and mass casualties have been reported. The President will address the nation tomorrow and is expected to ask Congress for a declaration of war."

Mom reached over and turned off the radio. No one spoke until Joyce began to sob.

"Does this mean I can't get baptized today?" she asked through her tears.

Buster spoke up to set her straight. "What do you think? The Japs are going to bomb your baptism? Maybe we should just throw you in Brush Creek. More than one way to get baptized."

Mom had heard enough. "Hush up, Buster. Of course, you will still be baptized, Joyce. We're almost there."

The car was quiet for a few blocks, until I put the question to my father. "What does it mean, Pap? What's going to happen now?" I could see the seriousness on his face as he spoke.

"I don't know, son, but it's not good, not good at all."

***

When the war began, Pap was too old for military service at thirty-three. Later, when they raised the age, he had four children at home. By the time that didn't matter, Pap's job had been "frozen," listed as vital to the war effort—keeping the trains running. In fact, business boomed on the railroad, with more trains, new routes, expansion in every direction, and a shortage of skilled workers.

As he walked into the Frisco yard one morning, Pap noticed a line of men looking for work, waiting to fill out applications. A scuffle broke out towards the end of the line. Four colored men had stepped in line to apply, and some of the white men tried to shove them aside.

"Don't need no niggers on the railroad, boy, unless you want to scrub toilets or carry garbage. You boys can go on, get outta here. These ain't no nigger jobs," the taunts rang out.

The black men stood their ground undeterred, without responding as the abuse continued. The disturbance threatened to turn violent as more men joined the confrontation. Just as punches began to fly, the superintendent came running down the stairs from the offices.

"Knock it off!" he shouted. "You men, clear out of here, the whole lot of you, you clowns that can't stand in line and wait your turn."

The white ringleader shouted, "The niggers started the trouble. Run 'em outta here, and we'll be fine."

Reluctantly, to keep the peace, the super pointed the black men toward the door.

One man voiced their protest. "Ain't right and it ain't fair. A man's got to work, and you got job's need fillin'. We can do our part in the damn war."

Nothing but catcalls and ridicule followed them out the door.

It struck Pap that those men were doing what any man would do, looking for work, not a handout. They likely had families, bills to pay, food to put on the table, the same pressures they all felt. Every man in that line, black and white, knew how it felt to be out of work, desperate and determined to provide for his family.

Pap also knew the unwritten rules of the railroad. The few Negroes who got jobs were limited to janitorial work or common laborers, while the skilled jobs and apprenticeships were reserved for white men. Management and the union agreed on this one issue and kept blacks and minorities out of the preferred jobs. The union steward sounded just like the boss on matters of race. Even a severe shortage of manpower could not open the doors to men like those forced to walk away that morning.

In 1942, after protests around the country, President Roosevelt signed an executive order that banned discrimination in all of the wartime industries, including the railroads. But regardless of the new law, the unwritten codes remained in place. Running the railroad was still a white man's job.

***

"What'cha doing Momma?" Joyce asked. "Another letter? Who are you writing all these letters to?"

Mom was sitting at the dining room table, her favorite place to write because she could enjoy her roses just outside her windows. Spread before her was a long list of names and a stack of small cards with a gold cross printed beside a single verse of scripture, Isaiah 41:10: "Fear thou not, for I am with thee: Be not dismayed; for I am thy God: I will strengthen thee; yea, I will help thee; I will uphold thee with the right hand of my righteousness."

Beside her coffee cup sat a box of pale yellow stationary, each sheet embossed with a tiny bouquet of yellow roses. Joyce ran her finger over the roses and shrugged like any bored twelve-year-old.

Mom laid aside her fountain pen and picked up her list. "I'm writing to our soldiers, letting them know that we're thinking of them and praying for them. Those boys are a long way from home and they like to get mail from back home."

Joyce picked up the list, not quite convinced. "Yeah, but do you even know all these boys? There must be fifty names on this list."

"Well, I started out just to write the boys from Parkway—Brent, Owen, Davy, and Stewart—but then I got some more names from the Red Cross, and now some of the ladies at church are helping me write to all the boys from Jackson County who are serving. Would you like to write to one of them?"

"Maybe. What would I say? Can I read one of yours?"

"Sure." Mom handed Joyce the letter she had just finished. "Be careful not to smudge it."

Joyce slumped into a chair and read her mother's words:

***

Dear Harvey,

My name is Verna Hill and I live in Kansas City with my husband and five children. I know this area is your home, too. Oscar is too old to serve, and my four sons are still too young to go to war, so I'm writing to you, another mother's son, to thank you for serving our country and to let you know I'm praying for you. I'm asking God to protect you and bless you and bring you home safe and sound. This Bible verse always comforts me when I am lonely or afraid. I hope it encourages you, too.

God bless you, Harvey. I look forward to meeting you when you return home.

Your prayer partner,
Mrs. Verna Hill

***

"That's nice, Momma. I'll give it a try." She reached for fresh sheet of stationary, and Mom pointed her to the next name on the list, Rex Harris. Joyce leaned back in her chair, holding her pencil to her chin, conjuring up her words. Slowly, she began to write, carefully lettering each word.

***

Dear Rex,

My name is Joyce and I am 12 years old. What is it like to be a soldier? Do you have to fight every day, even on the weekends? That would be hard. What do you eat for breakfast? I like pancakes best. I wonder where do you sleep? Do you sleep in your uniform or in pajamas? My little brother Buster has army men on his pajamas. My mom says we should pray for all the soldiers, so I'll pray for you at bedtime. When it gets scary, I hope you find a good place to hide. Come home soon.

Your friend,
Joyce Hill

***

Mom read Joyce's letter with a smile. "Come here, you," she said pulling Joyce close. "What a fine letter. It's just right. We'll send it off and who knows? Maybe he'll write back to you."

That prospect thrilled Joyce as she reached for another sheet.

Joyce soon became quite the little letter writer, telling bewildered soldiers all the adventures and struggles of her life as a twelve-year-old. In return, she received letters almost every week from soldiers who wrote back to her, adopting her as their kid sister.

Mom determined to do more than her letter-writing campaign. She led the neighborhood efforts to collect newsprint, rubber, and tin cans for the war effort. Like most women, she gave up nylon stockings and used an eyebrow pencil to draw the missing seam on the back of her legs.

At Parkway Church, a guest speaker from the Baptist World Alliance talked about the millions of refugees displaced and in need and the relief efforts that were underway. Mom stayed after the service to ask how our church could help with this crisis. Rather than try to send supplies herself, Mom determined to raise funds for the underfunded relief agencies already at work. So, as president of the Women's Missionary Union at Parkway, she led the church to raise extra dollars for refugees around the world. Mom especially liked putting on spaghetti suppers and bake sales, because that way she could be feeding people here *and* there—in the neighborhood and across the ocean. Just the thought of families homeless and hungry troubled Mom deeply and personally. Her hospitality at home extended as far as her hands could reach.

***

During the war and for several years after, Mom and Pap worked with the teenagers at Parkway, often hosting a dozen or more kids for meetings or meals in their home. One Sunday evening, all the kids came over for root beer floats. Guys and girls from the neighborhood joined in until the house bulged with teenagers, but I never knew my parents to run out of food, let alone ice cream. When the glasses were all used up, Mom spooned the ice cream and A&W into mugs and coffee cups, even cereal bowls.

Everyone was enjoying the evening until Mr. Weaver came to the door asking for his son, Tommy.

Pap knew by his expression something was wrong. "Is everything okay, Duane?"

Mr. Weaver shook his head and spoke softly, barely above a whisper. "We just got word, Oscar. Our older boy, Owen, got killed in Italy—Salerno. His tank was hit." His voice broke as he choked on the words. "I need to get Tommy home to his mother."

Pap put his arms around Mr. Weaver as he broke down, burying his face in Pap's shoulder. "I'm so sorry, Duane. So sorry."

In a moment, Mr. Weaver gathered himself and took Tommy out on the porch to tell him the tragic news.

When they had gone, a dark gloom settled over the house, with lots of tears and hushed conversations as the news scattered around the house. Pap sat down in his chair beside the fireplace, the glasses were all cleared away, and the kids gathered around him, crowding into the front room and covering the furniture, floor and piano bench.

Joy Baker began the conversation. "I can't imagine what the Weavers must be feeling. And then to think how many have died. We all know someone. My uncle Robert is in the Pacific, and we pray for him every night."

Several others mentioned their older family and friends who were serving. It struck me that our time might be fast approaching.

"Owen was just three years older than me," I said. "If this war goes on, it will be our turn to fight."

Others admitted the same reality.

Pap slowly rocked and smoked his pipe as the kids talked it through. Eventually, all the kids seemed to be looking his way, waiting to hear what he might have to say. When he did speak, his words fastened in our memory, wisdom we would revisit in many circumstances.

"I reckon we're all going to die someday, no choice about that. And, young or old won't matter much, whether we're eighteen or eighty. When we die, it's all the same. Our lives are just a mist, like the morning dew, the Bible says. We're here and then we're gone. That's the truth of it." Not a sound in the room as Pap continued.

"Now, what counts is how we live our lives, to love God and to love our neighbors as we love ourselves. Jesus taught us that to lay down our lives for others is a godly thing, the best thing. So I say, we have one life. I reckon we better make it count for something, make it count for others. A few of us may have a chance to make our life and death count for many. That's what Jesus did, and I guess that's what Owen did, too. God bless him."

The kids stayed at our house till nearly midnight, talking, praying for the Weavers, not anxious to go home or let the evening end. Not often did kids like us come face to face with the ultimate realities. A tragic loss and Pap's words put it in perspective.

***

The trains roared into Kansas City's Union Station most every hour of the day and well into the night. Early in the war, most trains headed east, freighters loaded with all the materials of war, from rations, blankets, and uniforms, to tanks, trucks, and heavy artillery. Troop trains rolled through packed with new recruits and draftees heading off to God knows where.

Later in the war, as Germany collapsed, the trend turned around to the west as the war in the Pacific raged on. As you might guess, trains were constantly in need of maintenance and repair, and nearly as many as rolled into Union Station also spent time in the roundhouse and railyards, as mechanics struggled to get engines in and out and back on the line.

Pap worked twelve- to sixteen-hour days, often seven days a week, and twenty-four-hour shifts were not uncommon. On those rare occasions when the workload lightened, Pap would be sent to wherever his skills were in short supply, short stents in St. Louis, Springfield, Fort Scott, Rolla, wherever a train broke down—Pap worked them all.

I remember going days without seeing Pap. He often left for work before we came down for breakfast. At night, I tried to stay awake until I heard him come up the stairs, too exhausted for anything but sleep. Mom kept the family together and managed as best she could.

One evening, we sat down for supper without Pap in his usual spot at the head of the table.

"Where's Daddy," Joyce asked. "Still at work again?"

We were all grumpy and tired of this strange family life without Pap.

Mom sat a bowl of creamed potatoes on the table with the pork chops and sat down. "Yes, he's at work. Do you kids realize how important your father's job is right now? The trains carry everything for the war, the troops and all their supplies and food."

Buster perked up and chimed in. "And all their guns and bullets and grenades."

Mom nodded. "That's right, everything they need to win the war, and your father is keeping those trains running. That's why he's working so much. That's why he's gone from us. Everyone has to do their part and each family has to make sacrifices, and this is our sacrifice for the war effort. It's not too much ask, is it, especially compared to what other families have to sacrifice? What about the children of our soldiers, not seeing their fathers at all?"

"Yeah, at least our dad's not gonna get blown up or shot down," Buster said, adding the obvious truth.

It made me proud to think of Pap working hard and so much depending on him, but we depended on him, too. We needed him more than anyone, even the railroad.

***

To the west of our house up the street was a vacant lot, the only level ground available for neighborhood ball games. Chick Elementary, seven blocks away, had a huge yard but was built on the side of a hill, not a good place to play unless you ran on the downhill side of things. So, the vacant lot became our stadium, with perpetual bare spots from our baseball diamond and a wide patch of dirt across the whole field from countless football games.

One bright October Sunday, Pap drove us home from church, and as we passed the lot a handful of boys tossed a football around. Kenny Nolan, our paper boy who lived around the corner on Jackson, held the ball and waved sheepishly, afraid he might be scolded for skipping Sunday School that morning.

Pap waved as we passed and pulled into our driveway. "Verna, can we wait dinner for a little while, maybe an hour?" Pap asked.

Mom nodded, knowing full well what Pap was thinking. "I suppose so. Kids, you heard your dad. We'll eat a little later today."

As Pap got out of the car, he pulled off his jacket and tie and handed them to Mom. Then he sat down on the top step to slip off his only pair of dress shoes and his socks, and rolled up his suit pants a couple of turns. "You boys want to come along, play a little football before dinner?"

We didn't need much encouragement as Buster, Dan, and I quickly shed our church clothes and pulled on our jeans.

We walked up the street and Pap hollered at the boys, "You need a few more? Can we play?"

Kenny's face lit up with surprise. "Sure! Mr. Hill's on my team!" The usual argument broke out and was resolved the same way as always—Pap and Dan on one team, Buster and I on the other. Fair enough.

If there's a better way to fill an October afternoon than playing sandlot football with your friends, it would be playing sandlot football with your friends and your dad.

After two hours or so, Mom sent little Jack up the street to call us to dinner. She wasn't even upset when we came in sweaty and dirty, Pap's white shirt rumpled and wet.

He kissed Mom on the forehead and gave her a squeeze, a little thank you for understanding.

Pap never said a word that afternoon about Sunday School, no lecture for Kenny or the other boys, not even a reminder—just playing football with the boys, and they loved him for it.

***

Mom's Uncle Harley was actually not a blood relation. Harley Atchison married Grandma Campbell's sister, Zora, to make him an uncle by marriage, but always family to us. Tall and gruff, with close-trimmed flat top hair, Uncle Harley scared us when we were little, but we soon saw his softer side. Harley served as a proud member of the Kansas City Police Department, a sergeant when I was a teenager. On more than one occasion, I escaped a well-deserved speeding ticket due to Uncle Harley's intervention. I appreciated his wise mix of law and grace, no nonsense and second chances.

When I turned fifteen, I wanted to learn to play a stringed instrument and set my heart on the violin. My music teacher at school loaned me a junior model that looked and sounded pretty rough, at least when I played it. I brought it home and practiced almost every day. My family soon decided that the ideal place for me to practice my violin was at the picnic table in the back yard, which was fine with me, until the weather turned and winter came on. Then I moved back in the house.

One evening, I sat on the piano bench practicing my latest assignment and making a mess of it.

Pap stood it as long as he could before he looked over the top of his newspaper. "Son, could you finish upstairs?"

I didn't argue or complain, knowing full well how bad it sounded.

Then one evening, when Uncle Harley and Dottie came over for dinner, Pap mentioned that I was learning to play the violin. Uncle Harley asked me to show him my instrument. He looked it over carefully and pronounced it the worst violin he had ever seen. Apparently, that was saying something, because to my surprise, Uncle Harley not only played several stringed instruments, he also constructed instruments himself by hand.

I had no idea. Mom and Pap had always known about Uncle Harley's love of music and unique woodworking skills, but it was news to me.

After insisting that I play a piece for him, Uncle Harley seemed pleased. "Mel, you're coming along just fine. We need to find you a standard-size violin, that's for sure. This one's junk, and you don't need that little model at your age. You just keep working at it. You have a nice touch and a good ear."

His kind words encouraged me, but I had no idea how I'd ever get a real violin to play.

***

Later that evening, the two men retired to the front porch for a smoke. Uncle Harley smoked La Prosa cigars, a cheaper Clear Havana brand, and before Pap could reload his pipe, Harley offered him a cigar.

"Try one of these," he said. "They're really smooth. You'll like 'em."

Pap laid his pipe aside. "Thanks, I'll give it a try."

As darkness fell and the local insects swirled around the streetlights, Harley raised the subject again. "Oscar, I'd be pleased to help you get Melvin a new instrument. I hate to think of him trying to learn on that little piece of kindling."

"Well, I've been meaning to ask you. What does a decent violin cost these days? I know they're expensive."

Harley nodded in agreement. "Yeah, real expensive. That's why I learned to make my own. I don't know how many hours I spent building instruments, all the time I could spare over about seven years."

Pap couldn't imagine such a project.

"I tell you what," Harley continued. "I've got a violin at home in my shop. It's almost finished. It's the third one I've made, and it's the best one I've done. I'd like to give it Melvin, as a gift, if you don't mind."

Pap objected out of hand. "Can't let you do that. That's really kind of you, but that's too much. I'll pay you for your work. That's only fair. What would you charge if you sold that violin?"

"Well, to tell you the truth, I'd charge at least $1500 for that instrument."

Pap almost choked on his cigar and shook his head. "I'm not sure I could pull together 150 bucks, Harley, let alone 1500."

"Oscar, just let me give it to the boy. I've got no kids to give it to, and Mel wants to play. It would make me happy to see him play it, a violin I made with my own hands."

Pap mulled it over for a moment or two, saddened to think he couldn't provide what his son needed. "Well, I reckon it will have to be a gift, because I can't pay you what it's worth." Pap's words caught in his throat. "I sure thank you. I appreciate it very much," he said, choked with emotion. "Mel will be thrilled, so pleased to know you made it for him."

Giving gifts came so naturally to Pap, but being on the receiving end felt awkward, humbling, uncomfortable.

Uncle Harley came to his rescue. "Don't you think a thing about it. I appreciate you letting me do for your boy what I'd do for my own, if I had one. Makes me feel like a proud father myself. So thanks for that, Oscar."

Pap puffed his La Prosa in peace, grateful for the gift and the giver.

Pap was right about me too; I loved my new instrument, admiring Uncle Harley's handiwork. The next year, when I played in the orchestra at Southeast High, guess who showed up at our spring concert? Uncle Harley and Dottie sat with Mom and Pap, proud of his craftsmanship, and proud of the kid playing it, too.

***

At work one day in the Frisco yard, Pap had a few minutes while waiting on some materials to be delivered. He found some long glass tubing and had an idea. Super heating one end, he shaped it down to a tiny opening. He fitted the other end with a rubber plunger on a metal rod. Then, after letting it cool, he filled the tube with water and inserted the plunger and rod like a giant syringe. Much to his delight, he had created a state-of-the-art water gun that would shoot a tight stream nearly thirty feet. Next, he filled a five-gallon bucket with water to allow for speedy refills and set up his new weapon in the undercarriage of the engine, out of view.

As he went about his work, he watched for unsuspecting targets coming within range. Several railroaders went home that day wet behind the ears and not sure why. As much fun as he had at work, Pap couldn't wait to take his new toy home.

Joyce's friend, Eva, came to our house one Saturday evening, one of her first visits to our home. Her first experience made her wonder what kind of family lived in the big green house down the street.

Eva Barnes was raised in a no-nonsense kind of home, with loving parents who Imagine her surprise when she walked into a full-blown neighborhood water fight, dozens of kids running around our house with anything that would hold water. Balloons were flying, and whole buckets of water splashed on whoever came in range. Eva hesitated at first, wearing a new dress and not wanting to get wet before dinner. were strict and conservative, not given to pranks or rough-housing. When she climbed the front porch steps, she couldn't believe her eyes.

There was Pap, an ornery grin on his face, sitting on a chair in the front doorway working his homemade water cannon, pumping with his right hand and aiming the long glass tube with his left, shooting a steady stream across the porch and into the yard.

Mom carried two pitchers while running back and forth from the kitchen, trying to keep Pap's five-gallon bucket full so he could keep up his attack on anyone who dared to cross the front yard.

"You girls better get in here," Mom called.

Joyce and Eva hurried inside and watched the rest of the battle through the dining room window.

This was Eva's first impression of my parents, the ringleaders in a huge water fight that engulfed the whole neighborhood.

***

My one ambition as a high school student was to become an architect. I enrolled in every math class offered at Southeast High School, along with the drafting and shop classes. From my third-floor classroom, I gazed across the football field toward the Kansas City skyline and dreamed of adding my own creations—magnificent bridges and towering buildings filling in the gaps—but during my senior year, my enthusiasm for architecture began to wane.

I knew for certain that I wanted to go to college, but graduating at just sixteen, I had no income or savings to pay for school. For the moment, the railroad offered the best job available, and Pap offered to take me on as his apprentice. Never thought I would work on the railroad, let alone with Pap, but I needed a job, and all that math and drafting might come in handy after all.

Pap was a demanding teacher. He typically explained something once, demonstrated it once, and then put me to work, expecting me to remember and do it correctly—no repetition, no practice, just see and do.

I learned quickly to give him my complete attention. Growing up, I had never given much thought to Pap's work, but seeing it firsthand, I was amazed at his skill, the calculations he did in his head, and the strength in his hands and arms. The way he maneuvered the heavy sheers, cutting and trimming the sheet metal, running pipe perfectly aligned and fit, it looked simple in his hands, almost automatic, but I soon knew better. Pap was a craftsman, a master mechanic. His standards soared beyond my novice skills, but he never let me be satisfied with inferior work, and he never repaired my mistakes.

"Do it again, son," he would say, "and this time measure from the edge, not from the weld. Mark it from the center and figure the angle of the cut to match the angle of the duct. It's got to be flush."

It was up to me to fix whatever problems I created, sink or swim. Some days I wondered if I'd ever learn to match Pap's skill.

When I got it right, he would run his hands over my work and say, "Now this is fine. That's a mechanic's work right there."

The only real problem between us boiled up at the end of the day. When the whistle blew and the men lined up to punch the clock, I wanted to get going as quickly as possible. Whether I planned to meet some friends or see Eva, I didn't want to stay at work one minute beyond the whistle, but Pap had an unshakable routine. He worked in the shop until the whistle, no picking up early. Then, he would put his tools way, everything in its place, and on to the washroom where he would clean up, change out of his dirty overalls and boots. Slowly and deliberately, he followed his end of the day ritual while I tried to hurry him along, but Pap would not be rushed.

"I have two speeds, son, and the other one is slower than this one."

Those words grated on me all the more as I waited each day to get going. Sometimes we didn't speak on the way home, equally annoyed with each other. By the next morning, when Mom handed us our lunch pails, all was forgiven for another day.

***

I wasn't around one afternoon when Pap took my little brothers downtown to Renner's to get some shoes. Having good shoes on our feet was important to my father, for some reason. Maybe he went without decent shoes when he was a boy after his dad died, but for whatever reason, he paid attention to our shoes and when they got ragged, he bought us a new pair.

So off they went, Pap, Buster, Dan, and Jack, who was just eight years old. Picking out shoes was not a complicated process with Pap—nothing stylish or flashy. He wanted something sturdy and economical, though he would pay a little extra for quality, the kind that could be re-soled if needed.

Buster wanted black shoes, while Dan and Jack went for the basic brown. The clerk tossed their old shoes in a bag and they walked out in their shiny new shoes.

The boys hadn't been home an hour when Pap stepped out on the porch and saw them playing 'kick the can' down the street, those new shoes already scuffed up. He called them up and questioned their basic intelligence to so mistreat their new footwear.

Then a solution came to his mind. "Come with me, boys."

They trapesed around the house and, as they passed the tool shed, Pap grabbed an axe and they continued down the path towards the woods below the house.

Jack and Dan were more than a little nervous about that axe. Could Pap really be that upset about messing up their new shoes?

Buster, being a little older, was not so worried.

Pap began to cut some branches from the brush and the low hanging tree limbs, branches that were mostly straight with a crook or a bend on one end, like a crude hockey stick. He cut four or five sticks and laid them in a pile.

"Pick 'em up, boys. Bring them along." Pap put his axe away and led the boys back to the street in front of our house.

"Now, let's see here. Can you play 'kick the can' without using your feet? Use these sticks. That'll be a lot more fun. We could set up a goal on each side, just a line to get across."

Buster was quick to expand the idea. "Whoever scores gets to whack you with the stick, right in the shin."

Thus was born the game of "Shinnie," the roughest game in the neighborhood. Their shins were black and blue, but their shoes looked real nice.

***

The news came on a summer evening, shouted up the street as Pap collected fresh tomatoes in the garden. Roy Hopkins just down the street heard the news first on the radio and couldn't help but holler to anyone who had ears. "The Japs surrendered! The war is over!"

Pap hurried in the house to tell Mom and turn on the radio. "Verna, the war's over. They just announced the surrender."

Mom stopped peeling potatoes for dinner and looked up in surprise. "Wonderful!" she exclaimed. "Finally, it's over. Praise God."

Instantly, we all gathered around the radio to hear it for ourselves, news almost too good to be true. With our hopes confirmed, the celebrating began in earnest.

Pap turned off the radio and gave directions. "Mel, put on that Tennessee Ernie Ford record, the second side, and turn it up nice and loud." Offering his hand to his surprised wife, he said, "C'mon, Verna, let's dance."

Mom rose and took off her apron, and away they went, across the floor and around the dining room table and around again.

Joyce grabbed her reluctant little brother, Danny, and danced along, though no one would ever recognize their steps.

Buster and I clapped with the music and cheered them on. Such sheer joy I had rarely seen, our parents beaming as they swirled around our house.

I quickly understood their feelings. I turned seventeen just the week before the surrender. Had the war dragged on, I would've soon been in uniform, followed by my brothers, one by one. Mom and Pap celebrated their family intact, their children safe and sound, in a world at peace. No wonder they danced.

After dinner, we piled in the old Chevy and Pap drove us downtown to Katz for sundaes and floats. People pranced about everywhere, the place packed, but no one got annoyed.

A citywide party broke out that evening and strangers behaved like long lost friends. Flags waved from rooftops and storefronts. Fireworks all around sounded like battle, but we all knew better. The fighting was finished. Peace came marching home like a parade.

Chapter 5 – All in the Family

"Families are messy.
Immortal families are eternally messy.
Sometimes the best we can do is to remind
each other that we're related for
better or worse... and try to keep the
maiming and killing to a minimum."
~ ***Rick Riordan***

I'd seen Eva around the neighborhood a lot since the Barnes's lived just down the street. She and my sister Joyce shared a locker at Southeast High. I would pass them in the hall or on the stairs, and Joyce ignored me, of course, but Eva always noticed me with a friendly smile, her brown eyes and long brown curls capturing my attention.

I started carrying Eva's books while walking home from school with the neighborhood kids, much to the irritation of my sister, who pestered me until I lugged her books too.

After youth group meetings at church or ballgames at school, I generally had a carload of kids to take home from all around the neighborhood. By then, I had my own car, a '37 Chevy coupe that I'd painted dark blue with some paint I got from work at the Frisco. I always made a place for Eva next to me, even squeezed between me and the door on my left if necessary, and I always dropped her off last with a goodnight kiss.

Still too young to go out on real dates, Eva's parents would only allow me to take Eva to church services. For months, she and I attended church all over Kansas City, all brands and all kinds—revival meetings, youth rallies, prayer meetings, gospel concerts. We scoured the religion page of the Star for any opportunity to spend an evening together. Sometimes I drove, but if the weather was nice, we took the streetcar and walked. Being together... that was all that mattered.

In just weeks and months, we fell fast in love, our excitement tempered with a sense that our being together felt natural, normal, even pre-ordained. Before long, we couldn't imagine life without the other. Eva and I were meant to be together.

We married in June of 1947 on my parent's twentieth anniversary. I was almost nineteen and Eva not quite sixteen, just kids really. Eva and I knew even then that, although the railroad supported us as we were married, we would be following a different path into the future.

***

I'd been working with Pap on the Frisco for nearly a year when my life began to turn in a new direction, one I never anticipated and struggled to define even to myself. On a warm summer evening after dinner, I found Pap on the front porch reading the paper. I sat down on the edge of the porch and leaned back against the cool brick post. When Pap laid aside the paper to light his pipe, I raised the subject, unsure of how he might respond.

"Pap, there's something that's been on my mind lately. Not sure how to tell you about it, but it has to do with my work on the railroad."

He nodded as he puffed his pipe. "What's on your mind, son?"

"Well, you know I've had lots of ideas about the future, things I want to do, jobs I thought I might like. And there's nothing wrong with the railroad. It's a good place to work, a decent living, and I've learned a lot already."

Pap listened intently. "What are you wanting to do, Mel?"

"I think God is calling me to preach, to be a pastor." I watched for a stunned expression to cross his face but saw only a gentle nod of his head, as if he had been anticipating this conversation for a long time.

"Can't say I'm surprised to hear that, son. It's crossed my mind before. Your mother and I have talked about it. If that's what God wants for you, that's the thing you should do."

I felt my anxiety drain out of me as I stretched my legs across the painted floorboards. "Sounds like you and Mom knew about this before I did."

He smiled and shrugged. "You've always had a good heart, a heart for God. We could see it. The railroad's not for everybody. You work hard and do the job, but it's not the life for you, I can see that. It doesn't suit you, and that's okay, son."

"Thanks, I'm glad you see it that way. I do plan to keep working with you for now, while I figure this out and decide what I need to do. I thought I'd go see Brother Herald and see what he says."

"Yeah, he'll know what you need to do to get started."

We sat listening to the cicadas and the kids playing kickball down the street.

After relighting his pipe, Pap continued. "It's a wonderful thing to be called by God, and it's a big job, more than I can imagine. On the railroad, I can teach you everything you need to know, but I'm afraid I won't be any good to you in this job, Mel. I don't know about such things. I won't be much help."

I could hear the resignation in his voice. "Pap, you and Mom raised us kids, teaching us right from wrong, living out your faith all my life. You've done more than anyone to help me find my own faith. I wouldn't care a thing about it if it weren't for you and Mom."

As the streetlights flickered to life, I stood and stretched and followed Pap to the door. Before stepping inside, he turned and put his hand on my shoulder. Face to face with brimming eyes, he reassured me of what I had always known. "I'll do whatever I can to help you, son. I'll always be in your corner."

"Thanks, Pap."

***

I stopped by the church after school that same week. Brother Herald welcomed me to his tiny study, lined with crowded bookshelves that left barely room enough for his desk and a couple of folding chairs. We sat down and I noticed his credentials in simple black frames hanging on the pale blue wall behind him—Certificate of Ordination, Bachelor of Arts, Master of Divinity—all of them faded yellow with the years.

"I'm glad you dropped by, Melvin. How's Eva and your folks? Is everything all right?" Brother Herald asked, curious why I made this unscheduled visit. I put his mind at ease.

"Sure, everyone's fine. We're doing well. Just needed to talk, if you have a few minutes."

"Of course." He settled back into his chair. "What shall we talk about?"

"Well, I've been thinking about my job and I just don't think I'm cut out to work on the railroad my whole life like Pap. And to tell you the truth, I've been thinking a lot about your job. Could you tell me how you know when you are called to the ministry?"

Brother Herald didn't seem any more surprised than Mom and Pap. "I wondered when we might have this conversation," he began. "I could see something of God's hand on you, Melvin. The way you see the world, the way you understand people, their thoughts and feelings, suggest to me that you may have a pastor's heart. When you went to work on the railroad with your dad, I prayed that it might help you discern what God has in mind for your life. I guess it did."

I was amazed that he could so easily read my thoughts and know my struggle.

"I had some other plans," I confessed, "At least I thought I did, but I can't shake this feeling that God is asking something of me, some kind of plan for me to be involved in his work. I never even imagined myself as a preacher. I'm no public speaker."

Brother Herald seemed to identify my feelings before I could express them. "I remember having those same feelings when God called me to be a pastor. I felt so inadequate and unworthy. Why in the world would God call me?"

"That's it exactly. Why me?"

"Why *not* you, Melvin? God can use anyone he chooses, can't he? Even ordinary people like you and me."

I left the church that day sobered but encouraged, with a sense that I was embarking on a journey that would lead to God knows where, doing God knows what. I was eager and fearful at the same time.

My fear turned into sheer terror when Brother Herald announced the next Sunday that I had been called into the ministry and would be preaching my first sermon the next Sunday. No waiting around—if you're called, get up and preach.

I spent the week feverishly poring over my Bible and a few borrowed commentaries, trying to find something I could say worth hearing. Mom and Pap encouraged me along, letting me bounce around my thoughts and practice my sermon on them when Pap would rather have read the paper.

Eva told her parents that I would be preaching on Sunday night, and they had decided to come hear me, too—all I needed: more pressure.

When Sunday night came a big crowd showed up, mostly to encourage me, only a few to watch me crash and burn. I didn't realize what a safe and supportive place I had to stick my toe in the water of ministry, and I appreciated their eager faces as I stepped to the pulpit and opened my Bible.

I can't remember what I said that night at Parkway, and I'll bet no one else does either.

Our senior deacon, George Johnson, shook my hand after the service and spoke with brutal honesty. "Melvin, you're a preacher. Not a very good one, but you're a preacher." I wasn't sure how to respond until he continued. "But that's all right. You'll go on to school, you'll study and you'll learn and you'll do better. But you're a real preacher."

I later told Pap what Mr. Johnson said, and he smiled and chuckled. "I guess that's the truth of it, son.

You did a good job tonight, but you'll do better when you get your education. It's like being my apprentice. You started out not knowing much, but you learned and improved every day. I guess now you're apprenticed to Brother Herald and other pastors who have been doing it a long time."

It made good sense to me.

My last day on the railroad conjured up a strange mix of emotions. The Frisco yard never felt like home to me, but I walked away saddened to think I'd never work alongside my father again. I'd never again be part of Pap's life on the railroad that meant so much to him. Yet, my melancholy was tempered with anticipation as I began my theological studies and began to look for opportunities in ministry.

As I left Pap behind in the railyard, I embarked on a new adventure.

***

"Oscar, it'll never happen again, I swear it. Hell, I don't know how it happened this time, but I can't lose my job over it. You gotta help me." Hank Evans was a desperate man. Normally a reliable worker and a better than average metal fabricator, he showed up for his shift one evening drunk, stammering and staggering around, until Sarge caught sight of him and sent him home.

The verdict had not yet come down from Mr. Stevens, but good men had been fired for less. Pap had been elected a union steward, giving him the job of filing grievances and representing workers in disciplinary matters.

Hank clung to Pap's shoulder as he pleaded his case. "Just don't let 'em fire me. Suspension's bad enough, but I gotta have this job. I got four kids and bills to pay. We've been livin' paycheck to paycheck. They just can't fire me over this."

Pap shook his head. "Sure they can, Hank. They have every right to fire you. There's nothing in the contract that says you can show up for work drunk. Now, I'll talk to Mr. Stevens, but I don't know what good it will do."

On his first break, Pap climbed the stairs to the railyard offices. Two women worked in the front office, their green metal desks facing each other. The walls were cluttered with faded railroad maps and schedules. Over the file cabinets hung pictures of every model of locomotive in the Frisco's history, with the new diesel in bright orange and white on the end.

Patty Austin, the older of the two, ran the office and for the most part the whole railroad or so it seemed. "Can I help you?" she asked without looking up from her typewriter.

"I'm Oscar Hill, union steward. I would like to talk with Mr. Stevens. It'll only take a minute."

Her expression was unfriendly despite her forced smile. "I know who you are, but I don't have you down for an appointment. Mr. Stevens is busy this morning." She had never tried to turn Pap around before.

He nodded and kept his voice low and polite. "I'm afraid it needs to be now. It's a disciplinary case. Won't take long."

Reluctantly, she rose to her feet and gently rapped on the supervisor's door. She returned a moment later with a terse invitation. "Mr. Stevens said he will give you five minutes. That's all the time he has for you this morning."

Pap nodded and thanked her for her trouble. When he stepped into Mr. Steven's office, he recognized the room from his first visit nearly six years before, that whole circus episode. Now he was negotiating for someone else's job.

Mr. Stevens sat at his wide mahogany desk strewn with files and paperwork under a green banker's lamp. Behind him a broad window gave him a bird's eye view of the north end of the railyard towards the river. He leaned back in his chair as he spoke. "So, what's on your mind, Mr. Hill? Something that can't wait?"

"I need to speak with you about Hank Evans."

"I'll bet you do. Let me guess. You want it put in the union contract that sobriety is not required around here. Hell, we might as well have happy hour before the evening shift, serve margaritas. Have a few beers at break time. Is that what you're after?" he asked, his words dripping with sarcasm.

"No excuses, Mr. Stevens. A fool thing like that put him at risk and would put plenty of other men in danger. We get enough men injured or worse around here. No excuses. We can't have drinking on the job or before the job."

Mr. Stevens shrugged and pointed at Pap. "Damn right. You want to be the one to tell him? He's done on this railroad. Union or not, he's finished."

Pap heard him out, standing in front of his desk with his cap in his hands. "What I'd like to do is see him suspended, as long as you like, without pay, and then bring him back. He's never been in trouble before, not on the job. Punish him, send the message, put him on probation for a year or two, but keep him on. I hate to see one foolish mistake ruin a man." Pap paused, waiting as the supervisor considered his words.

"Is this man a friend of yours? Why are you taking up for him?"

Pap shook his head. "No, not really. Hank's a railroad man with a family, like most of us. He's got four little kids who don't know what their father did. They need a roof over their heads and food on the table."

Mr. Stevens rose to his feet and shook his finger at Pap. "Don't put that on me, Mr. Hill. I'm not responsible for feeding that man's family."

Pap took a deep breath and spoke in a low voice. "I'm afraid you are responsible, Mr. Stevens, because it's your decision. You put a man out of work, you take food off the table, whether he deserves it or not. Kids get hungry just the same."

The supervisor's face flushed with frustration. "God damn it, he came to work drunk! He deserves to get his ass kicked out of here. It's plain as rain."

Pap nodded in agreement. "I reckon he does. I agree, but maybe that's not the best thing to do. If you give him a second chance now, suspend him, put him on probation, but let him keep his job, he'll be grateful. He'll work hard for you. You let him stay and you won't have any trouble from him from now on. I'd bet good money on it."

Mr. Stevens seemed unconvinced. "You think so? I guess you have a lot more faith in human nature than I do, Mr. Hill. I say a drunk is a drunk."

"I know what you mean, but plenty of people can turn things around if they get a second chance. Isn't it worth it to you to let him try rather than have to hire and train a new man? He's got the skills we need and they're hard to find. You know that."

Mr. Stevens stepped back and sat down in exhaustion. "Mr. Hill, if I ever get in trouble, I want you

to be the man who goes to bat for me. You wear me out."
He wiped his brow with his handkerchief. "All right, we'll do it your way for now—a month's suspension and two years' probation. If he is so much as five minutes late for his shift, he's done, you understand me?"

"I hear you. If it's okay with you, I'll tell him your decision. Thank you for your time and hearing me out." Pap extended his hand.

Mr. Stevens stood and shook his hand. "You tell him he's damn lucky to have a job today, and if he wants to keep it, he better toe the line. So much as a beer on his breath and he's finished."

Pap turned to go, relieved and anxious to clear out before the supervisor could change his mind.

Hank Evans was waiting for Pap when he came back to his shop. He couldn't stand the waiting, his job dangling by a thread. "How did it go with the old man, Oscar? Any chance I can stay?"

"It's a month's suspension and two years' probation, but you can keep your job. They'll be watching you close, so work hard and no more trouble, you understand?"

A wave of relief crossed Hank's face as he grabbed Pap's hand like a pump handle. "Thank you, Oscar. Thank you. I appreciate your help. No more problems from me, no sir. I'll be the best railroad man in the yard."

"You do that, and you'll be fine," Pap replied. "Are you going to be okay these next few weeks?"

Hank's face indicated he had far more questions than answers. "I don't know. I'm all out of credit at Milgram's. We can manage a few days, might have to go by City Union Mission. We could take the kids and eat there and sometimes they have groceries or commodities to give out."

I knew what Pap was going to say before he spoke the words. "Hank, you go by Dave's Market on Jackson and get the groceries you need. No booze. Tell Dave I sent you and to save me the bill. You can pay me when you get back on your feet."

Hank was surprised and touched, his eyes welling up. "Thanks, Oscar, I owe you. I owe you plenty. I'll pay you back as soon as I can." He meant it, I'm sure, but such debts were almost never settled.

But the children would get fed, and that's what mattered to Pap.

***

Nobody got in more trouble than my little brother, Buster. His mix of orneriness, stubbornness, and a bent toward violence made him more than a handful for Mom and Pap. Physically, Buster was a brute, one of the best football players in the city, and a punishing boxer who did most of his training informally. I always wondered why my little brothers were so much bigger and taller than Pap or me, and Buster was the bruiser. I had boxed in high school at Southeast, and I taught Buster what little I had learned as we sparred around the house. I worried even then that teaching Buster how to fight was not a kindness to the rest of humanity, a worry that proved to be well-founded.

As a teenager, Buster's disciplinary problems were rarely the result of his initiative. He never started a fight, or so he declared, but he always finished them, often with devastating effect. Blessed with his father's strong sense of fairness, whenever Buster saw anyone being mistreated, bullied, or humiliated, he would intervene, to put it mildly. He was not big on discussion or debate.

When such a situation came to his attention, someone was going to get a beating. He was a one-man gang—judge, jury, and executioner. Utterly fearless, more than once he found himself confronted by a gang of many, the only fights he ever lost.

When Buster was sixteen, he was involved in yet another altercation at school. Pap and Mom sat in the principal's office with Buster to hear the terms of his punishment.

The principal, Mr. Bowen, explained the situation. "As you know, Wednesday afternoon your son was in a fracas in the locker room after P.E., an argument that quickly turned violent. The other boy involved was seriously injured, a broken nose and black eye. I have interviewed Kevin's parents and they are not planning to press charges, but were insisting upon Buster's expulsion or dismissal from school. After some discussion, they have agreed that your son's apology for this whole episode would, along with a one-week suspension, allow your son to stay in school and graduate next year, assuming there are no more such incidents. He would in fact be on probation."

Buster responded before his parents could speak. "I didn't start the fight and I'm not going to apologize for something I didn't do. That kid's lying. He got the worst end of it, so he's saying I started it, but I didn't start nothing. He was asking for it, and he got it."

Mr. Bowen was not impressed. "You made choices, Buster, poor choices. There was no need for such violence. Kevin has been hurt, seriously injured. That is most certainly your fault. You need to apologize."

"Well, I won't," Buster said, with his trademark stubbornness.

"If you don't apologize, you will be dismissed from school. You will not graduate. Just apologize and we can put this whole episode behind us."

Buster slumped in his chair and shook his head. "Then I guess I won't be graduating. I didn't start the fight. I'm not gonna say I did."

Mr. Bowen's face flushed in exasperation. "Mr. Hill, please talk to your son. You know what he's done. Tell him to be reasonable and apologize."

Pap took a long look at Buster before he answered Mr. Bowen. "I know my son and I believe him when he says he didn't start the fight. I taught my children to tell the truth and to admit it when they've done wrong. I also taught them to defend themselves and to defend others when need be. I'm satisfied that's what he did, and I don't reckon he should be kicked out of school for that."

Mr. Bowen stood to his feet and leaned forward, his hands on his desk. "That's the end of it then. Your son is dismissed from this school. Young man, if you change your mind in the future, the terms of your readmission will be the same. I'm sorry it's come to this."

So ended my brother's academic career. He found a job the next week, determined to make his own way. Buster never graduated from high school but did get his GED.

Keeping Buster out of trouble and between the ditches became an ongoing struggle for Mom and Pap.

***

Somehow, at some point, my parents became Mom and Pap for the whole neighborhood. No one took neighboring more seriously than they did. Our home seemed to attract wayward kids, mostly boys with nowhere to go, no place to stay, some from horrific circumstances. Others moved in for short stays while they looked for work or finished their studies. Wherever the boys came from, whatever their circumstance, Mom and Pap welcomed them into our home—an open door, a warm bed, a bountiful table, and plenty of front porch wisdom for whoever needed a second home, kept them coming. Perhaps Pap's memories of helping his mother turn their own home into a boarding house made him more willing to take in strangers.

Mom had the idea that we should build some bunkbeds. She wanted them to be double bunkbeds, stacking two full-size beds. She and Pap moved out of the large front bedroom upstairs into the smaller room down the hall, to make space, and our custom-made bunk beds turned their room into a dormitory of sorts. Even though I had moved out and Joyce would soon follow, the house bulged with the rest of the family, plus assorted others, extra brothers finding a temporary home under our roof.

Jimmy was a foster child of Mrs. Hubbard next door, but he spent most of his time at our house. His mother had been murdered and his dad sent to prison. Pap became the father he had never known.

Hubert, without a job or anyplace to stay, hitchhiked to the city to take classes at the seminary. He found a home with us, though how he ever found a quiet place to study remained a mystery, not at our house where the dining room table doubled as our ping pong table.

Frank came home with me from school one day and never seemed to go back home. His mother was an alcoholic, and he had never met his father, so he moved in. One day, Pap took Frank and me downtown to Renner's and bought him his first new pair of shoes, brown wingtips with thick soles.

Luther had survived polio, but his right side wouldn't support his weight. He walked with a crutch and swung his bad leg around as he struggled forward. His dad died in France on D-Day, and his mother had three children to raise. Luther came home with Mom and Pap from church at Parkway, where he had come looking for some help. Mom put a thick cushion in the long window seat in the dining room, so Luther could sleep without navigating the stairs. When he needed a bath, Pap or Buster or whoever was handy carried him up the stairs and back down again.

Our young guests quickly learned that life with the Hills was no picnic. Everyone helped with chores—the cooking, the cleaning, the laundry, the yardwork, the garden. Living with the Hills was free, but it was not for freeloaders. Everyone pulled their weight by helping out. Mom and Pap treated every young man that came under our roof like their own kids, the same rules and routine, the same expectations.

How many extras spent time in our family through the years, I couldn't say. What they learned about life and family, love and grace, respect and responsibility, I could only estimate. How many families would eventually grow to affectionately remember "Mom and Pap Hill," I didn't know. I only knew the door was always open.

***

It's a strange thing when your best friend falls for your little sister. After high school, my buddy Howard joined the army. While he was away, my sister Joyce became his steady pen pal, writing back and forth, and when he returned, things got serious right away. They planned their wedding for June 20, 1950, Mom and Pap's twenty-third anniversary, at New Haven Baptist Church on Prospect at Thirty-Fourth. It would be my first wedding ceremony to conduct, a chilling prospect for me.

Mom suggested that Jack needed a haircut before the wedding, so Jack stopped by the barber college for a trim. The cost for a haircut depended on whether you wanted a near graduate or a newbie to cut your hair. Deciding to take the cost-saving route, Jack took the cheapest seat in the building. By the time he escaped thirty minutes and several restarts later, he had been peeled.

Joyce was mortified when he came through the door, but Pap took it all in stride. "How much did you pay for your haircut, son?"

Jack stood staring in the mirror over the hutch in the dining room, massaging what little hair remained. "A dime, and I got six of 'em," he said.

Pap burst into laughter, but Mom was not nearly so amused.

Before the big day, Pap had a private conversation with Joyce, the sex talk. Our mother could never bring herself to talk about such things, so it fell to Pap to have the talk. No big deal with his sons, but another matter to explain things to his daughter. Whatever Pap said to Joyce, she kept the details to herself except for one part she shared with me years later. It went something like this:

"It's a beautiful thing, Joyce, a gift from God. Nothing dirty or nasty about it. It's just another way to show our love for each other. We say so with our words, the things we do for each other, the gifts we give. Well, sex is another very special way to give our love to the most precious person in our lives, our partner for life.

"Now it doesn't always start out so great. It takes time to figure each other out, but it gets better, more wonderful as you go. It's like in school: you begin just putting down words and sentences, but eventually, you're writing poetry. That's it, if you ask me, a beautiful love poem between husband and wife."

Mom busied herself sewing the bridal gown, simple, but elegant. Then, Eva, who was six months pregnant, needed a dress as Maid of Honor, maternity style.

***

As Pap stood at the sanctuary door with his lovely daughter on his arm, satisfaction swelled his heart with no tinge of doubt or regret. Joyce had chosen a good man, a soldier, a hard worker, and any fool could see from the look on his face in that moment that he was crazy in love with her.

"Who gives this woman to be married to this man?" I put the question to Pap.

"Her mother and I," he responded with a broad smile. Pap kissed his daughter's cheek and winked at me before finding his seat next to Mom.

Looking back now, I never conducted another wedding quite like my first—my kid sister marrying my best friend with my wife as Maid of Honor.

It seemed that no sooner was Joyce out the door than she came back home. Three months after the wedding, the U. S Army called Howard back to active duty as the Korean War began.

Eventually, the newlyweds would move to El Paso, where Howard served as a communications officer, never having to ship out overseas.

When his service ended, he and Joyce moved back to Kansas City to settle and raise their family.

***

Though Pap loved baseball and football and followed the games in the paper and on the radio, we rarely had the money to go to games ourselves. Besides high school football, we only had two or three exceptions.

The Kansas City Blues, our hometown minor league club, was a farm team for the New York Yankees. This affiliation had its ups and downs. Because everyone wanted to play for the Yankees, the Blues had no shortage of young, talented players, exciting to watch and see them improve. The bad news came when the Yankees would call up these young stars to the major league club. As soon as somebody played really well, they were gone. No wonder my brothers and I grew up loving the Blues and hating the Yankees for stealing all of our best players.

So it was, on a cool, April afternoon in 1951, Pap, Buster, Dan, and Jack caught the streetcar to Blues Stadium at Twenty-Second and Brooklyn. Someone at church, maybe Mr. Roark, had offered Pap four bleacher seats, and my brothers were excited to come along. As an added treat, Pap picked up some sandwiches at Arthur Bryant's and carried them into the stadium wrapped in old newsprint, as was the custom. Smelling that sliced brisket and pulled pork as they walked up Brooklyn to the ballpark was torture for my little brothers, a rare treat.

The bleachers extended down the right field line and beyond the foul pole. Pap and the boys found seats in the lower level of the outfield seats. Buster was eighteen by then, so when Pap had a beer with his sandwich, he got one for Buster, too. Dan and Jack, fifteen and fourteen, were stuck with watery lemonade nowhere near as good as Mom's.

Looking over the scorecard and filling in the names, Dan quipped, "Yep, Mickey Mouse in center today and batting third."

Jack was quick to correct him. "You dope. It's Mickey Mantle, and he's no joke. Check it out. He's hitting .361."

"Just teasing," Dan replied. "But if he keeps hitting like that, he'll be gone. I'll bet you the Yankees call him up by the end of the month. You wait and see."

The boy's fears were justified. Young Mr. Mantle played forty-five games for the Blues that spring, before the Yankees did what the Yankees always did.

Years later, Pap would tell the story of the day he and the boys saw Mickey Mantle play baseball in Kansas City. By the time he told the story to his grandchildren, Mantle had hit two home runs, including the game winner in the bottom of the ninth. Nobody got an autograph that day, but the memories lingered just as well.

***

It rained for most of three months, May, June, and July of 1951, and when the floods came, they inundated much of the Midwest. The West Bottoms of Kansas City, where the major railyards were located, took the worst of it, and the severely damaged Frisco Railyard couldn't resume full operations for eleven weeks. They laid off the entire workforce, creating all kinds of hardship for the railroaders and their families.

In April, before the rains began, Pap had been elected Chief Steward of the union's local chapter. In the first weeks of the layoff, railroaders who had been living paycheck to paycheck besieged Pap with grievances and requests for relief, but union funds were woefully inadequate to meet the requests. By Pap's count, nearly half the Frisco workforce was at risk, unable to ride out the layoff without help.

Even contacting management proved frustrating since they'd shuttered the offices too. Pap finally reached the railyard supervisor, Harold Stevens, and requested a meeting, a hearing of sorts, to determine what if anything could be done to address the dire circumstances of the men.

Mr. Stevens agreed to the meeting, but he offered no assurances. "If the trains don't run, we're out of business. That's tough for everyone. We're not a charity, Mr. Hill. We're a railroad."

The meeting was called for that same week in some temporary offices at Tenth and Grand. Pap arrived at 6:00 PM sharp with an inch-thick stack of grievances and requests for relief. Mr. Stevens was flanked by the Frisco's chief labor negotiators, Otto Meyers and Daniel Gallagher. A secretary took minutes of the meeting. No one else was present.

"There's no guarantee in your contract for this kind of circumstance, Mr. Hill," Mr. Gallagher began. "The railroad cannot be responsible for these kinds of catastrophes. It's an act of God, really. It's not our responsibility. If we can't operate as a railroad, we can't pay our workers. You understand, don't you?" It wasn't difficult to pick up on the condescension in his voice.

"I understand the railroad has to run to make money. That's the bottom line." Pap laid out his case. "I'm just wondering if there's some way we can work together to get through this mess and not lose our people, because when we are back in business, we're going to need everybody back. You don't want to try to start up again short-handed."

Mr. Meyers chimed in. "No doubt about that, but in the meantime, you have to take care of your people. Isn't that what unions are for? When hard times come, you are responsible. That's why people join a union in the first place, isn't it? That's why they pay their dues."

"No, not really," Pap responded. "People join a union so that companies will do the right thing. Our union funds are nowhere near enough to meet payroll, even for a week, let alone two or three months. Seems to me, the only solution here is to find a way to get everyone back to work now."

Mr. Gallagher seemed puzzled and annoyed. "And how do you propose we do that?"

"Well, that's why we're here. Let me ask you, Mr. Stevens. What will it take to get the trains running again? What kind of work needs to be done?"

Mr. Stevens laid out the status of railroad operations. "Our inspectors tell us the damage is severe, although we didn't get it quite as bad as the Missouri Pacific, since we're farther from the main channel. But it's plenty bad for everyone. Even with the water receding, it will be another two weeks before all the inspections are completed. What we know so far is we've got wash-out all along the lines. Most of the tracks north to the ASB Bridge and south about 2.8 miles from the roundhouse are compromised, and who knows how long it will take to do the necessary repairs. There aren't enough roadbed crews to handle so much damage. It will take months. Then, there's damage in the shops and our other buildings, tools and equipment buried in mud and debris, and the offices are ruined. It's a grand mess. The last estimate I was given was January 1, and that's just unacceptable."

Mr. Meyers summed up the railroad's situation. "So you see, Mr. Hill, a few of your men having to tighten their belts for a while is the least of our worries right now. We've got bigger issues to address."

Pap nodded as he unfolded a sheet of notebook paper from the front pocket of his overalls. He put on his glasses and leaned forward in his chair as he began. "I made a few notes here, if you don't mind. I understand what you're saying. You don't have the people you need to repair the damage and rebuild the lines, so put us to work. Don't leave all these railroad men at home while you wait on more help. We could clean up this mess ourselves. Just put us to work. What if you doubled or tripled the number of roadbed crews, stretched them thin and then filled in with our men? They can learn the job as they go. They'll be supervised. We can all do the cleanup in the shops. Those are our tools in the mud. Let us dig them out. And, we can tear out the sheetrock, redo those offices in half the time, and you don't have to pay anything but the materials and our regular payroll. Put us to work. We all have a stake in this. It's our railroad, too. I'll bet we'd be up and running by September, a lot quicker than January. What do you think?"

No one spoke for a moment, rolling Pap's proposal over in their minds.

Mr. Stevens finally spoke first. "Do you think your people would be willing to do this kind of work? It's not in the contract?"

Pap smiled as he sat back in his chair. "You just let me make that call, and when the whistle blows in the morning, we'll all be here ready to work."

Mr. Stevens looked to Meyers and Gallagher for any objections and found none. Standing to his feet, he offered his hand. "All right, Mr. Hill, you made your point. We'll try it your way. It makes sense, and if it works like you said, we'll be back in operation weeks ahead of the competition at half the cost."

As he waited for the streetcar on Grand, Pap reflected on the conversation. One reality loomed large. On the railroad, the bottom line would always carry more freight than the needs of the working man—no surprise, nothing new. As he stepped on the southbound streetcar, Pap had no idea how many groceries he had just put on the table.

***

Mom had her own ideas about how to deal with the flood of 1951. At a meeting with her women's mission group, she led the ladies to consider several suggestions before settling on the idea of a free farmer's market for families displaced by the flood. They planned to contact the churches in the area, especially those closest to the worst of the flood, and work with them and all the families they might send to our free market at Parkway. Pastor Herald loved the idea and began to make calls to his pastor friends throughout the city.

The very next Saturday, Parkway's parking lot was spread with tables and tents, crates of garden produce, boxes of Mason jars filled with canned fruits and vegetables. Other tables held homemade baked goods, all kinds of bread and rolls, cakes and pies, even homemade donuts.

People began to arrive before the setting-up was complete. By 10:00 that morning, two dozen families had come through the market, leaving with bags bulging with all they could carry and put to good use. Most folks tried to pay or offer a donation, but any money they gave went into Parkway's benevolent fund.

One woman came with her baby wrapped in a bundle against her chest and a scarf around her face, despite the heat of the summer sun. She also had a little girl, perhaps three years old, and Mom tried to strike up a conversation, but neither the mother nor the child spoke English, nothing but yes and no, which didn't help much when they didn't understand Mom's questions. Mom tried her own sign language so the woman knew she was welcome to pick up what she needed at no cost.

As the little family was leaving, Mom smiled, pointed to the sky, embraced herself, and then pointed to the woman. "God... loves... you," Mom said.

Somehow the woman got the message and folded her hands in thanks.

As you might guess, no one brought more produce for the market than Pap. His soggy garden was not at its peak, but he had plenty of ripe fruit and vegetables to share. Neighbor kids lent their hands, and Dan and Jack helped out as well, wading through the mud, row by row. Everything that was ready to eat or can was picked and packed and carried to church.

By 2:00 that afternoon, just about everything was gone, only a few odds and ends remaining, but families kept coming by. Pap stayed at the church to sweep up after Mom and the others had gone home. Pastor Herald said to tell any latecomers to come back next Saturday, but what would these families eat in the meantime? Pap hated the thought of sending people away emptyhanded.

Just as Pap finished putting everything in order, a rusty black '37 Plymouth pickup pulled to the curb. A young man jumped out, leaving his wife and two little ones looking eagerly from the window of the cab.

"Excuse me," he called to Pap. "Was there a farmer's market around here? Are we too late?" The man was a muddy mess except for his hands and face.

"I'm afraid so. Everything went pretty quickly. I'm sorry, it's all gone."

The man put out his hand with a sad smile. "That figures. Walt Jefferies is my name. Would've come sooner, but the landlord said we had to get what we wanted of our stuff, before they bulldoze the place."

Pap noticed their pickup piled with a few sticks of furniture and couple of boxes of household stuff. "Oscar Hill is my name. Sorry to meet you in such hard times, Walt. We will have another market next Saturday."

Walt nodded and looked at his tired, worried family staring out from the truck. "Thanks, but that's the least of my worries right now. We got no place to go. My kin all live in Indiana and my wife's family's in Baltimore. Came out here for work and we were just getting by before this damn flood. Lost my job, lost everything but that old truck. That's all we got left."

Pap could see the desperation of a man at the end of his rope. "Walt, you got room in the back of your truck to give me a ride home? It's not far, and I was going to walk, but if you'll give me a ride, I'll make sure you and your family get some dinner and a place to stay tonight. How about that? Is it a deal?"

Walt glanced again at his little frightened family and turned back towards Pap with a look of relief. "Sure, you bet. Plenty of room."

Mom was surprised not in the least when Pap came through the front door with Walt and his family in tow. Amazingly, she acted as if they were special guests she had been expecting. Now, this was when Mom and Pap already had Dan and Jack still at home, and four extra boys boarding with them in their three-bedroom home, but that house never seemed to reach its maximum capacity. Within an hour, Walt's family had a hot supper and his children were headed upstairs for baths and bedtime. The boys doubled-up, with Dan claiming the couch and Jack sleeping on the roll away. Pap made some calls the next morning, and Walt started work on Tuesday as part of the Frisco's cleanup crew.

I couldn't help wondering how Walt's story would have read if, when he pulled his pickup to the curb at Parkway, with nothing left and nowhere to go, Walt had found anyone other than Oscar Hill.

***

I never knew Pap to forget a birthday or anniversary. He looked forward to those special days and always prepared some thoughtful expression of love. He had a way of knowing just what would please those he loved, what would excite his children, what would touch the heart of his one and only. Favorite flowers, favorite colors, favorite candy, favorite songs—he filed away these details in his mind for those special moments, a natural-born romantic.

My parents celebrated their anniversary each year as a major holiday, second only to Christmas in our family. Instead of getting a sitter and going out for a quiet, romantic dinner together, Mom and Pap always celebrated at home with their children, Mom cooking a special dinner and Pap preparing a huge fruit platter and churning homemade ice cream. It was a day devoted to love.

At Christmas, 1951, Pap pulled me aside to talk about a special project he had in mind for their twenty-fifth anniversary coming up in June. He showed me some pencil drawings of a large book to be made of copper with a hinged cover and two compartments inside, labeled across the top, "A Volume of Love." Pap planned to give it to Mom for their twenty-fifth, filled with thoughtful goodies—chocolates, little gifts, and a collection of Pap's own poetry—and then he would refill it every year on their anniversary, a gift that keeps on giving, a romantic heirloom.

Pap invited me to lend a hand, but I didn't have much expertise to offer. No one could cut and shape metal like Pap, so I helped him with the drafting, the details and dimensions of the project. Pap's standards had not changed since I worked as his apprentice: everything must go together perfectly.

In the months ahead, he often stayed after work to put his copper book together where he had all of his tools and could keep his surprise from Mom.

When Eva and I came back for a visit in the spring, Pap showed me and Joyce the finished product, as excited as Christmas morning. "A Volume of Love" turned out beyond my imagination, beautiful and so well-crafted, every seam smooth, no sharp edges, and the hinge moved perfectly, without a sound, made with love. On the top, Pap had outdone himself, fashioning a heart and a rose blossom from pewter embedded in the copper cover. I couldn't imagine the effort and skill such work required.

With the book completed, Pap began to plan the contents. Mom loved chocolate in any form, but everyone agreed that Price's Candy Company in downtown Kansas City made the most scrumptious chocolates around. Plus, at Price's you didn't have to buy a pre-packaged set. You could order exactly what kind of chocolates you wanted in your box. Over the years, Pap knew what tasty chocolate morsels Mom liked best, so he knew just what to order, especially the dark chocolate raspberry creams and milk chocolate hazelnut caramels. Who else would order three pounds of chocolate piece by piece? Only my father.

Pap loved poetry, especially story poems that he'd memorized in childhood. Through the years, he tried out his own words whenever he felt inspired, and Mom provided ample inspiration. On many evenings, as he sat on the porch for his after-dinner pipe, Pap would pick up a Big Chief tablet he'd borrowed from the kid's homework supplies, and scratch out a few lines, marking out words, sometimes starting over. In time, a new poem would take shape, and for their twenty-fifth anniversary, Pap had much to express.

Weeks later, finally satisfied with his effort, Pap printed his words as neatly as he could on a sheet of linen stationary.

***

By the Lake

As we stood in the night, on the lake shore there,
And I watched as the wind blew through your hair,
And the waves leaped high in their caps of white,
To splash on the shore with the sound of the night.

The wind blew cold, but I was warm inside,
For the love in your eyes you could not hide,
I thought of the joy that is ours to share,
And wondered again at the way you care.

I felt the warmth of your hand in mine,
And knew it was there through wisdom divine,
For God knew that to face the storms of life,
I would need the warmth and love of my wife.

He knew I would need someone to understand,
Someone when I failed to give me a hand,
Someone with a heart so kind and dear,
To brighten my life with laughter and cheer.

***

When the big day came, June 20, 1952, Pap couldn't wait for everyone to finish their dinner and for Mom to open her gift. He adorned the table with an arrangement of white gladiolus and blue aster, Mom's favorites. When the dishes were cleared away, the moment had arrived.

Mom opened the gift with a puzzled expression. She'd never seen anything like it, a copper box that opened like a book. Running her finger along the words "A Volume of Love," she suddenly realized without being told that she was holding Pap's handiwork in her hands.

"Oscar, what have you done? You made this for me?" Her eyes filled with tears.

Pap nodded and smiled. "Happy Anniversary, Verna." Mom opened her copper book to find her poem on top and paused to read it, wiping her eyes as she came to the end.

"It's so beautiful. You know I love you. Thank you so much."

Like I said, it was a day devoted to love. Is it any wonder that when I married Eva and when Joyce married Howard, we both chose June 20 for our wedding days? All of us hoped to find what Mom and Pap had, the kind of love, the kind of home, the kind of family worth celebrating. What a gift.

***

All of Pap's sons grew taller than their father. I was just an inch ahead of Pap, but my three brothers were all well over six feet. Jack, the youngest boy, outgrew Pap by four inches and nearly fifty pounds. As you might expect, this size advantage, even as teenagers, tempted us to test our father from time to time as we grew bigger—too big for our britches. Sometimes attitudes had to be adjusted, and Pap never hesitated to bring us back down to earth, sometimes literally.

One afternoon, Mom was putting up vegetables, canning and collecting dozens of mason jars for the shelves in the basement. The steps down from the kitchen were steep and uneven and Pap didn't want Mom carrying anything down those stairs. So, Mom relied on her sons to carry the jars down and stock the shelves for her. Jack was in the backyard with a buddy or two from the neighborhood when Mom stepped out on the back porch.

"Jack, I need you to carry these vegetables I've canned to the basement for me."

Jack nodded but didn't move in her direction.

About twenty minutes later, Mom opened the screen door and reminded him again. "Jack, I need you to come get these jars to the cellar so I can set the table for dinner."

"I will, I will," he answered, but nothing in his tone indicated he was anything but indifferent as he swapped stories with his friends.

Soon, Mom reached the end of her patience. She stood at the porch rail with her hands on her hips. "Jack, I need you to come right now and do what I asked you to do."

Again, Jack nodded and answered with typical teenage disdain. "Mom, I'll do it when I get good and ready."

I'm sure he said it showing off for his friends, but he failed to notice Pap coming around the corner of the house, just home from work. He had heard Mom's request and Jack's response and he never broke stride as he set his lunch pail on the picnic table, and with one quick swing, he hit Jack on the side of his face with his open hand, sending him sprawling in the grass, stunned and embarrassed. Pap stood over him and spoke low and slow.

"Are you ready now?" Jack looked up and slowly nodded, his ears still ringing.

"Yes, sir, I'm ready. I'll do it right now."

Pap spoke as he reached down to help him to his feet. "Don't you ever speak to your mother like that again."

We all learned a lesson that day at Jack's expense: disrespect Mom and you'll answer to Pap, no matter what your shoe size.

***

Everyone who knew Pap would eventually ask how he lost his finger. His right index finger, his "trigger finger," was gone down to his first knuckle, leaving a handy stub for tapping down his pipe tobacco or telling one of a dozen or so stories of how he lost it. One story involved chasing down Sitting Bull, who took his finger with his tomahawk. Another version involved wrestling a mountain lion back in the days when he road with Buffalo Bill. His favorite story involved "laying down the law to Verna" before she finally bit his pointing finger off at the knuckle, not something anyone could picture my mother doing.

The true story was much less dramatic but with the same end result. Pap was changing a tire on the old Pontiac when the car fell off the jack and caught Pap's finger under the wheel. He'd stepped on the porch with his mangled finger hanging by the loose skin, blood dripping on the floor.

Mom, not one to panic, wrapped his finger tightly in a kitchen towel, and then drove Pap to the hospital, where his crushed finger was removed and his remaining stub was stitched and bandaged.

Back home, his missing and bandaged finger captured everyone's attention for days. Pap's first grandson, Pete, was staying with the folks that next week. Pete was seven years old at the time and convinced that his grandpa was the person he most admired and nearly worshipped. After the accident, little Pete had lots of questions.

Pap couldn't resist having some fun with his grandson. "Pete, old Grandpa's lost his trigger finger, but that's all right. I'll just have to learn how to shoot with my left hand. I know you and I are partners, aren't we? Just alike, you and me."

Pete nodded his agreement with a proud smile.

Pap continued. "Well, since we're partners, maybe we should go have the doctor cut off your trigger finger so we can be just alike. Don't you think that would be a good idea?"

Pete's face clouded over as he pondered his grandpa's suggestion. Looking at his own tiny trigger finger, he changed his tune. "I don't want him to chop off my finger."

Pap couldn't help but tease him. "Well, don't you want to be like your grandpa? When we go the doctor, you just tell him that you and I are partners, and you want him to chop off your trigger finger just like Grandpa's."

Pete could only sit there on Pap's lap with a troubled look on his face, staring at his little index finger.

A few days later, Pap was headed back to the doctor for a checkup and to get stitches removed, and Pete had to go along for the ride. When they got to the doctor's office, Pete wouldn't get out of the car. Mom told him to come along, but Pete was not budging from that back seat. His grandma's pleading had no effect, until Pap returned to the car to put his mind at ease.

"Pete, I forgot to tell you. The doctor's really busy today, so he's not going to have time to take your finger off this time. He's only going to look at my finger today."

Reluctantly, Pete got out of the car, clinging to his grandma's hand.

Mom looked at Pap and shook her head. "What have you been telling that boy, Oscar? He's scared to death."

Pap chuckled to himself as he reached down and tousled the boy's hair. "It's okay, Pete. We're partners just the same. You can keep your trigger finger for now. If you change your mind and you want to be just like Grandpa, just tell me and we'll fix you right up."

Chapter 6 – Taking a Stand

"Life shrinks or expands in proportion
to one's courage."
~ ***Anais Nin***

That same year, a new housing addition was proposed for our neighborhood, about eight blocks from us, on the other side of Chick Elementary School. My sister, Joyce, went with Pap to the meeting in a packed gymnasium with the whole neighborhood assembled, an entirely white crowd. The proposed addition would provide modest, middle-class homes for families, including black families, many of which were returning veterans who qualified for VA loans. The opposition was boisterous and rude, unwilling to bend on the unofficial racial divide that kept blacks farther north and east and away from our school district.

The real estate developer and representative of the city council spoke in favor of the new addition, but dozens were ready to speak against the measure.

Mr. Murphy, a deacon at Parkway Baptist took his turn at the microphone. "People ought to live and go to school with their own kind, not mixing in with different folks. We don't need niggers on this side of town. They have their own neighborhoods, and I don't try to move in on them. I say, no, the niggers have no business moving into our neighborhood." The audience applauded in support.

Floyd Peters who we also knew from Parkway spoke next. "Think of our schools. Just imagine classrooms half full of coloreds. How's a teacher going to teach the white kids? What kind of education will they be getting? Taking recess together? Eating lunch together? Not my kids, no thank you. You let the coloreds in, I'll be moving out before the summer's over, and I'm not the only one, I'm sure."

Shouts of agreement came from every direction. The representative from the city council took the microphone and asked if anyone present would like to speak in favor of the proposed addition. People looked around, no takers, until Pap raised his hand. The representative motioned to him to come to the mic. It was deathly still as he cleared his throat and began to speak.

"Most of you know me. I'm Oscar Hill and I'm a mechanic on the Frisco. I've lived in this neighborhood nearly eighteen years. My kids go to school here. As the man was trying to tell us, most of the families that we're talking about, colored and white, are veterans. They've been off to Europe or the Pacific fighting a war, a war they won for us. Now, I never got called to fight, too old and too busy on the railroad, I guess. But I'll tell you, I'm not going to try to tell those veterans when they come home where they can live and where they can raise their families. I believe they have earned the right to go and do as they please as citizens. I'd be proud to be their neighbor. The way I heard it, on the battlefield, white and colored soldiers fought and died together. Now I reckon they ought to be able to live and work together, too."

The only sound as he moved back to his seat was the tramp of his footsteps on the wooden bleachers. Someone called the question and a vote was taken, overwhelmingly against the proposed new addition, but Pap had spoken his piece.

***

The next Sunday, Pap drove right past Parkway Baptist Church and headed north on Cleveland Avenue.

My kid brother Jack piped up right away. "Where are we going, Daddy? Skipping church? Are we going downtown?"

Pap slowed to a stop at 39th Street and turned his head to explain. "Your mother and I thought we might try a different church this morning. I know we all have friends at Parkway, but I think this is a chance to make some new friends."

"What's wrong with Parkway, Daddy?" Jack asked. "What happened? Are we leaving?"

Pap tried to explain. "Joyce and I went to that meeting at the school the other night. Remember? We heard what some of the folks from Parkway had to say. They want to pick and choose our neighbors by the color of their skin. I won't abide that kind of thing, especially at church."

Jack and Dan pondered his words in silence as they soon arrived at Garfield Baptist Church. Not sure why Mom and Pap chose this particular church to visit, the boys climbed out of the backseat and marched into the tall gray stone sanctuary like soldiers. The Hill family filed into the pew, Pap on the aisle, as the boys stared at the stained glass made bright in the morning sun, Jesus welcoming the children on the left and calming the storm on the right. Nothing like that back at Parkway Church.

People did seem friendly enough, and just as white as Parkway. What's the big difference, the boys wondered? On the way home they stopped at Katz Drug on Main at 39th, the cheapest place for Pap to pick up his no filter Camels.

Mom, relieved that her teenagers had not grumbled or embarrassed her at church, suggested a treat. "Oscar, how about some root beer floats? They're just fifteen cents on Sunday."

Unanimous enthusiasm from the back seat indicated their general agreement.

Pap opened the back door with a smile. "Sounds good to me."

They lined up on stools at the counter each with a tall fountain glass of foamy root beer and vanilla ice cream. Jack was ready to become a regular.

"So every Sunday, it's church at Garfield and Katz on the way home, right?" Jack said as he spooned the last bit of ice cream from the bottom of his glass. Nice try, but he knew better.

Our family quickly settled into Garfield Church. Before long, Mom and Pap found themselves teaching the teenagers on Sunday evenings. Dan and Jack were in their class and Buster occasionally showed up.

Mom joined the women's missionary society, and a short time later Pap was ordained as a deacon along with his son-in-law, Howard. Garfield felt like home, at least for a while, but appearances can be deceiving. Some matters that Mom and Pap had settled long before were still lurking beneath the surface, waiting for an opportunity to emerge.

***

No one witnessed the incident except the victim, Willy Roberson, and the three men who confronted him.

It happened in the locker room at the Frisco yard where employees stored their street clothes and cleaned up after work. Willy had recently bid a welding job in the main diesel shop, and was selected over two union members with more time on the Frisco but fewer years of experience as welders. What lit the fuse in these men was not hard to determine. Willy was a Negro and therefore not in the union. He was also the first colored skilled worker in the shop above the laborer's wage. It was a double dose of resentment that led Harry Welborn and two of his buddies to take down Willy Roberson.

As Willy told the shop foreman, Harry and his crew found him alone, changing clothes after work. They jumped him from behind, pinned him down, stripped him below the waist, and Welborn threatened him with a straight razor.

"There's no room for your black ass on this railroad, nigger. You get on out of here while you're still in one piece, while you still got your balls, boy. You never know, things could go bad for you. We know where you live, that pretty little wife of yours, where your nigger kids go to school. You don't need to be around here trying to steal a white man's work. Get on down the road or there's gonna be trouble. You hear what I'm saying, boy?"

Willy found the courage to report the whole episode to Sarge, who took it upstairs to the railyard boss. A hearing was scheduled for the next week. Harry Welborn and his accomplishes would have to answer for their alleged actions.

***

Pap was sitting in the lunchroom across from his fellow mechanic, Raymond Ward. Raymond had started on the Frisco in 1938, two years after the railroad had moved Pap to Kansas City. The two had become close friends through the years. When the folks decided to leave Parkway Church and find a new place to attend, it was Raymond who invited the Hills to visit Garfield Baptist, where he served as a deacon.

As Pap and Raymond finished their sandwiches, they were discussing the whole steam versus diesel revolution which had required them to retrain and retool themselves. The last steam locomotive, massive #4524, had left the yard in 1950. It was all diesel work now—far more durable and efficient, but without the same charm and lore.

Harry Welborn pulled up a chair and sat down at the end of the table between the two men. He looked to be a hard man, an aging veteran with a broad barrel chest and a partial flat top surrounding a wide bald spot.

The kind of man that didn't mind interrupting, he offered his hand to Pap. "You're Oscar Hill, aren't you? I'm Harry Welborn. I've seen you around, though I work the other end of the yard."

Pap shook his hand and nodded. "This is Raymond Ward. He's a mechanic, on the north end, the main shop."

Welborn shook Raymond's hand. "Yeah, good to meet you. Hey, Oscar, I got this union matter, been called on the carpet. It's a little dustup over nothing, but they're having a hearing. Everybody says you are the man for the job, the only union steward that the old man listens to. I need you to speak for me, represent me at the hearing. It's next week, Wednesday. Will that work for you?"

Pap leaned back in his chair and folded his arms across his chest. "Well, it will and it won't. I'll be there for sure, but I can't speak for you."

"Why the hell not?" Welborn said with obvious agitation.

"I'm representing another man at your hearing, Willy Roberson."

Welborn's face reddened as he realized what Pap was saying. "You can't speak for him! He's not a God damned member. I'm the union man," he said, poking Pap's chest, "and you're the fucking steward. You have to be on my side!"

"Yes, but not this time," Pap replied. "They told Willy to bring representation to the hearing. He can't afford a lawyer, so he asked me to help. I said I would. You'll have to find someone else to represent you, get one of the other stewards. I won't do it."

Welborn, enraged, stood to his feet, leaned on the table and glared down at Pap. "You gonna take his side against your own kind?" He grabbed Pap by the front of his shirt and pulled him close. "What kind of bullshit steward are you? I pay my fucking dues. I'm a member, God dammit. You won't even stand up for your own people, you nigger-lovin' son of a bitch."

Pap took hold of Welborn's hand at the wrist and applied his vice-like grip. Welborn winched and released Pap's shirt, trying to pull away, but Pap wasn't finished, and his grip tightened.

Welborn's expression went from rage to panic as the searing pain intensified. "Turn me loose! Let me go! Dammit, I'm sorry! I'm sorry!"

Pap finally relaxed his grip, a purple bruise already beginning to form on Welborn's swelling wrist.

Pap spoke in a deadly serious tone. "I reckon it's not so easy to bully a man when you stand alone, is it? I'll see you at the hearing."

Welborn left the breakroom still coddling his wrist.

Raymond sat there shaking his head in disbelief. "If that don't beat all. I swear, Oscar, you don't scare worth a damn."

***

They held the disciplinary hearing in the breakroom after hours, with representatives of management, the union, and the individuals involved in the complaint. As you might expect, Welborn's version of what happened bore scarce resemblance to Willy Roberson's account. Although Welborn's two buddies stuck to his story, no one seriously doubted which account was closest to reality. Some kind of disciplinary action would have to be taken.

Pap spoke to the matter. "No excuse for it. You threaten a man, threaten his wife and children, just for coming to work and trying to do his job. That's unacceptable. Is this a safe, decent place to work or not? I say, let them go. I hate to see any man lose his job, and I've never advised it, but these guys need to go. They should be fired, or at the very least suspended."

There was no response from those gathered there, no nods or words of agreement. When the decision came down, it was clear that racist threats were considered part of the norm, not part of the problem.

Sarge read the disciplinary statement. "One year of probation for all three of you. Any further verified complaint against you during the next twelve months will result in immediate dismissal."

Willy thanked Pap as they were leaving. "Thanks for standing up with me, Mr. Hill, and for what you said."

Pap shook his hand. "Just call me Oscar if you don't mind. I hope this puts an end to it, at least for a while."

Willy didn't seem optimistic. "I hope so too, but they could still come after me at home, on the street. They won't mess with me at work for a while, but what about the rest of the time?"

Pap reached in the chest pocket of his overalls for a pencil and scrounged a scrap of paper from the table. "Yeah, you better watch yourself. Here's my address. If your family ever needs to clear out, you can always come to my place. We're not too far from you, near Swope Park. Tell your wife. Anytime she doesn't feel safe. Our phone number is right there, too. Just use it."

Willy looked at the scrap of paper, holding it up in wonderment. "Thank you. That's real kind of you."

Pap smiled and put his hand on Willy's shoulder. "I reckon we're all working men just trying to do our jobs. That's the way I see it."

Willy offered a sad smile. "Yeah, me too. I wish more folks saw things your way, Oscar. Maybe we could get along."

***

On Christmas Day, 1955, Eva and I followed our usual exhausting custom: up at the crack of dawn with our kids, a little while to catch our breath and clean up the mess, and then loading up for the two-hour drive to Eva's folks, who had moved to Gladstone on the north side of the city. Otis Barnes, Eva's father, was born on December 25, 1900, so we combined an early Christmas dinner with his red velvet birthday cake.

Then, it was on to Mom and Pap's place on the south side for the evening and yet another Christmas dinner. By the time we staggered out on the front porch to get some fresh winter air, I was more stuffed than the turkey.

Pap settled into his chair and tapped down his pipe tobacco for an after-dinner smoke. The winter evenings never seemed to bother Pap. As long as he had his pipe, he was immune to the cold. "Sit down, son. You need anything?"

"A nap more than anything. No, I'm fine. It's been a good day."

Pap struck a match and puffed his pipe back to life. Leaning down, he picked up a section of the newspaper he had laid aside and handed it to me. "Didn't figure you still get the Star up there in Maryville. I want you to see this." He'd circled an article headlined, "Negroes Boycott Buses in Montgomery."

I scanned the brief columns. "What's this about, Pap?"

"Near as I can tell, colored folks down there got fed up with riding in the back of the bus. People are walking or hitching rides to get to work. The buses in Montgomery are running near empty, losing a lot of money."

This was all news to me.

Howard stepped out on the porch and pulled up a chair next to me.

I handed him the article to peruse. "Pap, you think something like that could happen here?" I asked. "The streetcars are open seating, but our buses are segregated, coloreds in the back—always have been."

"I know, son. That's why I take the streetcar to work. Who knows? It could happen here."

Howard was not so certain. "I don't know," he said, "There'd be a heavy price to pay if you asked me. It wouldn't go well in this town. I see it every day. Whenever a colored person crosses a line, uses the wrong door, or breaks somebody's rule, there's always hell to pay. I mean there's no such thing as a correction or a warning. It's just punishment, retaliation, an all-out attack. Remember those four colored men who decided they were going to play the whites-only golf course at Swope Park a while back? They pushed it and tried to play, but their tires were slashed, windows broken, ended up having to have an extra man guard their cars while they played. It didn't go smoothly then, and it's still pretty much whites only now."

"I never heard about that, Howard," I said. "Living up north, I'm out of the loop, I guess. I wonder what started the whole bus boycott in Montgomery?"

Pap took his pipe in his hand and leaned forward as he spoke. "That's what I wanted to tell you about. Sounds like it was just one woman, a colored woman on her way home from work. It says she was sitting in the colored section of the bus when more white people got on, and when the driver told her to give up her seat, she refused. I guess she'd had enough."

"What happened?" I asked. "Did they throw her off the bus?"

"Worse than that, they called the police and arrested her on the spot. Put her in jail, but I think she made bail later on. Before you know it, colored folks are calling for a boycott. You got to admire their moxie. That took some guts."

Howard shook his head, mulling it over. "I can't imagine Joyce being in a situation where she'd have to take that kind of stand, risk being arrested or beaten and left in some alley." His words hung in the cold air as we pondered such scenarios.

Pap expressed one more thought on the matter. "What struck me was just one colored woman, all by herself, saw the wrong of it and decided to do something, to keep her seat no matter what. I reckon that's courage if I've ever seen it."

On that, we all agreed.

I thought about it on the long drive back to Maryville that Christmas night. *How much of what is wrong in the world do we take for granted, assuming it can't be addressed, that the way things are is the way they will always be, until someone says, "No more. No longer. Not today." God bless her.*

***

One evening, Pap called to see if he and Mom could come see us the next day, a Tuesday evening, after Pap got off work. Fine with us, but we couldn't remember a time when the folks had made the two-hour drive to Maryville in the middle of the week. Hard to figure what would cause to them to come so far on a weeknight.

Eva fixed a meatloaf and potatoes and Mom and Pap arrived in time for supper. By this time, we had six children—Pete, the oldest, had just turned eight, and John, the youngest, just a toddler—and all six were thrilled with a surprise visit from Grandma and Grandpa.

After the dishes were cleared away and the kids finally settled down to their evening routine, the four of us sat around the table for coffee and conversation.

That's when Pap made a strange, startling request. "Eva, would you tell Verna how you felt when you were pregnant? Just explain how it feels to be pregnant. Will you do that?"

Eva and I glanced at each other, confused, bewildered.

Mom shook her head and muttered, "I know how it feels to be pregnant, Oscar."

"I know, I know," Pap said, "But just tell her, Eva, how you felt."

So, Eva, begin to describe what pregnancy was like for her, the initial symptoms and changes, and the longer she talked, the more Pap seemed to deflate before their eyes. He pushed his coffee cup forward, crossed his arms on the table, and put his head down on his arms.

Mom reached over and patted his shoulder. "I told you, Oscar. I told you."

The truth dawned on me and Eva. "Are you kidding us? Mom, are you pregnant?"

She smiled and nodded. "I am, but your father can't believe it."

"Neither can I. You guys are having a baby? My gosh. I'm twenty-seven years old and I'm going to have a baby brother or sister? We've got six of our own, for Pete's sake."

As the shock gave way to joy, Eva and I began to celebrate.

Pap still struggled with this new reality while Mom just sat and smiled, like a hen on her nest.

The next week, we got a letter from Pap, hand-written in pencil saying simply, "Well, the doctor must be crazy, too. He says we're going to have a baby next summer."

So it came to pass, on my twenty-eighth birthday, my mother, at the age of forty-eight, gave birth to a beautiful baby girl with blue eyes and curly blond hair. Our whole family rejoiced in little Sue, our bonus baby.

Pap couldn't help but think back to when he held me, his first child, in his arms on the porch of his mother's house in Springfield so long ago. He remembered wondering if he could be a good father to his firstborn. Now, here he stood, fifty years old, holding his baby girl and wondering if he could do it again.

***

The old timers called it "tornado alley," a broad path across two states frequented by the worst of storms. From central Oklahoma heading northeast into Missouri and on towards St. Louis, lethal storms regularly cut a swathe roughly a hundred and fifty miles wide across the Midwest. Tornadoes could pop up just about anywhere, of course, but some of the deadliest storms rolled across Oklahoma and Missouri.

Those of us who lived in tornado alley learned to accept these storms as part of life, even an occasion to stand in the yard chatting with the neighbors as dark funnel clouds formed in plain sight. We only ran to the cellar when debris began to swirl in the air above us, or the roar of the storm began to swell.

Then, it's time to run for your life.

On the evening of May 20, 1957, Pap stood on his front porch looking south at the coming storm. Joyce stood beside him, holding her baby boy and calling her girls inside. The dark sky took on a greenish tinge, eerie and foreboding, and the black funnel was clearly visible dropping from the clouds.

"Is it on the ground, Daddy?" Joyce asked.

"Can't tell from here, but it's a big one. I sure hope it's not touching down, but it might be." Both were filled with dread as the tornado moved from right to left before them. "God help them if it's on the ground."

The tornado Pap and Joyce observed had touched down near Williamsburg, Kansas, and would stay on the ground for seventy-one miles, cutting a path of destruction about seven hundred yards wide across south Kansas City. Forty-four people died in the storm, hundreds were injured, and thousands left homeless. The Ruskin Heights neighborhood got the worst of it, whole blocks swept clean, no structures left standing, only a few gnarled tree trunks stripped of their branches and bark.

The next evening, Pap and Buster drove south and east to Blue Ridge Boulevard, through Hickman Mills to Ruskin Heights. What they saw staggered them. Pap had seen plenty of storm damage through the years, but nothing like this. He had no words.

"Like a bomb went off," Buster said. "Like those pictures of Hiroshima. Unbelievable. The whole neighborhood, just gone, like it never existed."

They drove back to the house in silence, pondering the destruction they had seen.

Pap sat on the porch longer than usual that night, till the early morning hours. As he puffed his pipe, he thought about the scene he had witnessed, one block untouched and the next block obliterated, one family undisturbed while their neighbors were wiped out. How could he make sense of it?

"Oscar, are you coming up to bed? It's late," Mom called from the front doorway, already in her nightgown and robe.

"I'll be along after a while, Verna. Don't wait up for me. Goodnight."

"Goodnight. Better get some sleep."

Pap could hear her climbing the creaky staircase. He stood up, stretched his back, and pounded his pipe against the brick post. Sitting down again, he tapped down another bowl of Granger pipe rough cut and thought about the randomness of life. Does God tell the storm where to go? Does he choose which homes will be destroyed and which ones will be protected? Does God always decide who lives and who dies, or does it just happen? Is it really just about the weather?

A cool breeze blew in after the storm and Pap felt a chill in the air. He thought about the parable Jesus told, about the wise and foolish builders. The wise man who built his house on the rock survived, but the fool who built on sand perished in the storm. Is that what happened here? But this wasn't about wise or foolish, and not about who deserved to live or die.

Pap stepped to the edge of the porch and looked up into the night sky, crisp and clear after the storm. He studied the stars for any hint of truth, but it only made him feel small. The questions kept coming, questions without answers. Is it all planned out, chosen from the beginning, or are we living by accident and chance? Pap had never pondered such thoughts, but now he couldn't turn loose of them.

As he stared into the sparkling sky, he settled something with God that night, breathing a prayer. "Father, my life's in your hands, whether I live or die. I don't know if you know the day and the hour or if it's all up in the air, but either way, I trust you. You've always been good to me, always heard my prayers, and I'm grateful. And as long as you let me live in this world, I'll live for you. I'll do the best I can for you."

Pap wiped the tears from his eyes and felt the burden lift, the heaviness slip away. He had his answer. As long as this life lasted, better make it count.

***

In the fall of 1957, Mom inadvertently created an uproar at Garfield Baptist Church. As the president of the Women's Missionary Union, she planned a special Sunday to highlight Baptist mission work overseas, and with Pastor Keith's approval invited a guest speaker, a young seminarian from Nigeria.

The young man, Habib Adamu, had become a Christian through our mission efforts and hoped to return to his country as a pastor or evangelist. Tall and thin, with a compelling smile made brighter by his dark African complexion, Habib stood before the congregation and told his story.

As he began, Mom heard a rustling behind her and turned to see the Hammonds, the Smiths, Mr. Bolton, and a few others gathering their jackets and leaving by the rear door of the sanctuary. Habib did not seem to notice, but Mom was red-faced with embarrassment, as was Pastor Keith. Neither one had any inkling of what they had done.

Never before had there been a colored man in the pulpit of Garfield Baptist Church. An unwritten rule had been rigidly enforced from the congregation's beginning. We could pray for all kinds people and raise money to support our missionaries across the world, but the church's pulpit was reserved for white ministers. Pastor Keith, still relatively new to the congregation, had no idea that such protocols existed. The church's bylaws contained no such policy.

Those who remained to hear the young man speak were attentive and gracious, shaking hands and offering encouragement after the service. Mom and Pap invited Habib to come home with them for Sunday dinner, along with Pastor Keith and his wife, Dottie.

Habib showed everyone pictures of his family and was pleased to learn that the Hills had five children already grown, including a son in seminary and serving a church.

The phone calls started that evening, letting the pastor know in no uncertain terms that such things were just not done at Garfield Church. Some threatened to leave the church and others demanded that Pastor Keith resign. Any hopes that this would blow over were dashed at the next month's church business meeting, when Mr. Bolton made a motion to dismiss the pastor and specify in the bylaws that only white men would be allowed to speak at Garfield.

Pastor Keith looked pale and shell-shocked, with no idea how to respond to such a personal attack.

Mom felt mortified to think that her actions had led to such an ugly confrontation.

That's when Pap stood up to speak to the motion. "I can't support this motion for one reason. This is a church and a church is supposed to follow the teachings of Jesus. Now, if this was a country club, we could sit down and decide who's in and who's out, black or white or whatever, but this is a church, and we know how God feels about such things. He loves everybody, the whole world. Don't you see? If we give money to support our mission work all over the world, then I reckon we should be willing to welcome all kinds of people into our church right here at home. Otherwise, we're just hypocrites. We are a church, not a club. We have a fine pastor to lead us. I stand with Pastor Keith, and I hope you will too. Let's remember who we are and move on together."

The motion failed, but a handful of members left Garfield. After their departure, the atmosphere seemed to clear, at least temporarily. Pastor Keith continued to minister and serve there. Still, beneath the surface of things, trouble was brewing. Not everyone shared Mom and Pap's magnanimity.

***

The Pipefitters and Sheet Metal Workers Local held their meetings downtown in the old Masonic Temple at

Ninth and Harrison. The main auditorium provided plenty of space for the union membership, though rarely did all the men show up. The broad stage was framed by ornately carved columns and crowns painted a deep gold. Heavy burgundy curtains provided the background, with one small lectern, two fake ferns, and three folding chairs on the stage.

Norman Oakes, president of the union in those days, chaired the meetings, which were generally long and unwieldy. Oakes determined to keep the peace at all costs, fearing that any controversy might destroy the union or weaken its already tenuous negotiations with the railroads. No expert in Robert's Rule of Order, he sometimes dismissed out-of-hand motions that threatened to divide the membership or antagonize management. With this approach, Oakes struggled to preserve the status quo for nearly ten years. The rank and file grew increasingly frustrated with his high-handed leadership and his kowtowing to the office upstairs.

Pap, serving as Chief Steward for nearly five years, voiced grievances of the rank and file and constantly agitated for better working conditions and basic benefits. In the summer of 1955, the issue of health insurance took the spotlight—providing some minimal coverage for injury or illness, covering medicine and hospitalization, including maternity care.

Just months after management agreed to partially fund a basic policy, Pap and Mom stunned everyone with the news of their surprise pregnancy. As you might expect, the guys at work, from Sarge on down the line, teased Pap mercilessly.

"Sure, you got the boss to give us these benefits just so you could have one more bambino," they said.

"Oscar, it's time you found yourself a new hobby." I think it was Raymond who chimed in, "What do you know? The old steamer can still get down the line."

Pap took it all with a grin and a nod of his head, thrilled to welcome his baby girl, who was younger than nine of his grandchildren.

The first time he brought little Sue down to the yard, the whole shop came to a halt for her visit. Everyone wanted to see Oscar Hill's little toddler, her blond curls and dancing blue eyes capturing hearts. Even Mr. Stevens came down on the floor to offer Sue a piece of candy from the jar on his desk.

Later that fall, they held union elections at the Masonic Temple. Pap expected to continue his service as Chief Steward, but a rebellion was afoot. A growing segment of the membership had grown weary of Oakes' timidity towards management and commitment to the status quo. Many planned to replace him with someone who had the respect of the members and management, someone who would aggressively work for better wages and conditions for everyone.

Pap was as surprised as Oakes when they nominated him for president of the union. The vote indicated a clear majority, and without so much as a conversation, Pap found himself in that uncomfortable limbo, president of the union, the lightening rod between labor and management. As a steward, he had been able to raise questions and bring up important issues. Now he would often be deciding the matter, at least from the union side. I wondered how Mr. Stevens and his staff took the news, perhaps recognizing things would be different—no more easy accommodation, no buckling under in any standoff with management. Oscar Hill was a different kind of man.

What the rank and file never suspected on that day at the temple was that their new leader would push the union itself to address its own issues and inequities. Some of Pap's enthusiastic supporters would soon take issue with his agenda, question his leadership, and oppose his recommendations to the point of violence.

Looking back, how could they have been surprised?

***

On a steamy summer evening in 1958, Dan helped Mom clear the supper dishes before sitting back down with a glass of lemonade. The low hum of the window fan drowned out the cicadas and crickets outside. Mom busied herself with little Sue, washing her hands and face and removing a tiny scalloped potato from her curly blond hair after her best attempt to feed herself.

Pap and his fourth child, now twenty-two years old, had much to discuss. "Are you sure about this, son? It's a big decision. Serving in the military will be a lot different than going to college."

Brilliant and inquisitive, Dan never shied away from a challenge. Having finished his degree at Southwest Baptist College in Bolivar, Missouri, just north of Springfield, he had settled on the Air Force as his next step. "The recruiter said they need people with language skills. I'm solid in Russian and have a good foundation in French. They'll teach me the rest. Sounds like that's what I'd be doing, translating or decoding. That's exciting to me."

"Any idea where you would serve?" Pap asked. "I mean, where do you go to do that kind of work?"

Dan replied, "San Antonio to begin with, for basic training. After that, the language school is in Monterrey,

California, for maybe eight months or a year, and then I ship out. I guess in the Air Force, you take off instead of ship out."

Pap smiled, but Mom's face bore the signs of worry and fear. "You know, it's not wartime," she said, "but it might as well be. There's no telling what might happen. Plenty of young men join the military in peacetime, just looking for a job, and end up fighting the next war. It could happen to you."

Dan tried to calm her fears. "Mom, it's not like I would be flying a plane in combat. They need language skills. That's what I'll be doing."

Mom remained unconvinced. "You don't know that for certain, Dan. When war comes, everybody fights." She paused a moment to reflect. "Don't get me wrong. I'm proud of you wanting to serve your country like so many others have served, but I am your mother. I can't help thinking about such things. You should think about them, too."

Dan reached across the table and squeezed his mother's hand. "I know, Mom. I have thought this through, and I want to go. I want to serve."

Pap nodded in agreement. "Then, that's what you should do, son," he said. "You know your mother and I are with you and we'll be praying for you while you're away."

Dan followed Mom into the kitchen and hugged her as she dabbed her eyes. "I'll be fine, Mom. Don't worry, and when I get home, I'll have stories to tell."

It didn't turn out that way. Oh, Dan came home all right, safe and sound, but he had no stories to tell, not a word about his work, no details at all, except that it had to do with speaking and translating Russian.

Joyce and I decided he must have been some kind of spy, so cryptic about his work.

In his second year in Japan, he had to have his tonsils taken out, a miserable experience for adults requiring a general anesthetic. As Dan related the details, an Air Force officer had to be present while he was under, in case he unknowingly spoke about classified information. Mom and Pap never imagined Dan having a high-level security clearance, working on top secret projects, but apparently, he did. Mom worried to death about Dan's surgery so far from home, and wondered aloud what would happen if he did start revealing secrets while under the influence of the anesthetic. What would the officer do?

Joyce and I didn't make her feel any better, teasing her to break the tension.

"I suppose the officer would just have to shoot him, Mom," Joyce said.

I chimed in too. "Yeah, Dan better keep quiet or they'll have to shut him up. Unless he just tells our family secrets, like where he and Penny went on prom night, or where Buster got that black eye, or what Joyce wrote in all those letters to Howard. Plenty of secrets. No telling what he will say."

Joyce laughed. "Don't worry, Mom. They won't shoot him for that stuff."

Mom failed to see the humor in the situation. "Don't even joke about it. That's not funny."

But we had some laughs and were all relieved to hear the surgery went well and no one had been shot.

Never knowing the details about Dan's service in the Air Force did not dampen Pap's pride at having a son in uniform. Seeing his boy stride into Union Station in his dress blues, his service completed, brought the greatest joy of all.

Chapter 7 – Opening Doors

"You must never be fearful about what
you are doing when it is right."
~ ***Rosa Parks***

In the fall of 1959, Pap submitted a proposal to the union membership that included the following statement: "The United Pipefitters and Sheet Metal Workers Union Local 159 shall be open to all qualified and eligible workers regardless of race, color, religion, or ethnic background."

The hall was packed, nearly every member present, for the open debate.

Pap defended his proposal in both ethical and pragmatic terms. "A railroad man is judged by the work he puts in, the skill of his hands, his knowledge and experience, not by the color of his skin. No more "yellow dog" contracts. No more "whites only" unwritten rules. It's the man who can finish the job that deserves to enjoy the fruit of his labor. We have no business holding a man down because he's black, or promoting a man just because he's white. Let the man who can do the job, do the job, and get paid. It's only fair."

The roar of the crowd was a strange blend of polite approval and fierce opposition.

One man spoke up as the din subsided. "We've had coloreds on this railroad for nigh on twenty-five years.

Ain't nothing new. They got jobs, good steady work. What's the problem? Giving 'em a union card ain't gonna change a thing."

Murmured approval all around.

Pap raised his hand to make room for his words. "That's right. Just about every cleanup crew and custodian on the railroad is colored. Some of the unskilled laborers are black men. But we keep all the better jobs for white men. There's never been a colored apprentice on this railroad, no chance to master a skill or earn a decent wage. That's not fair."

A storm of protests engulfed his words.

"What makes you think niggers can learn a trade? Ain't good for nothing but pushing a broom or mopping a floor. They ain't got the smarts God gave a dog."

"Start their own damn union. Toilet scrubbers and garbage carriers local. That's the union for niggers around here."

"I'm not paying my dues to a union that lets a colored take a job from a white man. They're a bunch of scabs and strikebreakers. We've seen it right here in '49."

Pap had nearly lost control of the meeting before Raymond let out a shrill whistle that quieted the room.

He moved on to his second point. "That's right. Railroads and other companies have hired colored men to break strikes. They need work the same as we do. They've got families. For some, it's the only chance they get, and if we don't let them in the union, they'll always be around for management to hire when we strike. If we bring them in, then the boss won't have any choice but to negotiate with us in good faith. Don't you see, we're all better off if we stand together, black and white."

The opposition had not anticipated this tack, but the plain truth was indisputable. Union bigotry was providing management with a ready-made workforce, strikebreakers by necessity. Integrating would strengthen the bargaining position of the union in any work stoppage.

Pap struck the gavel on the podium, giving him some semblance of attention as he summed up the situation. "You better decide where you want the colored man to be—crossing the lines against you, or standing with you when push comes to shove."

The meeting rolled on with heated conversations breaking out throughout the hall. Someone called the question, and a vote was taken by a simple show of hands, with Pap's proposal soundly defeated. All the logic in the world stood little chance against generations of ingrained prejudice, as plain as black and white.

A reporter from the city desk at the Kansas City Star called Pap for a comment. "I'm disappointed about the vote, but we'll come together and move on. We always have."

The article heralded the union vote as the first major vote on integration in Kansas City history, and its defeat as an omen of increased racial conflict ahead.

***

Disheartened and disgusted, Pap thought about resigning as president. He and Mom talked it through. She tried to encourage him, but his mind was made up.

"I can't look the other way," he said. "I won't lead a union that's not open to everyone. It's bad enough to be a member, let alone the president."

Mom remained unwavering and pragmatic. "Oscar, you've been in the union a long time and you've made some progress. Maybe you moved too quickly. If you give it more time, I'll bet they'd come around."

Pap wasn't so hopeful. "I saw it in their faces. Their fear and hatred run deep. Not sure men like that ever change. I guess it can happen, but I've never seen it."

Pap went to bed that night, restless and depressed, pondering the prejudice that sets some men above others, the way even decent, church-going folks can harbor hatred and disdain for those that God loves, people created in the image of God. Could it ever change? What was the use?

Later that week, a letter came in the mail hand-addressed to Mr. Oscar Hill with an Independence return address on north Delaware. Pap opened it to find a hand-written note from the then-retired 33rd President of the United States.

***

Dear Mr. Hill,

I read with interest the story in Wednesday's Star regarding your efforts to integrate your union local. I know you must be disappointed with the defeat of your proposal. I was reminded of my own experience in 1948 when I integrated our armed forces by executive order. I did it because I knew it to be the right thing even though I had not one friend in government who advised me to do so. The Joint Chiefs opposed my decision as did my own Secretary of War. After I issued the order, I was called every name in the book and one or two I had not heard before. I was burned in effigy at military schools in the South and here in

Missouri. I confess I watched my back for a week or two.

Bigotry is a devilish beast that is not easily overcome. Only the brave will take it on. Mr. Hill, let me encourage you to stay in the fight, keep at it. One of these days that beast will be put down. In the meantime, please know that you have this old man's respect and admiration. Keep up the good work.

Sincerely,
Harry Truman

***

Pap read the letter over and over, to Mom, to himself, and to me on the phone savoring every word, a potent transfusion of encouragement. No coach ever gave a better halftime speech, and Pap was back in the game, as stubborn and determined as a Missouri mule. That same night, he made a list of key union members that he could work on before bringing up integration again in the coming spring.

He left for work the next morning with a spring in his step and glint of purpose in his eye. There would be no giving up, no turning back.

***

Pap never anticipated the storm of criticism and resistance in the months following the vote on his proposed integration. He had struck the hornet's nest of racism on the railroad, and his enemies were attacking from all sides. Many of the local rank and file came after him swearing they would never tolerate Negroes doing a white man's work. Some men threatened the safety of any Negro who took a promotion, even if the proposal passed. Any colored apprentice would be a target, and any white man who took on a colored apprentice would be a marked man, too. It was clear to Pap that a significant number of the union membership were determined to oppose integration by any means necessary. He couldn't be sure what percentage might be more open to change.

Within weeks of the vote, Pap was called by the regional and national union leadership. They questioned him thoroughly about the proposal itself and what strategies or motivations were driving him. Apparently, no other large union local had voted on full integration, and the national leadership was miffed that they had not been informed in advance of the vote.

Pap shared his rationale for the proposal, citing his primary arguments, but it quickly became obvious that had they known about Pap's agenda, they would have squelched it before the vote.

The next week, a letter arrived from the union headquarters directing Pap to cease and desist in his integration efforts until a decision could be made by the union leadership at the national level. There was no suggested timetable for their decision. The none too subtle implication was that Pap would be removed as president of the local if he didn't abide by this directive.

Pap knew the union charter and handbook by heart, aware that only the local membership could remove a chapter president from leadership. For all their bluster, the national leadership had to know the truth. They could push and threaten all they wanted, but they could not control or remove Pap. Union structure was bottom to top, not top to bottom, in those days.

Pap wrote a respectful letter in reply, laying out his arguments once again, and stating his intention to let the local rank and file decide the matter, probably in the spring. So, most of his worries remained at the local level, where he would have to convince enough of the membership to support his leadership and the integration proposal that he refused to withdraw.

***

One evening, as Sue was helping Mom finish with the dinner dishes and Pap was enjoying his pipe on the porch, the phone rang. Mom wiped her hands on her apron and answered with a friendly hello.

The angry voice on the line was unfamiliar and threatening. "Mrs. Hill, you better tell that nigger-loving husband of yours to remember his own kind and stop this integration vote. We ain't having niggers in the union—not now, not ever. You tell him. This is going to get ugly if he keeps it up. Somebody's gonna get hurt. You wouldn't want that, would you?"

Mom put her hand over the phone and spoke softly to Sue. "Go get your father. Run quick."

Sue seemed puzzled but scooted toward the front door.

Mom tried to gather herself, speaking as calmly as she could muster. "Who is this? What is your name?"

The voice on the other end was losing steam. "Never mind that. You just remember what I said. We won't have it, no niggers in our union. You tell him what I said." The phone went dead in her hand as Pap came in the door.

Mom leaned back against the kitchen counter and began to weep.

Pap took the phone from her hand, and put his arm around her shoulders. "Who was it, Verna? What's happened? Is it one of the kids?"

Mom dabbed her eyes with a tea towel and shook her head. "It's not the kids. It was a man. He wouldn't tell me his name. He said to tell you to stop trying to integrate the union or somebody is going to get hurt. He was threatening our family, Oscar."

Pap pulled out a chair for Mom and she sat down. "Trying to scare us, I guess," he said.

"Well, it worked," Mom said tearfully. "They know where we live, Oscar. Everyone knows where we live." Her voice trembled as she spoke. "What about Sue? She's four years old."

Pap tried to put her mind at ease. "I'm not going to let anything happen to you or Sue or anyone. I'll take care of it, and hopefully this will all be over soon."

Mom would not be reassured. "So you're going to drop the integration proposal? Is that what you are saying?"

"No, I can't do that. We're going to vote. There's no stopping now. We have to get it done," Pap said, more angry than afraid and determined to finish what he had begun.

Mom was not so steady. "So what are we supposed to do around here? Just hope for the best?"

Pap reached down and picked up Sue, who nestled into his shoulder. "I'll call Buster. He can stay over here when he's not at work, and keep an eye on things. Let's keep Sue here close, in the house, or over at Joyce and Howard's, at least for a while, a few weeks. Jack and June will be coming for Easter. Maybe you and Sue could go back with them for a visit. Take the train back after things settle down. Would you feel better about that?"

"What about you? What are you going to do? You're the one they're trying to stop."

"Verna, I'll not be bullied by cowards who try to scare women and children. You have to stand up to them. It's the only way."

Mom stood up and put her arms around Pap. "Just promise me you'll be careful. You don't have to be a hero. Just make sure you come home every night, will you?"

He pulled her close and kissed her. Pap had not showed Mom the angry letters he had received. More threats and intimidation, but they might as well have saved the postage. There was no turning back once Pap decided what was the right thing to do.

The next evening, without telling Pap, Mom called Raymond Ward and asked him to ride to and from work with Pap, to make sure he was never alone.

Raymond was happy to help though he didn't seem too worried. "Oscar's tough as an old boot. I'm sure he'll be fine, but I'll ride along anyway. If anything happens, Oscar can protect me."

Pap was embarrassed at first and frustrated with Mom for dragging Raymond into this situation, but she soon convinced him to get used to the arrangement, at least until this was settled.

***

I heard most churches only offered Sunday School classes for the children and teenagers, but Baptists are funny about such things, believing that small group Bible study is an important spiritual discipline for all believers, from the cradle to the grave. So most of the adults at Garfield attended a class if they weren't teaching the children or youth. For a few years, Mom and Pap attended a couples' class, but after Mom started teaching boys and girls, Pap settled into a men's class taught by Horace Sanders, a retired cabinet maker. Generally, the first fifteen minutes of class consisted of friendly conversation, catching up on the week's news and whatever stories the guys had to tell.

On one March Sunday, Donald Mills had a burr under his saddle from the moment he sat down. "Were any of you downtown yesterday? I hear it's been going on all week. I'm telling you, there's going to be trouble."

Raymond Ward shrugged and asked, "What trouble? What are you talking about?"

"It's all over downtown, Macy's, Jones Store, Kline's, and Peck's. The coloreds are protesting again, crowding into the lunch counters, acting like white folks," Donald explained. "There's going to be trouble, I'm telling you. There's plenty of white people that won't abide that kind of thing. What do you think, Horace?"

Horace laid aside his Bible for the moment and responded, "I heard about it. It was in the paper. I think it started back east—Carolina, I think. Some colored college boys got it in their heads and marched right into Woolworth's and parked themselves at the 'whites only' lunch counter. Nobody knew what to do."

"Seems like they never can leave well enough alone," Donald chimed in. "I mean, there's always something they're complaining about."

Raymond saw things differently. "If you ask me, it doesn't sound all that unreasonable. I mean, if we all go to war together and we all work together, what difference does it make where we eat our lunch?"

Donald leaned back in his chair and shook his head. "People should know their place, that's all I'm saying, and those colored boys should know better."

Raymond turned to Pap, and for a moment it seemed everyone was turning their attention to Pap, waiting to hear his thoughts still forming in his mind.

"What struck me about the report from Carolina," Pap began, "is that those college boys didn't fight back. A mob of people came at them right there in the stores, screaming at them, attacking them, and they just sat there, taking it. I reckon those colored folks here did the same. That says something, I think."

Donald said, "It says they're stubborn fools who might just get themselves killed."

Horace picked up his Bible and lesson book, signaling an end to their open discussion. "We better get started on the lesson, men. We're working our way through the Beatitudes in Matthew 5. This morning we're looking at verses five and six: 'Blessed are the meek, for they will inherit the earth. Blessed are those who hunger and thirst for righteousness, for they will be filled.'"

Only Pap seemed to notice the irony.

***

It wasn't like Mr. Henderson to come calling. Neighbors for over twenty years, the Hendersons mostly kept to themselves, spending summer evenings on their own broad front porch rather than venturing out for a visit.

Pap stood up in surprise when George Henderson strolled up the front steps as the evening sky faded to dusk. "Good evening, George. Good to see you," Pap said with a smile and a firm handshake. "How have you been? Care to sit down?"

George stepped to the porch and pulled up a chair. "Hello, Oscar. It is a nice evening, isn't it?" Settling into his chair, he gave a deep sigh and, holding his cap in his hands, wiped his brow with the sleeve of his canvas jacket. "We're doing pretty well, Alice and me. Not getting any younger, that's for sure."

Pap relit his pipe and shook the match to put it out. "I reckon you're right about that, George. Little different than twenty years ago, when our kids were little."

George shook his head with a sad smile.

"That's what's on my mind, Oscar: my kids—well, just my son really. You know Terry, my oldest boy. He just came back home. He's been gone a while." He paused for a moment, then decided to continue. "To tell you the truth, he's been in jail. We didn't talk about it, but that's the truth of it. Terry's been locked up for four and a half years. Some of the neighbors thought he ran off and joined the military, and we never corrected them. Just easier to let them think what they will."

Pap puffed his pipe and rocked slowly in his chair, listening intently. For a long moment neither man spoke, letting the words hang in the air with the pipe smoke.

Pap broke the silence. "Good to have him home, I'm sure."

"Yeah, it's good. I mean, we're glad Terry's out of jail. It just seems strange. He's not the same, Oscar. He's not the son I raised," George said, shrugging in resignation.

"I'll bet he is, George. He's your boy. But being in jail changes a man, maybe for the worse, sometimes for the better. Four years is a long time."

"Yes, it is, plenty long."

The men watched the stars come out in the night sky without comment.

George pulled a cigarette from his jacket and bummed a match. "I might as well tell you. It'll get around eventually. Terry got to running with some bad apples. He should've known better, but he didn't. They robbed some businesses, did some damage. Nearly killed a night watchman who walked in on them. Not Terry personally, that's what he says. To hear him tell it, he was just in the wrong place at the wrong time, but that ain't so. He knew better. He earned his jail time, every day of it."

Pap heard him out, knowing full well the disappointment a father feels when a son goes wrong. "I'm sorry," Pap said. "I know that's hard to take, when a kid goes wrong and forgets everything you tried to teach him."

"Thanks, Oscar. I know you had your own troubles with Buster, and he did his jail time. You made no secret of it."

Pap nodded as he relit his pipe. "Yeah, Buster's had his troubles, always getting in fights. It's a wonder he didn't kill somebody. Sure broke his mother's heart to see him go away for a while."

"Violet, too. Nearly killed her when Terry went to jail. I could've killed him myself, so angry I was. How could he do such a thing? How could he be so dad-blamed stupid?" George gathered himself, struggling with his emotions. "And what do I with him now? I got no use for him around here."

Pap had no answer, just rocking and reflecting. "George, I need some coffee. Would you drink a cup?"

"That would be fine, thank you," George replied.

Pap stepped inside and found the coffee pot still hot with the evening brew and poured two cups, then returned to the porch. "Here you go, George"

"Thanks," he said. Pap settled back in his chair as George spoke up. "Tell me, Oscar, is it ever the same—I mean... with you and your boy? Not sure I can ever get past this. What am I supposed to do?"

Pap sat his coffee cup on the porch floor beside his chair and scratched the back of his head. "I don't know, George. When Buster got in trouble, all I knew was he's my son. He'll always be my boy, no matter what he does or how much trouble he gets into. I drove Verna down to Jeff City to see him, as often as we could. Sometimes we took the train. I knew he'd be all right. Buster could take of himself, even in prison, but I wanted him to know we weren't going to turn loose of him."

George leaned back in his chair, letting Pap's words soak in.

After reaching down for a sip of coffee, Pap continued. "All I know to tell you is, when these things happen and our kids get off track, all we can do is hang on to them, hang on no matter what. Hang on even if he won't give you the time of day. And when they do finally come home, you got to let them in. Let them know they still have a family, a mother and father who care about them and still believe there's good in them."

George put out his cigarette in his coffee cup. "I'm not sure I can do that at this point. I don't know. Vi's already forgiven him, like nothing ever happened, but I can't let go of it. It's not so easy for me. I know I should, but it don't seem right. The way I look at it, the prodigal son, he should've had his ass kicked off the porch."

Pap laughed out loud. "Well, he had it coming. You got that right, George. My boy, your boy, you and me, I guess we all had it coming. There's been plenty of times I needed a little grace along the way. How 'bout you?"

George nodded in agreement. "Yeah, I know. Me, too. I reckon so. Thanks." George got to his feet.

Pap stood to see him off. "You tell Terry I'd be pleased to see him. Maybe I can help him find some work, get him started again. Will you do that?"

George shook his head. "Who's going to hire a convicted thief? Nobody, and who could blame them?"

"I don't know," Pap answered, "but somebody's going to have to vouch for him and somebody's got to give him a second chance. What he does with it is up to him. I know Buster's done real well for himself, a new start. I'll bet Terry can do it too."

"I hope so, Oscar. I'll tell him what you said. Goodnight."

As Pap watched his neighbor walk home by the streetlight, he thought about fathers and sons, the grace we give and the grace we need, and all the prodigals on God's porch.

***

Mom and Pap loved their church and served however and whenever asked. For nearly seven years, they had been a part of Garfield Baptist after their older kids were grown, and now brought the little one, Sue, who was four years old. Pap was a deacon, serving in worship and caring for benevolent needs in the church and community. An older congregation, they had a number of widows who needed help and attention, and Pap was good to drop by, to run errands, or do some home repair. He could fix just about anything. Mom led the women's group that kept up with the mission work and raised money at Christmas and Easter. Together, Mom and Pap often hosted the teenagers on Sunday night, for socials or special studies.

Through the years, Pap and his pastor, Keith Hudson, became close friends. Perhaps knowing something about my ministry gave Pap a better window into the life of his pastor. In time, he became Pastor Keith's chief encourager and confidant. After Keith's father passed away, Pap provided a source of strength and comfort, someone to lean on. Their close friendship made Keith's call to a new congregation painful for Pap and Mom.

Garfield Baptist was just beginning to transition with the community, with a few black families beginning to visit the services. Pap was confident that under Pastor Keith's leadership, the congregation could welcome their new neighbors and not resist the changes happening in their community. But with Keith's departure, how would the church respond?

The church elected a search committee to find a new pastor, the way Baptists do things. Pap got the impression that the roster of the committee had been somehow manipulated, chosen in advance, without nominations and pushed forward for speedy approval. Thus, neither Pap nor Mom was asked to serve. As the committee went about their work and within a few months presented a candidate, Pap's worst fears were realized.

Rev. Jerry Bedford, short and overweight, boisterous and loud, arrived from rural Mississippi to lead the congregation. He seemed friendly enough and certainly sincere, though perhaps an odd fit for the Garfield church. After a few months, he began to come clean about his personal views and agenda for the church. One sermon in particular expressed his views.

"God loves all the people of the earth, red and yellow, black and white, as the children sing for us. God loves all kinds of people, even people very different from ourselves. In Genesis, we read that God scattered the different peoples all over the face of the earth. He called out the children of Israel to come out and be separate, set apart from the other tribes and nations. That's God's intention for all people, for all races—to be separate, set apart from one another. And that's what we should do today—separate—the same kind with the same kind, and let those that are different keep to themselves.

"There are churches for all kinds of people. This is a white church and I believe that's what we are called to be. There are plenty of Negro churches and I don't think we should bother them, and I'm sure they won't bother us. Different churches for different kinds of people, that's God's way."

A black family towards the back slipped out the main door.

Pap wanted to go with them, but he was not leaving without saying his piece. As he shook the Pastor Jerry's hand at the door, he asked him directly, "I want to make sure I heard you right, pastor. You want to keep this church all white and not welcome any black members?"

Pastor Jerry wiped his sweaty brow with his handkerchief and said, "Yes, I do. God doesn't approve of the mixing of races. We are supposed to be separate, as the Bible says."

"You do know our neighborhood around the church is changing and that it's not going to stop." Pap was holding up the line of those wanting to shake hands with the pastor on the way out, but he had to know.

"That may be true, Mr. Hill, and if necessary, we may need to think about relocating our church. Many churches are taking that approach."

Pap was incredulous. "So, you would sell this building and move before you would welcome a black member?"

The pastor nodded in the affirmative.

Pap looked at Mom who must have been on the same page. "It's not my place to judge you, Pastor, but I won't attend a church that doesn't open its doors to all people. We'll be staying just long enough to find new people to cover our duties, and then we will be moving on. I appreciate your honesty." And with those words Mom and Pap walked out the door.

A few weeks later, Mom and Pap found themselves back at Parkway Baptist, their neighborhood church that they had attended before Garfield. In their absence, good things had happened at Parkway, with the call of a new pastor and new lay leaders stepping up. Several of their close friends in the neighborhood also attended Parkway, as did some of Sue's playmates.

Within a few months, Mom and Pap found themselves as busy at Parkway as they had been at Garfield.

***

Changing minds on the railroad proved more difficult for Pap than repairing locomotives, but one by one, man to man, Pap's efforts began to have an effect. The vitriol faded and real conversations took place in the lunchroom, in the shops, and after work. Before long, Pap had made a serious dent in the opposition.

Ralph Stinson, a forty-year-old diesel mechanic, changed his attitude in one lunchtime conversation. "I don't need no black man trying to take my job," Ralph began. "There's enough competition for work as it is."

Pap laid aside his sandwich and stated the obvious truth. "Ralph, there's going to be the same number of jobs around here whether the men are black or white. The competition for jobs will be the same either way. You bid the job you want. Maybe you get it or someone else has more seniority and he gets it. That's the way it works. And what do you care? You'll have more seniority than all the new men coming in anyway, so you really have nothing to lose. But let's make it fair for everybody. The best man with the most experience gets the job. Isn't that the way it should be?"

Ralph pondered Pap's perspective, likely one that had not occurred to him. "I hadn't thought of it like that. I guess it's what we've been doing all along."

"That's right," Pap said. "It's the same process, only this way it's open to everyone, whoever can get the job done. No special favors, just a fair deal."

Ralph nodded. One more mind opened just a crack.

Pap didn't hesitate to remind some of his union brothers of their own employment issues, the times they had been called on the carpet, hoping for fair treatment or reasonable discipline. Back then, they needed union support, and who had gone to bat for them? Oscar Hill, the same man who pushed for the integration proposal. "Every man who puts in a good day's work deserves that same support, a fair deal on the job. That goes for every man, black or white."

***

The vote came in April, 1960, as the redbuds and dogwoods were blooming and Pap's garden came to life. The auditorium at the Masonic Temple was nearly filled since every union member knew what was on the agenda. It had been seven months since the proposal to integrate the union was defeated by an overwhelming majority. Now it was time to see if any minds had been changed. The railroads had employed Negroes for decades, almost always as unskilled laborers, and never as union members with access to apprenticeships and the higher paying jobs. As a result, the only chance that black men had to earn a decent wage on the railroad was to either "buck the extra board" for temporary jobs, or to be a strikebreaker, a ready-made workforce for management to call in—scabs, as the union called them.

Pap's proposal would change this long-standing arrangement, making Negroes eligible to become full union members with all the rights and opportunities of their white brothers. He understood that deep-seeded racism would never be changed, but an appeal to self-interest and basic fairness might sway those not completely blinded by bigotry. All winter long, at the lunch tables, in the shops, across the yards, Pap and a handful of like-minded men had tried to push for fair treatment and equal opportunity for everyone, black and white, hoping to change attitudes and open minds.

Only now could the success or failure of their efforts be gauged.

Pap called the meeting to order, and after the obligatory minutes and housekeeping matters, he presented the proposal once more. As Pap began, an immediate objection was raised.

An older member, Dalton Coffey, with a gray beard that hung down over the bib of his overalls, waved his hand and interrupted. "I object, Mr. President. We have already heard this proposal, we discussed it, and we voted it down by a large majority. You mind telling me why in hell we are considering this proposal again?"

Other voices chimed in. "There's no sense going over this again. No niggers in the union. We already voted. That's the rule."

Pap struck the gavel and spoke as the room quieted. "It's not at all unusual, as you all well know. How many times did we vote on that proposal about health insurance before it was finally settled? And if management makes any changes or the rates go up, we'll have to bring it up again. That's the way it is, the way we do things. We voted last year on this proposal, and we voted it down. Now we need to know where we stand this year. So we'll vote."

Pap's words seem to calm the room as Mr. Coffey sat down. A few others spoke to the motion, about an even split of support and opposition.

Just before the question was called, Pap gave one last plea. "I reckon you men know where I stand on this, how I feel about it. I believe it's the right thing to do, and I think deep down you probably know it is, too. I could ask you to vote for this proposal because it the right thing to do, it's what's fair. If that's not enough for you, I could ask you to vote for it for your own sake, for your own interest. Do you want the black man working with you or against you, on your side or on the boss's side? And if that's not enough for you, if you still want to vote no, let me tell you something you might not have thought about. It's coming. You think this whole talk about civil rights and equal opportunity is just about our union? No, it's everywhere—in our schools, in the government here locally, in our stores. It's coming, I'm telling you. This train is going to leave the station whether you get on board or not. I think it's time to get on the train. Do the right thing for these working men, and do it for yourself, because sooner or later, change is coming. Let's get on board."

The vote was taken by ballot and counted by a group of union stewards. Members milled about the main hall, subdued and tense as they waited for the result. When Pap called the room to order, a deathly silence descended like a cloud.

Pap put on his glasses to read the handwritten tally. "On the proposal to open the union to all qualified employees regardless of race, religion, or color, the vote is 311 in favor, 243 opposed." Pap choked up, cleared his throat and stammered out, "The proposal is adopted."

The room erupted in a storm of boisterous cheers and angry shouts, but it was done, approved, completed. What had seemed unthinkable just months before had come to pass.

As he left the meeting that day, Pap was thanked and threatened, blessed and cursed, but his conscience was clear. He felt deeply gratified. Finally, they'd opened the door.

Chapter 8 – Homefront

"It is through this mysterious power that we too have our being, and we therefore yield to our neighbors, even to our animal neighbors, the same right as ourselves to inhabit this vast land."
~ ***Sitting Bull***

In the spring of 1963, it happened—what everyone had been dreading, everyone except Mom and Pap. The Weaver's house had been for sale less than a month when it sold to a black family. As Pap left for work one morning, he noticed a large panel truck and a pickup out front. By the time he came home that evening, the truck was gone and the new folks were settling in.

Mom had baked bread that afternoon, so she and Pap wrapped up a loaf and walked down the street. Pap knocked on the door.

A woman opened the screen door with a cautious smile and said, "Can I help you?" She wore a simple blue house dress, her hair pulled back, an apron around her slim waist.

Pap spoke up first. "Good evening. I'm Oscar Hill and this is my wife, Verna. We live just down the street in that green house, 4408. We noticed you moving in and want to say welcome to the neighborhood."

The woman just stood there, tilting her head as she tried to make sense of her unexpected guests. A tall, broad-shouldered man appeared behind her putting his arm around her waist. She glanced at his puzzled expression and extended her hand to Pap. "I'm Stella Jenkins and this is my husband, Leroy. It's nice of you to come by."

Mom held out her bundle. "I baked some bread this afternoon. I'm sure you've had a long day."

Stella took the bread with a smile. "Thank you. That's kind of you. I was just making some sandwiches and this bread will be fine."

Mom nodded and smiled. "Do you have any little ones? Our little girl, Sue, is seven years old."

Stella turned her head in surprise, assuming Mom was well past raising little ones, except perhaps grandchildren. "Really? Seven years old. Our son Henry is eleven and Rachel is nine years old."

Mom noticed her surprise. "Yes, our daughter is seven, but we also have five grown children and sixteen grandchildren, so you might notice lots of kids in our yard. Sue was an extra blessing, you might say, and Henry and Rachel are always welcome to come play."

Stella cleared her throat, touched by Mom's friendly welcome. "Thank you, Verna. Sue is welcome here, too, anytime. Thank you."

Pap extended his hand to Leroy, who took it with some hesitancy. Pap just smiled. "It's good to meet you, Leroy. We're right down the street if you need anything. Anyone else stop by today?"

Leroy shook his head. "Yeah, but not so friendly. Two cars rolled by and yelled at Stella and my boy, didn't say a word when I was out front. Said they don't need our kind in this part of town. Better stay where we belong, they said. You don't need to hear the rest. It's a dead-end street so they must live around here."

"I'm afraid so. I could probably guess, but there are some folks on this street that don't want you here."

Leroy didn't hear Pap's words with any measure of surprise. "No kidding. We didn't expect no welcome mat, but I do appreciate you and your wife coming by. Nice to have a neighbor."

"There's some good people around here," Pap said, "but they've got some things to learn about getting along. I'm hoping they'll come around."

Leroy was not so optimistic. "I counted three 'For Sale' signs on this street. Did that just happen? Is that because of us?"

Pap shrugged and replied, "I don't know, maybe so. I reckon people have to make their own choices. They have to live with themselves, too."

Mom and Stella rejoined the conversation as they said goodbye. "Good to meet you all," Mom said. "Just holler if you need something. I'm usually at home."

As she and Pap strolled back down the street, they noticed the newly lettered "For Sale" signs on 54th and wondered how many more would soon be posted.

***

Pap had just said the blessing over dinner when he heard a knock at the door. Pap answered, surprised to see two of his neighbors, Eugene Cunningham and Herb Davis, on the porch. The men said hello as Pap stepped out on the porch.

Eugene, tall and thin with a large Adam's apple that people couldn't help but notice, got right to the point. "Oscar, we've been talking to folks in the neighborhood and it's pretty much unanimous. We don't need nor want no coloreds on our street or anywhere around here. That's the consensus, a strong majority anyhow. We got up a petition and twenty-two of us signed it, all homeowners in our neighborhood. Now, it ain't personal. It just says we don't want their kind around here."

Then Herb chimed in. "Most folks know how you feel about all this, Oscar, and we respect you and your opinion, but we can't just sit by and watch our homes and our schools turn into Niggertown. Anyway, we got this petition, and we took it over to the Weaver place where that family moved in to show it to them, but nobody's home. We couldn't even find them to give them the damn thing."

Pap looked over the petition with disgust. As he handed the clipboard back to Eugene, he said, "Our new neighbors are the Jenkins, Leroy and Stella, and they're not home, all right. They are having supper with us. Why don't you join us? We could all get acquainted. You're welcome to come in and have some dinner, but that clipboard will have to stay on the porch."

The men stood there openmouthed.

"No, no, thanks, but no, ah, some other time. Oscar, whatever possessed you to do such a thing?" Eugene asked.

Herb backed away with his own mumbled excuses.

Pap reminded them as they stepped off the porch. "Do you remember when you moved in back in '42, Eugene? We invited you over. You and Dorothy sat at my dinner table, and we got acquainted. It was same for you, Herb, you and Mildred, right here on the porch. It's just being a neighbor. You know how it works or how it's supposed to work. You welcome your neighbors. You don't run them off. What are you thinking?"

Pap came back in the house with a sick feeling in the pit of his stomach, a premonition of what was to come.

***

The girls were playing in the front yard, Sue, Joyce's daughter, Elaine, and Leroy and Stella's daughter, Rachel. Joyce had come over for the evening and she and Mom finished up the supper dishes while Pap enjoyed his pipe on the porch.

The warm September sun hung just above the rooftops across the street, so Pap couldn't quite make out Stella as she climbed the front sidewalk stairs.

"Good evening, Oscar. I've... I've just come to collect Rachel." Her voice sounded raspy as she clutched a wadded tissue, dabbing her eyes. "I need to get her home."

The girls began their usual ploy. "Can Rachel spend the night?" Sue asked as she scratched the chigger bite on her knee.

"Please, Mama," Rachel added. "Can I stay over? Mrs. Hill said it was fine with her."

Stella shook her head. "Not tonight, Rachel. I need to get you home. We better go."

Pap could see something was troubling her. "No need to rush off. What's wrong, Stella? Are you all right?" Pap asked.

Stella tried to compose herself. "Didn't you hear the news, down in Alabama, what they did to those little girls?" She began to cry, her shoulders shaking.

Pap stood to his feet and helped her find a chair on the porch.

The girls scattered, delighted to have a little bonus time to play.

"Tell me again, what happened?"

Stella wiped her eyes and cleared her throat as best she could. "I thought you might've heard," she said. "Maybe it wasn't in your paper yet. They bombed a church... in Birmingham... they killed four little girls." Her tears fell freely. "They was all dressed up for Sunday School, and somebody bombed those little children. People so filled with hate. Can't they just let us alone? Little girls like my Rachel, murdered in God's house."

Pap struggled to take it in, much less find any words to speak. He reached to put his hand on hers. "I'm so sorry," he said.

For a few long minutes they sat on the porch together listening to the crickets and locusts and the sounds of happy little girls playing in the yard.

As Stella collected herself, she began to think out loud. "What makes white people do such things? They don't want us in the neighborhood, they don't want us working the same jobs, I know all about that. But littles girls in Sunday School, my God." She sobbed as she spoke. "Leroy's so angry. I don't know what he'd do if somebody hurt Rachel, and who's to blame him?"

Pap listened to her questions without any answers to give. "I don't know. I've seen it all my life, since I was a boy, so much hate in the world. I get to thinking that people can learn to get along, to know better and do better, and then something like this happens. I guess some folks would rather die than change."

Stella nodded as she wiped her eyes and rose to her feet. "They'd rather kill than change, Mr. Hill. They'd rather kill."

***

Before the first frost of autumn, half of the neighborhood had moved out. Five other families were waiting for their houses to sell. The moving companies worked the neighborhood, and it seemed like the same trucks kept coming back nearly every week. Mom and Pap said goodbye to friends who had been their neighbors for over twenty years. Some of them gave Pap a cool farewell, knowing his decision to stay and feeling judged for moving out. It didn't matter that Mom and Pap never lectured or berated anyone for deciding to leave. Still, a troubled conscience will find someone to target, so they blamed their new Negro neighbors and the handful of white folks who welcomed them. This led to lots of awkward goodbyes in the old neighborhood.

On the happier side of the equation, there were plenty of new neighbors to welcome each month, mostly black and a few Hispanic families, with lots of children. Mom and Pap sent Sue up and down the street with cookies, cakes, or homemade bread. In the warm evenings, Pap always had new friends on the front porch, and whoever came by took home a share of Pap's abundant garden produce.

In the spring of 1964, Fred and Mona Sadler moved into the house directly across the street from Mom and Pap's. For some reason, Pap always made a big deal out of May Day, May 1st, and enjoyed cutting fresh flowers and making baskets combined with some of Mom's cookies or bread to be delivered to friends and neighbors. Since Fred and Mona had just moved in that week, Pap fixed them a basket and sent Sue across the street to leave the basket with a note on their doorstep.

Later that evening, Fred and Mona came across the street as Pap was loading his pipe on the porch.

"Mr. Hill, I just want to thank you folks for the nice basket," Fred began.

Mona was quick to add, "What a lovely surprise. That's so kind of you." They stood at the base of the porch steps.

Pap stood to welcome them. "Come on up and have a seat. Let me call Verna."

In a few moments, they were all enjoying some of Mom's lemonade and getting acquainted.

"How old are your children?" Mom asked.

"Richie is our firstborn, he's thirteen. Sammy is ten and Frieda is seven. I'm sure you'll be seeing them. We'll try to keep them out of your way and off your property and such."

Mom was almost indignant. "Your children are welcome here anytime. Our Sue is about the same age as your Frieda and she'll be happy to have a new friend to play with. And we're used to boys around here. We have five older children, four of them boys, with families of their own now. Little boys are nothing new to us. In fact, we have a bunch of grandkids that come around, too."

"That's real kind of you," Mona said. "Your daughter is welcome at our house, too. Freida will be excited."

Fred sat in the metal lawn chair next to Pap, still a little uneasy, unaccustomed to being welcomed by white neighbors. "Have you lived here a long time, Mr. Hill? To tell you the truth, we didn't even know there were white folks in this neighborhood. Mr. Dorsey down the street told me about you and your wife, said you stayed when every other white family moved out."

Pap smiled and nodded. "Fred, it would be fine if you call me Oscar. We've lived here since '36, so soon be thirty years. It's been a good neighborhood to raise a family, and it still is. We're still getting to know our new neighbors."

Fred's curiosity was not quite satisfied. "Don't mind me asking, Mr. Hill—ah, Oscar—what possessed you to stay? You must've thought about leaving when everybody else did."

"We thought about it, talked it over," Pap said. "I never thought the color of a man's skin was reason enough to move away. We decided to stay and try to be good neighbors to whoever moves in. I reckon that's what God has in mind for all of us."

"That's the truth. Love your neighbor as yourself, that's what the book says, ain't it? Don't matter the color."

Pap had found a kindred spirit in his new neighbor across the street.

Fred became a lifelong friend, the kind of neighbor that feels like family.

***

As the racial transition of Kansas City crept farther south and east, the neighborhoods around Swope Park grew much more diverse. As the transition continued, the flight of white families accelerated. In the midst of this tide of change stood Parkway Baptist Church. Black families began to visit, and the church was divided about how to respond. Pap and Mom and a handful of like-minded folks were very welcoming, and a few black families began attending regularly. Even so, several white families quietly slipped out the door, never to return. The pastor, young and idealistic, fresh out of seminary, did his best to encourage openness and love for all of our new neighbors, but some were not having it. Within a year, only three white families remained in the church.

Mom and Pap invited Bert and Polly Noland and Charlie and Gladys Brooks over for Sunday dinner on a warm summer afternoon. After the roast and potatoes, everyone settled into the living room for coffee and conversation. The subject focused naturally on the coming and goings at church.

Gladys and Mom debated their latest project, the annual church picnic. "Where do we go this year?" Gladys asked. "We can't use the main shelter at Swope Park like we always have before. Most of our church is not allowed to use that shelter."

For years, nobody seemed to mind that the park was segregated, but now it mattered. Suddenly the unfairness was obvious.

"I don't know where to go," Mom replied. "Are all the parks still segregated? I heard they opened the city pools."

Bert raised his hand to offer a solution. "Shelter #5 at Swope Park. That's the spot. Alvin said something about it the other day. It's the only shelter in the park that black folks can use. It's tucked over there between the zoo and Starlight Theater. It's not very big, but we can make do."

Pap nodded with approval. "That way, we'll be the ones breaking the rules, and I'm okay with that."

Bert had more to say. "Me too, but you know, this is just the beginning. Everything's changing and it's not all for the better. Polly and I are in no hurry to rush off, but it does make you wonder what's going to happen. I mean, what's our neighborhood going to be like in a few years? Our kids are grown, so the schools aren't the main thing for us. I'd just like for our house to still be worth something when it comes time to retire."

Gladys, who always seemed to speak for Charlie, shared their thoughts. "Charlie's always worked hard, and he's made a good life for us, and having good neighbors like you all has been a real blessing. The last thing we want to do is to move out and start over somewhere else. We've been in our house for thirty-two years."

Polly spoke up. "Bert and I were married at Parkway. Our children were baptized there by Brother Herald. It's our home. We love Parkway but, honestly, it's not like it used to be. You would have to agree, it's changed a lot."

Pap had been keeping his counsel just listening, trying to gauge the feelings of each person. Mom refilled the coffee cups and sat down on the piano bench opposite the stone fireplace while Pap loaded and lit his pipe with his Granger Roughcut.

Charlie decided to speak for himself. "Oscar, what are you going to do? Are you and Verna going to stay here? You've still got a child in school. Sue's in second grade?"

Pap nodded in agreement.

"Well, I'd say you have the most to lose here, the most at stake. It's not just property values for you. You've got your family to worry about."

Pap laid aside his coffee and leaned forward in his chair so he could see everyone face to face. "I never thought the color of a man's skin was reason enough to hate him, and I never thought the color of my neighbor's skin was reason enough to move off. Same goes for church. I reckon if God made all kinds of folks, I can worship with all kinds of folks. Now, lots of our friends have moved away, but we've made lots of new friends, up and down this street, wonderful people, good neighbors. And I have to believe that there are some values that are more important than property values."

Pap let his words hang in the air a moment as he puffed his pipe. Then he continued. "Our church has changed in lots of ways, but it hasn't had a fight. We haven't gone to war over these changes, at least not yet. Most of the churches around here have either split or moved or closed up shop entirely. I can't think of one church that's been able to work through this change from white to black in a peaceful, respectful way. I'm determined that Parkway will be the first."

Bert held up his hands as he asked, "How do we do that, Oscar? How can we control what happens at Parkway?"

"It's pretty simple, Bert. We stay there. We don't leave. We don't make a fuss. We welcome new folks, and we let them take the lead. We don't insist on our own way. Someday before too long, this church will call a black pastor, and we'll need to be just as supportive as we've always been. Just like before."

"So," Polly said, "we just pretend nothing's happened. Is that it?"

"Not exactly," Mom answered. "We know things have changed, but we need to forget about color and be brothers and sisters in Christ like we've always been."

Pap waited for the quiet before he laid the matter before them. "Verna and I are staying at Parkway, and I hope you will too. I believe if the six of us determined to stay, if we decided to see this through, we could see something beautiful, a church that stays together, welcomes everyone, and tries to live out what the Bible teaches." He paused as they pondered his challenge. "What do you think? Can we make this commitment together today? Will you stay?"

Charlie waited for a nod from Gladys before he spoke. "We'll stay at Parkway for now, Oscar. We're not sure what we'll do about our house, but we won't leave Parkway. I've got five and half years left before I retire, and after that, all bets are off. But we'll stay for now and help hold things together."

Pap smiled and turned his gaze toward Bert and Polly.

"Okay, Oscar," Bert said. "We'll stay and help get the church through this time of change. We're looking to move, maybe out to Raytown or Ruskin Heights, but we'll stay at Parkway at least for a while." Bert leaned back in his chair shaking his head. "You know, you're a hard man to turn down."

Everyone laughed, echoing those same sentiments.

"He sure is, Bert," Charlie said with a smile. "It's tough to argue with Oscar Hill. Besides, more often than not, he's right."

More laughter as Pap shrugged his shoulders.

"Don't tell him that," Mom said. "He's not always right, even if he thinks he is."

Bert put his arm around Mom's shoulder and nodded in agreement. "Not every time, Verna, but he's right this time. That's good enough for me."

***

When my baby sister, Sue, turned eight years old in 1964, she wanted to have a birthday party. By then, all of her older siblings were long gone, out on their own. I was living in Maryville, Missouri, with Eva and our eight children. So Sue was almost an only child, keeping her parents young and wearing them out at the same time. On this birthday, she had her heart set on taking all of her friends to Fairyland Park, Kansas City's first and only amusement park. It featured a huge steel roller coaster, the Wildcat, said to be the largest steel roller coaster in the world, but who knew if that was true? Sue was still too little for the Wildcat, but there were plenty of merry-go-rounds and other rides for just her size. Though not expensive by today's standards, twenty-five cents to get in the gate, an outing to Fairyland represented a major sacrifice for Mom and Pap.

But that was not the biggest problem. Little Sue had friends from church and from the neighborhood, white friends and black friends she wanted to invite on her birthday outing. Mom had to explain to Sue that her black friends were only allowed to go to Fairyland one day each year, and that one day was a month past her birthday.

Sue was crushed, so disappointed that her friends couldn't come to her party at Fairyland. After thinking it over, she came to Pap with a solution in mind. "Daddy, can I change my birthday? Could I have my birthday in September? Then we could all go to Fairyland."

Pap smiled and scooped her up on his lap and gave her a hug. "Well, that would be a sweet thing to do, Sue, but I think birthdays are pretty hard to move. Once you're born, you're born. But if we want to celebrate on another day, I guess we can do that."

Sue nodded and kissed her daddy's cheek. "Okay, let's have my party in September so we can all go to Fairyland."

So in '64, Sue marked her eighth birthday with a cake and a few cards and presents from her family, but no party, looking forward to a special day after Labor Day.

Sue circled the date on Mom's kitchen calendar and announced her plan. "Today is my birthday, but September 8 is my birthday party." Not a tinge of regret, Sue was perfectly content to put off her celebration so she could share it with her friends.

The problems began in August, when Sue's homemade invitations were delivered. Mom got calls that weekend from the parents of three white boys and girls who received invitations.

Alice Hopkins' response expressed the gist of all three calls. "Mrs. Hill, do I understand this invitation correctly? This is Sue's outing to Fairyland and we're going on the coloreds' day?"

Mom tried to explain. "Yes, that's right. Sue put off her party until now so that all of her friends could go, black and white."

"So you mean the whole park will be full of colored kids? I'm just not comfortable with that. I can't send my Margie to Fairyland on the coloreds' day. What would she think? Where would she eat or use the restroom?"

Mom calmed herself and responded. "There's a nice picnic area at the park, Shelter #5. We'll bring along some sandwiches and chips and cookies. It will be fine. The kids just want to play together."

"I'm sorry, Mrs. Hill. I'm not sure that's such a good idea, letting our boys and girls mix like that. I'll be keeping Margie at home. I hope you all have a fine day."

By the time the big day arrived, four of Sue's white friends had sent their regrets. She was disappointed, but still excited about the day, one she had so long anticipated.

When we arrived at the park, a bigger disappointment was waiting for us. Pap went to the ticket booth to pay the admission for eight boys and girls and three adults.

The cashier explained the problem. "This is colored day at Fairyland. It's only for colored kids, not white folks."

Pap tried to explain. "It's my daughter's birthday party, just eight boys and girls, black and white. They are all friends. We waited until today so they could all come together."

The gate manager had stepped up behind the cashier and heard Pap's plea. "I'm sorry, sir. There is one day for coloreds and that's today. There is no day when both whites and coloreds are admitted to the park. No mixing. That's the rule."

No matter how Pap protested, the keeper of the gate was adamant. In exasperation, Pap asked, "Is there anywhere in this city where kids can play together?"

He walked back to his eager little party and proposed a change of plans. Under normal circumstances, ice cream at the Velvet Freeze would have brought cheers, but this day it brought only disappointment. The sadness on Sue's face as Pap tried to explain broke his heart. In her innocence, she couldn't understand the rules and attitudes that drew lines between blacks and whites, separating neighbors and friends.

***

Mom came from the kitchen with two bowls of popcorn and settled into her favorite chair in front of the television. It was a Sunday night and Mom and Pap wanted to watch the program, "Judgment at Nuremburg," recounting the Nazis on trial for war crimes. Pap had followed the trials in the papers after the war, and he wanted to see the drama unfold on television.

Mom had sent Sue upstairs for an early bath and bedtime, not anxious to fill her eight-year-old imagination with images of such atrocities.

The film had an all-star cast: Spenser Tracy, Burt Lancaster, and Marlene Dietrich. The trial scenes dripped with emotion as the dialogue probed issues of good and evil and what the prosecutor referred to as "crimes against humanity."

Nearly an hour into the broadcast, ABC interrupted the film with a special news bulletin from Selma, Alabama. Six hundred Negroes marching peacefully for the right to vote had been attacked by Alabama state troopers, local law enforcement, and a large crowd of white townspeople. The graphic footage was shocking in its brutality. Troopers on horseback ran people down, whips and billy clubs struck, and the violence raged on through the tear gas and gunfire.

My mother wept as she watched in horror the troopers relentlessly pursuing the marchers as they ran for their lives.

The sheer brutality shocked Pap, as he anticipated some intervention, waiting for someone to make it stop and put an end to such violence, but on and on it raged. The peacekeepers were the perpetrators.

For Pap, the comparison could not have been clearer: Nazi genocide and Southern bigotry; Hitler's Brownshirts and Wallace's blue shirts; hapless Jews and helpless Negroes.

"Look at that. How can people do such things? Look, some are just kids, and the women... he's beating that woman. I can't believe it." Pap wanted to turn away, but he had to see it, burn it into his memory alongside other heartless, senseless images.

He thought back to his boyhood, that piece of bone in his hand. He remembered that awful day in St. Joe, the stench of burning flesh. He thought about all the hatred and bigotry he had witnessed in his life.

"I'm tired of it, Verna. I'm sick of it. I reckon God's sick of it, too. When will it ever stop?"

***

By this time, Eva and I were still living in Maryville, a couple of hours north of Kansas City. I was the pastor of a small congregation, and Eva scrambled to care for our rowdy household of eight children. Pete, our oldest, was in high school, and the little guy was about ready to start kindergarten.

In addition, I was trying to finish my seminary studies, commuting to North Kansas City for classes when we could scrounge my tuition from our modest income. I had managed to turn a three-year degree into a fourteen-year marathon that had no end in sight. Any extra expense, repair, or medical bill would mean dropping out and waiting until the next semester or the one after that. When Christmas came around each year, I cringed to think how little we had to spend, how meager our Christmas would be. And every year, my fears would prove unfounded. A not so mysterious intervention made up the difference, filling the gaps, and bringing Christmas to us in wonderful ways.

You must know by now, no one loved Christmas more than Pap. It began with his own faith, his love for the one whose birthday we celebrate, but Pap loved all of Christmas—the stories and the music, the traditions and the nostalgia, the decorations and the food—but above all, he loved the giving most, giving to his children and his grandchildren. Nothing else brought him such joy, such an expression of satisfaction on his face, as Christmas morning with his family.

You may recall that Pap loved poetry and even wrote a few lines himself through the years. He also memorized several story poems that he loved to recite for his grandchildren: "Casey at the Bat," "Paul Revere's Ride," "The Ballad of Casey Jones," "The Charge of the Light Brigade," "Abdul Abulbul Amir," and "Annabel Lee." Our kids would gather around his chair mesmerized by his words.

Best of all was Pap's annual telling of "The Night Before Christmas." Hearing those familiar words captured by Pap's imagination made many a believer for Santa Claus, a favorite memory of every child and grandchild to sit on his lap and hang on his words.

One Christmas Eve after we finally got the kids calmed down and off to bed, Eva and I set in the light of our Christmas tree fretting about the morning ahead. One inexpensive gift for each child from Santa, and a little something from a sibling, would have to do it this year. Most of the gifts were things the kids needed, things we would have to buy anyway. It was all we could do. We filled the stockings with an apple and an orange and a peppermint stick. I had nothing to put together, nothing to assemble that night.

It was almost 11:00 when the phone rang. Eva took the call in the kitchen, and returned curious and confused. "That was the man at the bus depot. He says there's a crate that just arrived on the late bus addressed to you. You better go pick it up."

"A crate? That's strange. I'll go get it." I bundled up and drove to the depot in our '59 Chevy wagon. The town was quiet as light snow fell and the lights twinkled in the windows on First Street, a few late-night church goers the only ones about.

The crate was huge, about six feet long, three feet wide, maybe eighteen inches deep, and plenty heavy. The man at the depot helped me load it into the car, and I could barely close the tailgate. It was all Eva and I could do to get it in the house, pushing the couch and coffee table out of the way to make room.

"Look, there's the return address: 4408 54th Street Terrace. It's the folks," Eva said with surprise in her voice.

I used a hammer and a screwdriver to pry the lid from the box and, after pulling away a layer of newspaper, we stepped back to take it in: all of Christmas in one crate.

The crate was packed solid, every crack and crevice filled with Christmas candy, nuts, and fruit. A huge ham was packed in the center, surrounded by a bag of sweet potatoes and three jars of Mom's canned green beans. The gifts were not wrapped but they were labeled for each child and signed from Santa Claus: a scooter for Jim, a toy farm for Jerry, a tricycle for Drew—all kinds of things straight from their wish lists.

I stood there in amazement. "How did they know? We didn't tell them. How do they always seem to know when we are running short?"

Eva looked up as she scooped candy and fruit from the bottom of the crate. "I don't know, Melvin. I just can't believe it. It's so much. It's wonderful."

I gave her my hand as she stood to her feet and kissed me. "Merry Christmas, after all." I surveyed all the gifts spread across the floor. "I guess I have some things to put together, after all. I better get started."

It was nearly 2:30 when we finally got to bed, but everything was wrapped or assembled, the food was stowed away, and the crate was on the back porch. As I laid awake reflecting on that Christmas Eve, I remembered Pap's words on the porch the night I told him that I felt called to be a pastor. *'I don't know much about being a pastor, son, but I'll do whatever I can to help you.'*

Always a man of his word.

***

In those days, most Southern Baptist churches set aside one Sunday in January called Baptist Men's Day, featuring a service led by laymen rather than the pastors. (I don't ever remember a Baptist Women's Day.) Often men would share testimonies, tell a little bit of their life's story, rather than struggle to put a formal sermon together. The congregation relished the occasion, savoring a reprieve from the usual sermonizing and enjoying a "regular" person's story.

Pap's turn came in January of 1966. Never one to seek the spotlight, he reluctantly agreed after Pastor Silas asked him the second time. For three weeks, Pap struggled to write down his thoughts, but when the day arrived, he laid aside his notes and spoke from the heart. By then, the congregation reflected the changing neighborhood, with only three white families remaining. Silas Walker, fresh out of seminary, had come to Parkway in October, the first black pastor in the church's history.

When Pap stepped to the pulpit and scanned the faces before him, he didn't feel like a stranger or a minority. It felt like family, his church family, brothers and sisters in the faith. Anyone who knew Pap could probably guess what Bible story he would choose as the theme of his testimony.

Taking a deep breath and trying not to stammer, Pap began. "Well, the pastor asked me to tell my story. I don't mind sharing my testimony, though there's not much to tell. I'm an ordinary working man, like many of you fellas, doing the best I can. God's been good to me, though it hasn't been an easy road.

"I hardly knew my father. He was killed when I was just a kid. I had to grow up fast. My mother made a home for us and kept us together and warm and fed. Hard times. Tell you the truth, I don't know how she managed it. Call it faith or just plain grit. She's a godly woman and she lives her faith every day.

"Where I come from, the old ways died hard. I've seen it my whole life, meanness and cruelty, rich men lording it over the poor, the boss man grinding down the working man, white people hating black folks, doing all manner of evil to keep them down, like they were less than human.

"Once, I saw a black man die. A mob hung him from a tree and burned him alive, white folks standing around cheering them on. White folks like me."

Pap's voice broke as he struggled to find the words. "I heard his screams.... I'll never forget it." He cleared his throat and gathered himself. "I think about Jesus on the cross, nails in his hands and feet, while a mob of his own people stood around mocking his pain, just watching him suffer and die. People today are no better—so much hate in this world.

"You know the story of the Good Samaritan. When Jesus told that story, he talked about a Samaritan that took pity on a Jewish man. Now, the Jews hated Samaritans just like some white folks hate Negroes, but it was the Samaritan who put aside his prejudice and rescued a dying man. It was no accident Jesus told the story that way, teaching us how to be a good neighbor to all people, especially those not like ourselves. The truth is, we are neighbors in this world, we're all living on the same street, all of us children of God."

The congregation responded with calls of "Amen! That's right. Preach it."

Pap had one more story to tell. "One day, I was coming home from work on the streetcar. I watched a black man sitting there, and all I saw was a filthy man without enough decency to clean up after work. But God spoke to me right there, not out loud, but in my heart. The Lord said, 'I died for him, just like I died for you.' Three times I heard those words, a black boy begging on the sidewalk, a tired old woman on the streetcar. 'I died for her, just like I died for you.' Sure as I'm standing here, I'll never forget those words.

"Seems to me, that's the truth of it. God loves the whole world so much that he gave his only Son to be our Savior. Christ died for all people, just the same. God don't play favorites, and nobody's left out. I reckon if I've learned anything in this life, that's what I know. He loves us all just the same."

After clearing his throat one more time, Pap finished his thoughts. "Verna and I been coming to Parkway for a long time. 1936, I think it was, the first time we came here. A lot has happened since then, some good and some not so good. We got off track a time or two and forgot what being a church is all about. But God's been good to us and seen us through. I love this church and I've never been prouder to be a member than I am now, looking at your faces this morning. We love every one of you. That's all I got to say."

Pap stepped down to his seat beside Mom, while folks clapped and called out their encouragement. If any of the newcomers ever wondered why that older white couple stuck around Parkway, now they knew the answer.

Pastor Silas pulled Pap aside after the service. "Thank you, Oscar. I never heard such a testimony. Powerful words. Can you teach me to preach like that?"

Pap shrugged his shoulders, more than a little uncomfortable with such compliments. "Just living, Pastor. I reckon the years teach us what we need to learn, if we're paying attention. Took me about forty years to give that talk."

Pastor Silas nodded his agreement. "I guess that's right," he said. "Well, I'm glad when the time came, I was around to hear it. Bless you, Oscar."

***

"Good morning, boys. You ready for some breakfast?" Pap asked standing in the doorway of the upstairs back bedroom.

Two of my sons, John and Jim, ten and twelve years old, came sleepily to life. Eva and I farmed out our eight children every year while we attended the annual Baptist convention, and this year the boys had hit the jackpot—an extra week with Mom and Pap.

"Sure," Jim said with a stretch. "What's Grandma fixin'?"

John pulled on his jeans and reached for the same socks he wore the day before. "Smells like bacon to me. You better get down there."

The boys rushed past Pap and headed down the stairs. Nothing matched breakfast in their grandma's kitchen. Jim and John squeezed into their kitchen chairs without pulling them back.

Mom greeted them in her cotton house dress and apron, her long hair tied up in her usual bun. "Good morning, boys. What would you like for breakfast?"

There it was, that wonderful, magical question, music to their ears. They had choices, and whatever they wanted, their grandma would cook for them—pancakes, French toast, biscuits and gravy, eggs anyway you liked them, bacon or sausage, you name it. Back at our house, breakfast for the ten of us was of necessity kept simple—cereal, toast, oatmeal—so a hot home-cooked breakfast tasted like heaven.

"How about pancakes with lots of syrup?" John asked, still not sure his request would be granted.

Mom just smiled. "All righty. What about you, Jimmy?"

Savoring the choice nearly locked him up. After a long moment's thought he came to a decision. "Could I have scrambled eggs with cheese and French toast?"

"Of course, you can. Coming right up. Mom poured the orange juice and went to work rustling up a breakfast that would have made any classic diner proud.

Pap poured himself some coffee and sat down with the boys. "After breakfast you boys can finish up the back porch. Your brushes and what's left of the paint are on the picnic table. Try to get the paint on the porch today instead of each other."

Jim and John nodded in agreement. Somehow doing chores for their grandpa made the boys feel like little men able to do grown-up jobs.

"And if you get the porch finished up, you two can come to work with Grandpa this afternoon. Would that be all right with you?"

The boys sprang to full attention, wide-eyed, gripped with excitement.

"Yeah, that'd be great, Grandpa," Jim said for both of them.

You must understand, for my five sons and my many nephews, there was no greater thrill than going to work with their grandfather. It rose above ballgames or carnivals, almost like Christmas morning—for the boys, the coolest place with their favorite guy. Sure, it was loud and dirty and sometimes scary, and that's why the girls weren't much interested, and if they did go, once was enough. But the boys would've gone every day if they could.

"Okay then, get your work done this morning and Grandma will bring you down to the railyard this afternoon. See you there."

Mom handed Pap his lunch pail and with a kiss sent him on his way.

***

When Mom pulled up to the railyard that afternoon, Jim and John scrambled out of the car too excited to wait any longer, but Mom wasn't quite ready to turn them loose. "Wait a minute, boys. We better wait for your grandpa. He'll be coming right along."

The boys gazed past the tall chain link fence across a river of railroad tracks toward the shops and the roundhouse. Jim spotted him first, walking towards the gate in his bib overalls and chambray shirt rolled up above his elbows.

"There's Grandpa! He's coming," Jim said pointing to Pap. "See him?"

"I see him," John answered.

Pap's enthusiasm matched the boys' as they waved to their grandma and walked together across the yard holding Pap's hands and staring in every direction at once. As they entered the shop, all the guys welcomed their young visitors.

"Hey, Oscar. Who you got there? Did you find some new railroaders?"

"Welcome to the Frisco, boys." Raymond Ward stepped up with a smile. "Did you guys come to give your grandpa a hand today? Well, we better put you to work around here."

Pap handled the introductions. "These are two of Mel's boys, Jim and John, and they want to be real railroaders."

Raymond smiled and nodded to Pap, remembering how this was supposed to go. He and Pap had been working all week overhauling big Frisco diesel #2015, and they finished the job that morning.

Raymond put his hands on his knees to talk to Jim and John eye to eye. "Boys, I'm glad you're here today. We've got a job to do, and we could sure use your help. See that big engine over there? Your grandpa and I got it running again and we need some help moving it out of the shop. Did you ever drive a train? You think you could help us?"

Jim and John nodded in astonishment.

"I guess so," Jim said while John stood there speechless.

The boys had never been up close to a diesel locomotive.

John finally found his voice as Pap boosted him up into the cab. "It's so big. It's huge."

Jim climbed up behind him and Pap followed.

"Yes, it is, young man," Raymond said as he sat him down beside Mason, the tall, gray-headed engineer.

"Would you like to blow the whistle when it's time to move out?"

John said, "Yeah!"

Raymond lifted him up so he could reach the pull line for the whistle.

Pap spoke to Mason, who smiled and nodded. Then, the engineer turned to Jim standing beside Pap. "Young man, you think you could drive this train for me?"

Jim stood there with a nervous grin.

"Well, climb right up in my chair and I'll show you what to do. Before we fire it up, your brother better blow that whistle."

Right on cue, John pulled the cable long and loud. The deep-throated blast startled and thrilled the boys as the engineer brought the huge diesel up to power.

The roar of the engine forced him to shout his instructions to Jim and place his little hand on the levered throttle. "Nice and easy now, push it forward!" he shouted, with his big hand over Jim's, and together they moved the lever ahead. The big locomotive groaned and shook and slowly crept toward the turntable. Too loud for conversation, but the sheer wonder on the boys' faces brought big smiles to Pap and his partners.

When Jim and John finally climbed down from the train, Raymond gave the verdict. "Yes, sir, you two are real railroaders now, just like your grandpa."

Those were the words they longed to hear and would always remember—just like your grandpa.

On the way home with Pap, two more stops made the day complete. First, they swung by the old Sears building at Fifteenth and Cleveland, and Pap pulled up beside Maurice's sidewalk tamale stand. At least once a month, Pap would pick up a sack of greasy, spicy tamales for the family. Nobody liked them as much as Pap, and his grandsons ate them only because Pap convinced them how wonderful they tasted—anything to be like Grandpa. The second stop was much more popular with the boys–Velvet Freeze on Gilham Road, the best ice cream in Kansas City. Pap picked up a gallon of Gold Coast Chocolate, the family favorite.

A day to remember, two little boys' dream come true, a grandfather's delight, and a song to sing all the way home: '*I been working on the railroad, all the live long day....*'

Chapter 9 – Fighting Fires

"Fury spends itself pretty quickly
when there's no fury facing it."
~ ***John Lewis***

In the years that followed the vote to integrate the union, it became apparent that changing policy had not automatically changed behavior. Dozens of Negroes joined the union, but their job prospects on the railroad seemed mostly unchanged. Blacks continued to fill the same custodial and unskilled jobs as before—not a single black apprentice, no chance for advancement—even though on the books, blacks had the same opportunities as everyone else. It became an unwritten rule, a code of silence that kept all the higher paying jobs for whites, while the blacks and other minorities found only rejection and disappointment.

Pap repeatedly tried to address the issue with the other union officers and stewards and with management, but was met with blank stares or stony silence. Anyone who tried to buck this unwritten policy was liable to be harassed, or worse, by the same union members who had opposed integration from the start. After five years, only a paltry number of decent jobs had gone to black members of the union. Pap began to despair that all of his efforts had been useless, a waste of time, if no real progress had been made.

In the winter of 1966, Pap decided to take on a new apprentice. He had struck up a friendship with a young black man who worked on the cleanup crew in the main yard. His name was Darrell, tall and strong, quick-witted and friendly.

One afternoon toward the end of the shift, Pap called him aside for a conversation. "Darrell, did you ever think about learning a trade, being an apprentice?"

The boy furrowed his brow and tilted his head in response. "Not much, Mr. Hill. You know they ain't gonna to let a guy like me be apprentice around here. No chance of that."

"Sure, I know, but what if you got the chance, let's say to work alongside me and learn to be a mechanic, a sheet metal worker or a pipe fitter. Does that sound good to you?"

The boy brightened as he pondered the idea in his mind. "Well sure, Mr. Hill. That would be fine, but I just don't see that happenin'."

"Maybe not," Pap said, "but if I could bring you on as my apprentice, it wouldn't be easy, and I'm not just talking about the work. Lots of folks around here don't like the idea of a Negro apprentice. They'll be rough on you, give you plenty of grief, and they'll be watching to see you make mistakes, wanting to see you fail, so they can say, 'See, coloreds aren't any good at white man's work.' So, you need to know from the beginning, you'd have to work extra hard and put up with a lot of people who don't want you around."

Darrell took it all in as if he already knew the score. "Nothing new to me. Been that way all my life."

"So, if I can work this out, are you willing to be my apprentice? That's a full three-year commitment and lots of hard work. I won't put up with excuses. Here every day, on time, work hard and learn fast—that's what I expect from my apprentices. I'll teach you, I'll show you, and then I'll expect you to do it yourself and do it right. Can you handle that?"

Darrell smiled at Pap with a glint of determination in his eye. "I'll be the best apprentice you ever had, sir. If you can get me the chance, I won't let you down."

Pap smiled at the young man's enthusiasm. "All right, then. That settles it. Let me see what I can do."

Later that same week Pap told Sarge that he was taking on Darrell as his apprentice. As he expected, Sarge hit the roof.

"Oscar, why do you always have to be upsetting the apple cart, turning things up-side-down, pissing everyone off? You know the way we do things around here, and we do it that way to keep the peace. Everybody's happy. Everybody's working."

"Not everybody, Sarge. How would you like to be nineteen years old and know that all you are ever going to do is mop floors and clean toilets? Not too happy, I reckon. This young man needs a chance to learn a trade and I aim to give him one."

Sarge shook his head. "You know there'll be hell to pay. Never been a black apprentice on the Frisco, and if you take this boy on, you'll never be re-elected president. Think about it, Oscar. Don't you think you can do more good leading the union than by training one black apprentice?"

Pap heard him out and knew Sarge was speaking the truth. For nine years, Pap had led the union, but what good was that if no real progress had been achieved?

He'd made up his mind. "Sarge, I think maybe the best thing I can do for the union right now is take on Darrell as my apprentice. I'm going to do it."

Sarge shrugged in resignation. "Of course, you are, Oscar. Of course, you are."

***

Darrell's first week on the job with Pap was rough, worse than either one anticipated. Pap's position as union president and his history with many of the men kept them from attacking him personally. As a result, the men heaped all the more scorn on young Darrell. Pap kept the young man close to him all the time, rarely sending him on any errands around the yard, afraid of what he might run into. He gave Darrell careful instructions to avoid isolated areas around the yard, and even as he traveled back and forth to work each day.

One evening, as the day shift was lining up at the time clock ready to go home, Darrell was standing in line with his lunch pail, while Pap was still cleaning up in the locker room.

Roy Cooper, one of old guard in the shop, couldn't resist a chance to grind his axe. "Hey, boys, you know there's a nigger in line ahead of you? See him standing there like he's good as us, Oscar Hill's own slave hand. Wish I could get my own nigger to do all my work for me. Yessir, that'd be fine, but I'd still make him stand at the end of the line. Don't be puttin' on airs, boy."

"Shut your mouth, Roy," Pap said, walking up to the end of the line. "I don't want to hear another word, you hear me?"

Cooper retreated back into the line.

Pap wasn't finished. "What kind of fool are you? You want to work on this railroad or find your big mouth out on the street. Darrell works for the Frisco same as you, and on most days, better than you. Get used to it. If you can't handle it, move on."

The young apprentice proved to be a quick study, paying close attention and picking up the ins and outs of working with sheet metal and pipefitting. By the end of his first year, Pap had enough confidence in Darrell to turn over whole projects for him to complete. And by that time, most of the workers in the yard had grown accustomed to seeing a black man doing the work of a mechanic, a skilled craftsman. A few persisted with their slurs and demeaning talk, but most of the men didn't seem to mind Darrell's presence in the lunchroom or standing in line to punch out when the shift was over. In time, he had become a working man like any other, no longer a black man out of place.

Pap was proud of Darrell's progress and pleased to see the changes in how he was treated as the months and years went by. During Darrell's third and final year as an apprentice, two other young black men began apprenticeships on the Frisco. The line had been crossed with Pap and Darrell blazing the trail.

In November, Pap decided to stand for re-election as union president, though he felt certain he would lose the vote this time. Yet when the ballots were collected and counted, once again he had been re-elected. The rank and file, by a slim majority, decided Oscar Hill was still the man to trust with the working man's best interests. The support of Negro union members likely made the difference.

***

As Pap arrived home from work on a chilly March evening, Fred Sadler ambled across the street. "Hey, Oscar, how you doin'?"

Pap sat his lunch pail on the front step and offered his hand. "Evening, Fred. Doing well. How about you folks?"

Fred shook Pap's hand and put his hands on his hips as if his tall, lanky frame needed extra support. "Doing fine, thanks. Hey, don't know if you been followin' bout the big game on Saturday, the college basketball championship. Gonna be on TV. Some of the neighbors are coming over here to watch and you're welcome to come, too. I hear it's gonna be something to see, if you're not busy."

Pap didn't need a second invitation. "That sounds good to me. Thanks."

Fred smiled and nodded. "Great! 'Bout two o'clock it starts."

Pap had no idea who was playing, but Fred's enthusiasm captured him. "I'll be over."

On Saturday, Mom baked a double batch of her date and raisin oatmeal cookies for Pap to bring along for an afternoon snack.

Mona, Fred's wife, greeted him with a warm smile. "Come on in, Mr. Hill. Whatcha got there?" she asked, pulling up the foil from Mom's cookie plate. "Oh my, those look good. Nobody bakes like Verna." She moved to the kitchen, where a few other snacks were gathered on the table.

"Come in, sit down, Oscar," Fred called, motioning Pap to his own favorite chair, a black vinyl recliner.

Pap found a spot at the end of the couch, so Fred could have his usual place. "Leroy, Alvin, good afternoon," Pap said, acknowledging two more friends from the neighborhood.

Alvin was the oldest resident of 54th St. Terrace, pushing eighty years old, and Leroy was one of the youngest dads, in his early thirties.

"Hello, Mr. Hill," Leroy said, still uncomfortable calling Pap by his first name.

Alvin didn't mind at all. "Hi, Oscar, good to see you. Ready for a ballgame?"

"Sure am," Pap answered. "But I haven't been following the tournament this year. Who's playing?"

Leroy couldn't wait to fill Pap in on the details. Leaning forward, he talked with his hands as well as his voice. "You know Kentucky, they're always at the top or close to the top. They're playing for the championship again. Rupp's still the coach, a legend really, but the thing is, he doesn't recruit Negroes for his team, won't allow it. Rupp only recruits white boys from Kentucky, and he makes no secret about it."

Fred jumped into the conversation. "Think about it. It's been almost twenty years since Jackie Robinson broke in with the Dodgers, and right after him came Doby and Thompson and a bunch of Negro ball players. And here we are after all this time, and old Rupp's still pretending only white boys can play basketball."

Alvin struggled to follow the conversation, his hearing fading with the years, but he got the jest of it. "You see, Fred, Rupp's been around a long time, like me," Alvin explained. "When he started coaching, black folks couldn't even come watch the game, let alone play it. After that, they let us watch from the worst seats, the back end of the gym. And now, Negroes want to take the court and play against white boys? Well, that's more than people like Rupp can tolerate. Can't say I'm surprised."

No wonder his friends cared about this game, Pap thought to himself. "Yeah, I understand. Who's Kentucky playing, anyway?"

Leroy almost burst with the news. "Mr. Hill, that's the best part. They're playing Texas Western, a little school nobody ever heard of down in El Paso. And get this, their team is mostly Negros. They got this young coach, a white guy, and they're saying he may send out five black starters to play Rupp's all white team. That's never happened, ever. Five black players going for the national championship."

The men paused to take in the wonder of those words, before Fred spoke up. "No one knows what's going to happen. They're playing in Maryland, College Park. At least they're not playing in Kentucky. I'm not sure the white folks there would allow it. There'd be trouble, real trouble."

Pap had no idea. "Fred, you said the game would be something to see, and you weren't kidding. My, those boys are making history."

"Yes, they are," Alvin added. "And if they can win it, it might just change some things, things that needed to be changed for a long time."

Pap and his friends settled in to watch a game they would not soon forget, a black and white game on Fred's black and white television. As rumored, Coach Don Haskins of Texas Western sent out five Negro ball players to start the game. No white players entered the game that day against Kentucky, and when the smoke cleared and Mom's oatmeal cookies were gone and the final whistle blew, Texas Western had defeated Kentucky, 72-65, to become National Champions, the first NCAA title for an all-black starting five.

The four men clapped and cheered, hugged and wept, as the unthinkable unfolded before them.

Pap watched Coach Rupp, red-faced and ungracious in defeat, leave the floor with his team, unwilling to acknowledge his opponent's victory as Coach Haskins and his team waited for the postgame ritual. Time would tell how much that game would open the minds of those who witnessed that glorious scene.

As Pap crossed the street, feeling wrung out from the excitement and emotion, he thought about what that game meant to his friends in the neighborhood. Young as Leroy or old like Alvin, the victory moved them far deeper than basketball or even the championship. What mattered to those men was basic human dignity, an acknowledgement of their full humanity as black men. Coach Haskins' players had no idea how much self-respect they carried on their shoulders as they played that day, but some of it found its way down 54th Street Terrace.

***

One Thursday evening after dinner, Walter Cronkite interrupted CBS programming to announce that Martin Luther King, Jr. was dead, murdered in Memphis, gunned down on a motel balcony. The news sent shockwaves across the country as many enraged blacks took to the streets to give vent to their anger. Pap spent much of the night among his neighbors, offering what consolation he could, moved by their tears, their anguish and despair. When he came back to the house, dozens of people were in the yard and on the porch, still dazed and wondering what might happen next.

Gratefully, no violence erupted in Kansas City on that fateful night—no protests, no demonstrations. Two peaceful marches were held on the weekend, vigils of grief attended by thousands of blacks and whites.

On Monday evening, April 8, the Kansas City school board decided not to dismiss classes on Tuesday for Dr. King's funeral. Other surrounding districts had already announced their closures, but the superintendent, James Hazlett, thought it best to keep the teenagers in class and off the streets where trouble might arise. It proved to be a fateful miscalculation.

When the announcement was made on Tuesday morning at Central High that classes would not be canceled for Dr. King's service, the students walked out in mass. The same scenario played out at Lincoln and Manual High. Soon, hundreds of students were gathering and marching north towards downtown and city hall, to protest this perceived insult to Dr. King. Mayor Davis met the students at 17th and Paseo and joined them in their march toward city hall. At Truman Road and the Paseo, they met a wall of police officers, barricaded and wearing gas masks. The mayor's presence did not forestall the violence, and tear gas cannisters were fired into the crowd of students. That's when the chaos erupted.

The violence raged for three days. Fires swept through many neighborhoods, whole blocks of businesses were destroyed, and looting and vandalism were widespread. Mayor Davis declared a state of emergency, and more than a thousand national guardsmen and state troopers eventually restored order. Hundreds were injured, dozens hospitalized, and six were dead—five black men and a black teenager, all unarmed.

Pap worked that fateful Tuesday and didn't hear about the violence until he finished his shift that evening. The men coming in for the next shift told him the news of violence and rioting all over the city. As he drove his old white Ford Falcon toward home, the smell of smoke hung heavy in the air. Streets were closed and police barricades blocked his normal route across 31st Street. He could see the fires raging on Prospect, the sky glowing orange above the charred buildings.

As he pulled into his driveway, the whole neighborhood stood in the street and front yards, milling around, gathered in groups under the streetlights and trying to make sense of all that was happening.

As he stepped on the porch, a man called his name. "Oscar, what's going on downtown?" Fred Sadler hurried across the street. "Can you tell me what you saw?" As he came up the walk Pap could see the worry on his face.

"It's bad downtown, Fred. Fires, police everywhere. Kids running wild. I'm afraid it's going to be bad. Nothing good can come of it."

Pap's words did nothing to put Fred's fears to rest. "It's Richie. He went to school this morning and he never came home. Someone saw him walk out with the rest of the students at Southeast, but nobody's seen him since, so far as we know. Mona's worried sick. I want to go find him, but where do I look? The police aren't giving any information and the mayor says for everyone to stay home. Anybody out and about could get arrested."

Pap shook his head. "No, you don't want to go downtown right now, Fred. There's no talking going on, just fighting, and they'd send you off to jail or something worse." Pap set his lunch pail on the porch and put his hand on Fred's shoulder. "You stay here with Mona. Let me go find Richie. Maybe I can get some answers. He'll turn up, I'm sure. Probably on his way home right now. I'll go look for him."

"Oscar, I can't put that on you. You just got home from work. You've got no business down there either."

"Sure, I do. I'll find your boy. That's Buster's car in the driveway, so maybe I'll take him along. Just let me talk to Verna a minute."

"I appreciate it, Oscar."

Thirty minutes later, Pap and Buster drove up Prospect Avenue towards the smoke and the barricades.

Buster held one of Richie's school pictures that Mona gave them as they left the house. He was not optimistic about their chances. "Those cops aren't going to recognize one black kid over another. All the same to them, especially in the dark."

"Then we will just have to find him ourselves," Pap said. "The radio says there was a bunch of kids at that church downtown, that Catholic church, Holy something. I think it's on Southwest Boulevard."

"Yeah, I know where it is. Let's try it," Buster replied.

Pap knew Kansas City like the back of his hand, but that night the city convulsed and contorted, a strange landscape of sirens and fire and smoke. A block from the church, the police stopped all traffic. Pap and Buster could see police surrounding the building and kids pouring out of a basement door. The burning stench of tear gas hung in the air.

Buster was stunned. "Tear gas in a church? Those bastards. They're just kids. Goddamn."

Most of the teenagers were running for their lives. Others stumbled to the ground heaving and struggling to breathe. Police grabbed and cuffed as many as they could, and lined the sidewalk with young blacks. None of the fewer white protestors had been accosted. Two officers were taking names down the row, when Pap and Buster approached them.

"This is a restricted area. You can't be here," the officer shouted.

Pap responded with a nod and a loud call.

"Richie Sadler, are you here? Can you hear me, Richie?"

The officer was obviously annoyed. "What do you think you're doing? You've got no business here. This is a police matter."

Buster, who was always more likely to speak up too quickly and say too much, couldn't hide his disgust. "A police matter? Gassing kids in a church basement? No wonder you don't want anybody around to see it."

Pap held up his hand to silence Buster. "Just one boy, officer, a friend of ours, Richie Sadler. Buster, take a look around."

Buster hustled across the church lawn and moved through teenagers gasping on the ground, calling out for Richie.

Pap kept the police officer distracted and thoroughly irritated with his questions. "Are all those kids being arrested? What did they do? Why would you fire teargas into a church building? What about first aid for those kids?"

The officer had heard enough. "You two need to clear out of here. This is a restricted area."

Buster called from across the lawn towards the backside of the church. "Over here! He's over here!" Buster found Richie near the wall behind the building, rolling side to side on the ground, wheezing. Buster helped him to his feet, but Richie could barely walk. After a few steps, Buster scooped him up like a child and headed toward the car.

The same officer came running towards them shouting as he came near. "You can't take him until he's processed and questioned and signs a statement. He stays here."

Pap stepped near the officer and spoke quietly and deliberately. "If the boy gives a statement, so will I, every word of what I've seen here tonight. If you don't want to take it, I reckon some reporter will—gassing these kids, roughing them up, no medical treatment. They were in a church, for God's sake. So it's up to you, officer. Do you want the boy's statement or not?"

The officer stepped back, hesitated, then nodded. "Take him and go."

Buster put Richie in the back seat, and Pap drove off, weaving their way through the burning city back home.

***

By the time my sister, Sue, twenty-eight years younger than me, began her freshman year of high school, our alma mater had changed significantly. Southeast High School, with its castle-like construction and looming tower, had transitioned to mirror its changing community. By 1971, nearly ninety percent of the student population was black, and a strong majority of the faculty as well. Sue, with her pale complexion and long blond curls, stood out more as an oddity rather than a minority. Frequently, she was the only white person in her classroom, but for Sue, it felt no different than her own neighborhood or the church she attended. She felt remarkably comfortable at Southeast, and several of her friendly black classmates looked after her, even walking her from class to class. Mom and Pap were adamant about keeping Sue at Southeast.

As the latter years of the Civil Rights Movement began to wane, a more strident, militant approach to racial injustice came to the forefront of the national debate. Several of the young educators at Southeast were students of Malcolm X, rather than Martin Luther King, Jr. While many students at Southeast were accepting or at least tolerant of their few remaining white classmates, a more militant minority looked for opportunities to "stick it to the man."

In January, 1971, Sue attended a school assembly remembering Martin Luther King, Jr. One of the speakers that day was a young black coach and civics teacher fixated on the evils of "the white man." He spoke with anger and passion, encouraging active resistance, even violent revolution, if necessary, to secure equal rights and opportunity for black citizens. Two men representing the Black Panthers also attended the assembly.

When the program ended, Sue thought it best to go home early. She called Mom, who was not at home, and her older sister, Joyce, who was also unavailable. Those being her only options, she went back to class.

After school that day, Sue followed her normal routine and walked from Southeast High about two blocks down to Swope Parkway, and then over to the Junior High, a more convenient place for Mom to pick her up, avoiding the traffic. As she made the corner on Swope Parkway, Reggie, a classmate, ran past her and then turned, looking back. Before Sue realized it, she was surrounded by more than dozen black students she didn't recognize.

A girl grabbed Sue's long hair from behind and pulled her backward to the ground. All of them rushed forward and beat and kicked Sue from every direction, pulling out handfuls of her blonde hair.

Across Swope Parkway, three park workers were in a truck and saw Sue pulled to the ground. When they finally got across the parkway and pulled up to the curb, all of Sue's attackers scattered. The men helped Sue get to her feet and gather her books.

Mom pulled up then to see what was keeping Sue.

"Momma, look what they did to me," Sue said through her tears. "Look at my hair."

Mom held her there on the sidewalk as she cried. After helping her to the car, Mom turned to thank the men who had intervened.

Sue's painful questions had no answers. "Why would they do this to me? I never did anything to hurt them. Why do they hate me? Just because I'm white?"

Pap didn't take the news well. He was protective of his baby girl and angered that anyone would lay a hand on her. He knew that such things happened at Southeast and all over our end of the city, but usually not to students who tried to get along and be accepting of everyone.

After dinner that night, Sue took a long hot bath and Mom doctored her scalp as best she could. Pap was sitting in his chair by the fireplace reading the paper when Sue came downstairs in her robe and pajamas. She took the paper from Pap's hands and, for the first time since grade school, curled up on her daddy's lap.

Pap held her close while the fire burned low, reassuring her without words that she was safe. Try as he may, Pap couldn't stop the painful questions grating on his mind.

All these years, standing up for the black working man, insisting on a fair shake, a decent chance to make a living and be treated like a human being, and what do I get for it? My baby girl has a bloody scalp and a bruised face. How can children have such hatred?

***

The next Sunday, Sue didn't want to go to church with Mom and Pap at Parkway. She holed-up in her room most of the weekend, embarrassed by her bruises and tattered hair, and brokenhearted by the brutality visited on her by her classmates. Mom encouraged Sue to come along, and when Pap called up the stairs, she opened the door and came down without a word. She wore a white blouse and pink sweater with her black skirt, her hair brushed gently to her shoulders. A little makeup nearly covered her bruises on her chin, cheek and forehead.

Pap tried to encourage her. "You look fine, Sue. Just fine."

She swept past him and out the door with a nod. "Don't say that, Daddy. I know better."

When we arrived at Parkway, Sue didn't want to go to her Sunday School class, embarrassed and unable to explain what had happened to her. She determined to sit on the back row of the sanctuary until time for the worship service. Mom and Pap let her stay there, but things changed soon enough.

Along came Pearl, a third grader with a special fondness for Sue. Her smile lit up the day and Sue couldn't resist smiling back at her little friend. Pearl did as she always did, reaching up to touch Sue's hair, gently this time, as if she knew to be careful. In a moment, she had Sue by the hand leading her down the hall to the classrooms.

When Sunday School was over, Mom and Pap returned to the sanctuary and were visiting with friends when Sue came in accompanied by all the girls in her class, along with Pearl.

Mom saw her first. "Oh, my. Look at you. Oscar, look at your daughter."

Sue was beaming as she entered, her hair up as if she were queen of the prom. Her friends, with a little help from their teacher, Mrs. Hudson, had decided to take a break from their lessons and show a little love to Sue. So, in a one-hour makeover, her patchy scalp had been covered in a lovely hairdo, fit for a bride.

"How do you like my hair, Daddy?" Sue gushed.

Pap choked up as he tried to answer her. "It's, it's beautiful, Sweetie. You look beautiful."

Sue's whole demeanor had been transformed.

Mom wiped her tears as she turned to the girls, Mrs. Hudson, and little Pearl. "Thank you, thank all of you. You're so kind."

As the worship service began, Pearl squeezed into the pew next to Sue, grabbed hold of her hand and stretched up to whisper in her ear. "We're sisters, ain't we. We're sisters, you and me."

Sue kissed her on the forehead. "That's right, Pearl. You'll always be my little sister. I love you."

"I love you, too, Miss Sue."

***

That same week, Pap got a call from Mr. Roark, a friend from Parkway Baptist and the assistant principal at Southeast High. He wanted to come by and visit with Mom and Pap about Sue and the attack at Southeast.

The next evening, Mr. Roark arrived with two more friends from Parkway, Ezra Dorsey and Cora Washington. After some cake and coffee, Mr. Roark came to the point.

"Oscar," he said, "we know how you feel about staying in our church and our neighborhood and in our schools. We love you and respect you for your convictions. We've been doing our best to keep an eye on Sue at Southeast. Cora's girl, Jeanie, and Ezra's kids watch out for her, sometimes walk her to class. I try my best to keep watch, to keep her safe, but there's nearly three thousand students, and never more than a hundred white students. Most of the kids are fine, but you know there's trouble, more and more every year. We've been talking, and while we respect your views, we think it's time to move Sue to a different school. The truth is, we can't protect her anymore, and we would hate for anything like this to happen again. I know you don't want that."

Pap and Mom took in his words in thoughtful silence. It was a question that Mom had raised before. *'When do our beliefs have to give way to the safety of our daughter? We can't sacrifice our daughter just to prove a point.'*

Pap nodded as he smoked his pipe. "These attacks, how often does this kind of thing happen?" he asked.

Mr. Roark filled him in on the state of things at Southeast. "It's almost every week, Oscar. A few years ago, if a white student was friendly and respectful, like Sue always is, there wouldn't be any trouble. She'd be fine. But now, nobody's safe. There's a gang of our black kids that are angry and militant, and they prey on our white students. I don't want any white kids coming to our ballgames without their parents. I'm afraid they might not make it home. We've hired more security, put more teachers on duty, but we can't stop it. We can't control it. It's bad, Oscar. I'm sorry to say so, but it's bad."

"My Jeanie feels the same way," Cora added. "She loves Sue and it would break her heart to lose her, but she said it herself. It's time for Sue to go. There's too many of them all filled with hate, and they take it out on the white kids."

Mom said, "We appreciate the way you all have tried to watch over Sue at school. It's still hard for me to believe how much things have changed since our older kids went to Southeast. It's sad, what's happened."

"I wish I could tell you it's going to get better," Mr. Roark said apologetically, "but we don't have the people or the funding we need to fix these problems. For right now, it's not a safe place for white students." Those words hung in the air for a moment. "If you decide to move Sue, I'll help you with the transfer, make some calls, make it as smooth as we can for Sue."

Pap answered. "Thank you for your concern and wanting to help. Verna and I will talk this over. We'll let you know what we decide. Thanks again."

As their friends went on their way, Mom gathered the cups and plates while Pap put the chairs in place.

Mom didn't waste any time coming to the point. "You know how I feel, Oscar. I've always been fine with Sue going to school with all of the kids in the neighborhood, but this is different. If she's not safe, we have to move her. We can't let these things happen. We didn't know how bad things are, but now we know. We have to do something."

Pap followed her into the kitchen, poured a cup of the leftover coffee, and sat down at the kitchen table. "I guess it's not just about race anymore."

Mom reached for his hand on the table and spoke with gentle but firm conviction. "We have to keep her safe."

Pap sipped his coffee and leaned back in his chair as if he'd come to a decision. "She'll want to go back and say her goodbyes. She has a lot of friends at Southeast, some she's known since kindergarten."

"Not as many as you think. Most of the kids she knew back then are gone."

Pap admitted the obvious truth. "Verna, why don't you call over to Southwest and see what we need to do. That sound all right?"

"I will. I'll call Mr. Roark and let him know what we're doing."

Knowing this was a necessary step and the right thing to do didn't make it easy for Pap. It troubled him deeply to think that black and white children couldn't be accepting of each other, that Sue could be so victimized despite not having one prejudice bone in her body. Whether white flight or black power, the racial divide seemed just as wide from either side.

Hatred breeds hatred, and God help the innocent bystanders on both sides.

Sue finished high school at Southwest, much to the consternation of her older siblings who had always considered Southwest their archrivals.

***

It was a Christmas Day our family would never forget, for a number of reasons. We left Eva's folks in Gladstone right after lunch so that we could get down to Mom and Pap's before the game started. The Chiefs were playing the Dolphins in the 1971 AFC playoffs to decide which team would advance to the AFC Championship Game. Joyce, Buster, and Dan were there with their families, while Jack was still on the road from St. Louis. The game began at 3:00 PM, and Mom had planned for Christmas dinner at 6:00, allowing ample time for the game.

We all crammed into the family room around the only TV in the house. The dining room, kitchen, and living room were all set with tables and chairs for the dinner to follow. Serious football fans may recall that this particular playoff game was, and continues to be, the longest game in NFL history, playing well into a second overtime, or sixth quarter, before the outcome was decided.

By 6:15, Mom was annoyed, making regular trips from the kitchen to the family room, standing with her hands on her hips, her apron over her Christmas dress, to remind Pap that dinner was ready. No one paid attention to her since the tension of the overtime game gripped everyone.

By 6:45, Mom was thoroughly frustrated, trying to keep the food warm without overcooking it, and fighting a losing battle. Again, she entered, and the typical gentleness was gone from her voice.

"Oscar! Dinner is going to be ruined if we don't come to the table."

Pap held up his hand to hush her without ever looking up from the television. The gesture was not well-received.

At 7:15, Mom had had enough of watching three days of preparing and cooking being wasted because of a game that refused to end.

She spoke from the doorway in command mode. "It's time to eat. Everyone please come to the table."

No one else had the nerve to resist, but Pap was mad anyway because the game was slipping away, and he snapped. "Verna, we'll eat when the game is over and not before," he nearly shouted. "Now hush up. We're trying to hear the game."

No one made a sound. None of the grandkids had ever heard Mom or Pap raise their voice to the other. I hadn't heard such an exchange between them in many years.

Mom retreated to the kitchen and a pall settled over the holiday. When we did finally eat at nearly 8:00, the mood was sullen and subdued. The Chiefs had blown the game on a couple of missed field goals, so that didn't help matters. The one silver lining to this cloud over Christmas was that Jack's family actually arrived in time for dinner, something that never happened.

I never did hear the apology, but I'm certain it was offered. Even as strong and stubborn as Pap could be, he realized he had crossed a line into rudeness, and he could not live with knowing he had hurt Mom's feelings. The day after Christmas, a bright bouquet of white gladiolas and blue asturs, Mom's favorite flowers, occupied the center of the dining room table. The Chiefs may have been eliminated, but Pap was forgiven.

Chapter 10 – Sunset

"I had an inheritance from my father,
It was the moon and the sun.
And though I roam all over the world,
The spending of it's never done."
~ ***Earnest Hemingway***

In February of 1972, Pap had finished his bacon and eggs and sat down to read the Saturday morning Star when the phone rang. Mom took the call in the kitchen. The administrator of the nursing home in Springfield called to say that Mae, Pap's mother, had passed peacefully in her sleep. The news, though not unexpected, felt sudden just the same.

Mom and Pap had made the trip to see his mother just a week before. Nearly every month, they rode the Frisco to Springfield to visit his mother, to patiently answer her questions and assure her that all was well. Her dementia had worsened over the past few years, often leaving her anxious and confused, but she always recognized her son, her Oscar. Though her memory waned, her strong will persisted as she barked orders to her caregivers, kind but firm, and always in charge. This was my grandmother's way.

The move from her little white frame house on Pacific Street had been traumatic and confusing for my grandmother. For weeks, she would awaken in the night frightened, crying out, not knowing where she was. During the day, she often felt agitated and restless, wanting to get back to her house, her home.

When Mom and Pap visited her, sometimes she would beg Pap to take her home. He hated to disappoint his mother and tried his best to help her understand. Leaving her after each visit broke his heart.

For eighty-eight years, Mae Hill had made her way in this world, fifty-three years as a widow, on her own and fiercely independent, tirelessly working to do whatever must be done to survive, to care for Margaret, to see to the needs of her family. Besides her unshakable faith in God, her one constant was her second son, Oscar, from those frightening days after her husband's tragic death until she came to the end of her journey.

Never once did my grandmother complain about her lot in life, the cruelty of her loss, the unfairness of her plight, the tiresome burdens that she carried on her tiny frame.

I wondered how much of her stubborn determination had been passed on to her son, and perhaps in smaller measure to me as well.

We laid her to rest in Nevada, Missouri, next to her long-lost husband. I brought the eulogy and Pap had prepared a beautiful spray of roses from his own garden for his mother's casket. As I stood at the graveside on that fading February afternoon, I tried to imagine that rainy November day so long ago when Pap, just eleven years old, stood beside his mother in this same spot as his father's casket was lowered into the ground. I thought about my grandfather, whom I never met, and how happy he must be in eternity to see his young bride again. And I pondered the pride he must feel in his boy, Oscar, who in so many ways filled his father's shoes.

***

When his last day on the Frisco arrived in the summer of 1972, Pap sat down for breakfast with a sad smile.

Mom scooped scrambled eggs on his plate and then her own. "Well, Oscar, today's the day. Nearly forty-seven years of eating breakfast and then heading off to work on the railroad. One last day. How does it feel?"

Pap sat back in his chair and smiled. "Is this my last breakfast, too? I'm sure gonna miss these eggs."

Mom rolled her eyes and passed the bacon. "When I packed your lunchbox, I was remembering when we lived in Monett, and you were working that job in Oklahoma City. Remember that coffeecake I used to make and pack in a shoebox for you to take with you each week? Remember that? So long ago."

Pap nodded and reached for her hand. "I think I still have that box around here somewhere, but the coffeecake is pretty stale."

Mom just sat and smiled, lost in her memories.

When Pap arrived at the railyard, he soon realized this would be no ordinary workday. Everyone had something to say, men dropping by from all over the yard, at times a line forming in Pap's shop. His old friend, Raymond, came and made a day of it. His foreman had given him the nod. After thirty years of friendship, it was worth one day's work.

Darrell, Pap's former apprentice, came by for a few moments and brought along his new apprentice, Martin. "That's right," Darrell explained. "If it wasn't for Mr. Hill taking me on, I wouldn't be here taking you on, you understand? We'd still be scrubbing toilets."

Martin extended his hand to Pap as he replied, "I appreciate it. Thank you, Mr. Hill. Thanks for what you done for Darrell and me."

Pap shook his hand and nodded, choked with emotion.

None of the management staff remained from Pap's early days on the Frisco. Pap had outlived most of them. Harold Stevens, who had called Pap on the carpet for skipping work to take his kids to the circus back in 1938 was in his nineties and living in a nursing home. Nonetheless, the present group had been around long enough to know Pap's history of union leadership. They understood that Pap still carried more weight with the rank and file than anyone, even years after his final term as president expired.

The present railyard supervisor, Ron Marshbanks, asked Pap to stop by the office sometime during the day.

After enjoying his lunch complete with cupcakes baked by Raymond's wife, Pap climbed the stairs to the offices. For all the years, the main office remained much the same. The two green metal desks still faced each other. The faded pictures and charts hung on the same nails. Only the names and faces had changed.

Mr. Marshbanks greeted Pap warmly, shaking his hand and offering him a seat in a leather armchair. "This is a big day for you, Oscar. How's it feel? Forty-seven years... I can't imagine. I'm just forty-five years old myself."

Pap laughed. "Now I really feel old," he said.

Mr. Marshbanks moved to his desk and picked up a small package wrapped in shiny silver paper. "Some of us went together and got you something, just a token of our appreciation and respect for you, Oscar. Open it up."

"Thank you, sir. That's kind of you." Pap opened the package and unwrapped a pocket watch, an old-style Hamilton that looked strangely familiar.

Mr. Marshbanks explained. "Raymond had to help us on this. I hope we got it right. You said your father died in an accident on the railroad when you were just a kid, and you have his pocket watch crushed in that moment. I've never seen it, of course, but Raymond has—you showed it to him. So we tried to get you exactly the same watch. It's not a new one. They don't make them like that anymore. It's an antique. Anyway, we found one in good shape, had it fixed up, and we want you to have it, not to replace your father's watch, but to keep your legacy going. We had it inscribed on the back."

Pap ran his fingers over the watch, recognizing every detail, his father's watch come back to life. He turned it over and read the words. *"Oscar L. Hill, Frisco Railroad, 1925-1972."*

"I don't know what to say. That's real kind. Thank you for this. It is just like my father's watch."

Mr. Marshbanks gave him a broad smile. "I'm so pleased to hear you say that. We wanted it to be just right. I'll bet your father would be very proud of the railroad man you turned out to be." He stepped forward and extended his hand once more. "Good luck, Oscar, and God bless."

When it was time to clock out, Pap started toward the west door carrying a bundle of everything that had accumulated in his locker through the years, along with his lunch pail. Instead of the usual single file approach to clocking out, a long double line stretched past the offices and across the main yard. A young black apprentice took his bundle and lunch pail and followed along behind him. Everyone was in line, the office staff, the clean-up crews, the brass from upstairs, and all the railroaders from the full length of the yard.

When Pap walked to the end of the line, the foreman shouted from the front, "Oscar Hill, forty-seven years on the Frisco, moving on down the line. Godspeed, Mr. Hill."

At that moment, the steam whistle from the massive diesel #2015 sounded, loud and long, and the cheers went up.

Pap walked slowly between the lines as his fellow railroaders clapped and whistled, reaching for his hand or offering a pat on the back. Even the youngest of the crowd had heard his story, and every black man in that line knew the truth. This old man had made the difference.

In his last several years at work, everyone except Raymond called Pap, "Mr. Hill," no matter how many times he said, "Call me Oscar." It had nothing to do with his age or seniority. Nor was it because of his skills as a master mechanic. It was respect, plain and simple, the respect that is due a man of integrity, a man who lives by his convictions and stands up to what's wrong in the world, a man who is unafraid to stand alone. And so they cheered Pap down the line and on his way into retirement.

When he pulled his Ford Falcon into the driveway, Mom was sitting on the porch waiting for him. There was no banner across the doorway, no big celebration planned, just dinner with Joyce and Howard and their kids—nothing out of the ordinary. Still, it was the best moment of a wonderful day, when his partner through thick and thin met him at the top of the stairs with love in her eyes, a kiss and a hug.

"Well, Oscar, you did it. You finished the job. Welcome home."

***

Pap's retirement began in a flurry of activity. His old 1948 Chevy pickup sat in the driveway half-buried with accumulated junk. The engine had not been started in fifteen years or so, and the tires were rotten and flat. Pap determined to get the old truck on the road again, a necessity for his many projects to follow.

He and Buster spent days overhauling the engine, picking up some cheap used tires, and replacing the exhaust system, which was blowing clouds of smoke directly from the manifold into the cab through the rusted-out floorboards, a quick fix for a sheet metal man.

When the engine finally turned over with a cloud of blue smoke, it did not inspire confidence, sputtering and wheezing like a dying man. It never did run well, but it ran well enough for Pap's purposes, hauling huge loads of fertilizer, mostly horse manure, for his second big project.

In recent years, the back half of Pap's four and half acres had become an overgrown thicket of brush and hedge wood. Pap called in a bulldozer and had it cleared off, burning a huge brush pile as the whole neighborhood looked on. Then, with the help of a few neighbors and grandsons, he planted fruit trees, dozens and dozens of trees of all varieties, everything he thought might do well in the extremes of a Kansas City climate—peach, plum, pear, cherry, nectarine, apple, apricot, mulberry.

Along with the planting came the fertilizer, fragrant in the summer heat, shoveled to every hole as the trees were planted. Joyce's youngest and our youngest, Bob and Drew, were drafted into Pap's army that summer, provided wheelbarrows and shovels, and assigned fertilizer duty. Every day for a week, Pap would drive the old pickup to the nursery, with Bob and Drew along for the ride, and get a half ton of horse manure dumped in the bed of the truck, weighing it down to the axle. The harrowing ride across the city as the old truck staggered under the load filled the boys with dread, deciding each day they would never make it back, but every day another load had to be shoveled into wheelbarrows and wheeled around back to the trees.

One evening as the boys were hosing out the truck bed, Pap noticed a lump of coal, big as his fist, that had somehow come with the load of fertilizer. He stood on the porch and held it up with a grin. "Boys, don't you know some old mare must have kicked up a fuss when she passed this thing. Mercy!"

The boys laughed with their grandpa, who knew how to humor his middle school grandsons.

Pap's new orchard, in addition to his vegetable garden and rose beds, made the transition from the railroad to small-time farming complete.

He devoted his evenings to his artistic side, taking an oil painting course and then signing up for a cake decorating class. He wondered what the boys in the railyard would think of him pursuing such interests. After all, the only other man in his cake decorating class was a pastry chef—no other railroaders around.

What possessed an old pipefitter to learn such skills? Those who knew him best, his wife and grown children, were not surprised. The same man who engineered and shaped sheet metal for the Frisco carefully tended and arranged his roses and crafted his

May baskets each spring. The master mechanic who repaired huge diesel locomotives also wrote romantic poetry for his sweetheart. Oil paints and frosting provided Pap with more gifts to give, fresh ways to appreciate beauty and express love.

***

In the fall, Pap and Mom left home on their first cross country adventure. One of the best perks of a railroad retirement was a rail pass for two, anywhere, anytime seats were available. As you might expect, my parents loved to travel by train, and to travel together at their leisure promised to be a wonderful, relaxing treat.

Buster drove them downtown to Union Station, where Pap had arrived in Kansas City so many years before. On this day, Mom and Pap were departing the familiar site for the longest train trip of their lives, catching the Texas Chief on its way from Galveston to Chicago, where Dan lived. Mom and Pap looked forward to several days with their most distant son.

Then, just as the trees were beginning to turn, Mom and Pap headed west aboard the Empire Builder, getting off for a few days at Glacier National Park, before continuing to Seattle. For a day, the folks traded the rails for the water and enjoyed the Seattle Water Tour to Blake Island, taking in all the sites along the coast. For landlocked Midwesterners, the ocean spray in their faces and the gentle rocking of the waves, which might have annoyed other travelers, only added to Mom and Pap's enjoyment. Pap finally gave up trying to catch a good picture of the dolphins swimming and leaping in the distance, a novelty for them.

Next, Mom and Pap climbed aboard the Coast Starlight with service from Seattle to San Diego, though they were going only so far as Los Angeles. Heading south, the snow-capped Cascades took their breath away before the rails descended to the Pacific coastline, conjuring sunsets over the ocean like they had never imagined. Mom and Pap sat in one of the new dome cars, where they could take in the entire vista—mountains to the left, the ocean to the right.

Late in the afternoon, a young couple sat down across from Mom and Pap to take some pictures, and Pap couldn't help but strike up a conversation. "Good evening. Would you like me to take a picture of the two of you with that nice view behind you?"

"Sure, that'd be nice. Thanks," the woman answered, handing her Kodak Instamatic to Pap. She and her partner looked like a storybook couple, beautiful and obviously very much in love.

"Smile," Mom said, but they didn't need any encouragement.

Pap tried his best to capture their expressions and the evening sun on the mountains behind them.

As he returned the woman's camera, she offered to return the favor. "Can I take a picture of you two?"

Her long brown curls and kind, round face reminded Pap of the first time he saw Mom when they were just kids.

"That would be nice of you," Pap said, handing her his camera and pointing out the focus and the shutter on his old Kodak Brownie.

Mom and Pap smiled the carefree smile of those who have left behind the daily burdens of life, enjoying this moment at their leisure.

As the young woman returned Pap's camera, she couldn't contain her news. "We're on our honeymoon! It's so exciting. This is my husband, Kenneth. That sounds so strange, 'my husband, Kenneth.' I can't believe we're finally married. I'm Julie. What's your name?"

Mom smiled and handled the introductions. "I'm Verna and this my husband, Oscar. We're newlyweds of forty-five years, still on our honeymoon, too."

"That's so sweet. Wow, forty-five years. That's wonderful. Where are you all from?"

"Kansas City. Oscar just retired from the railroad, so this is how we like to travel."

"Yeah, see the country like this. It's so beautiful," Julie agreed.

Kenneth had been sitting back, savoring the view, but suddenly seemed interested in the conversation. "Didn't your dad grow up in Kansas City, Babe? I remember him talking about it. He had some stories to tell."

Julie's expression saddened as the subject changed. "That's right. My daddy grew up there, but he had a terrible childhood. It's not a pleasant story. When my daddy was still just a little boy, his mother was killed, murdered, and his father went to prison. Daddy was raised by a foster mother, an older woman who did the best she could for him, but times were hard."

Mom and Pap knew all about hard times, no explanation needed.

Julie hurried on to the happy ending of the story. "But, he made it. I mean, it's amazing. If you met my daddy today, you'd never know what he went through. He worked his way through college and became a teacher. Now, he's the principal of an elementary school in Cleveland."

"Your father sounds like a wonderful man," Mom said, reaching out to squeeze Julie's hand.

"Yes, he is. I wish you could meet him." Julie said.

Kenneth thought there might be more story to tell. "Babe, Oscar's retired from the railroad. Tell them about the neighbors. Remember, the family next door that your dad always talks about. Didn't that neighbor man work for the railroad? You know, the one who helped Grandma Hubbard and took your dad under his wing. Remember?"

Mom and Pap sat there, stunned as the realization dawned on them, the possibility so far-fetched and yet, who else could it be?

Mom had to know. "Julie, what is your father's name?"

Julie answered proudly, "Dr. James Hanson."

"And his foster mother, Mrs. June Hubbard?"

Julie and Kenneth's faces went blank with shock.

Julie slowly found the words. "That's right, Grandma Hubbard was always sickly. She's been gone for a long time."

Pap nodded as Mom answered. "Mrs. Hubbard was our neighbor in south Kansas City. Jimmy was one of our boys."

Julie began to weep as she soaked in the truth of it. Kenneth put his arm around her shoulder.

"You are Mom and Pap Hill?" she asked through her tears.

My parents smiled and nodded.

"We loved your daddy," Mom said, dabbing her eyes. "He was part of our family, too."

By then, even Pap and Kenneth fought back the tears.

Julie stood and took Mom by the hands, and helped her to her feet before the two embraced in a happy cry.

Then, turning from Mom, she reached for Pap. "Can I give you a hug?" she asked. "The way Daddy tells it, you are the only real grandfather I ever had, and we never met, until now."

Pap stood to his feet and held little Jimmy's daughter against his shoulder for a long, sweet moment.

Over the next four hundred miles, a strangely reunited family celebrated, enjoying meals together in the dining car and filling in the gaps in their stories, all centered around little Jimmy, Dr. Hanson.

In Santa Barbara, the four of them crowded around a phone booth as Julie called her dad and told him the astonishing news. Pap stayed on the line the longest as Julie's dad recounted those childhood days and explained to Pap how his wisdom and mentoring had been put to good use in his life.

Kenneth and Julie said goodbye in San Francisco and continued their honeymoon, but vowed to stay in touch and to visit Kansas City sometime soon.

Deeply humbled and gratified, Mom and Pap resumed their journey down the coast, pondering the mysterious ways life unfolds and the blessings we give and receive along the way.

They caught the Super Chief in Los Angeles, which brought them east past the sites of the Southwest, through the Rockies, and across the plains to Kansas City.

Joyce picked them up at Union Station and drove them down Paseo Boulevard, where the maples lined the way in full autumn glory.

"Look, Oscar, we didn't miss it," Mom said. "The trees are so beautiful. I'll travel anywhere you want to go, but don't let me miss Missouri in October."

Pap patted her hand and smiled. "I'll make sure you don't miss a thing."

More trips and travels would follow for Mom and Pap, including an overseas journey to Amsterdam for the famous tulip festival. But for Pap, no car or plane or ship could match the satisfaction and sheer joy of riding the rails.

***

In June of 1977, Pap's neighborhood underwent yet another transformation, a balancing of black and white to a degree unseen since 1963. We all wondered what might be the precipitating event for such a dramatic reversal.

Mom and Pap marked their 50th wedding anniversary, and my brothers and sisters and I tried to make the day truly special. All the grandchildren and great grandchildren happily showed up to celebrate, along with dozens of my parents' old neighbors and friends, folks from Parkway and Garfield churches, people whose lives they had blessed through the years. Even some of those stray boys that had boarded with Mom and Pap decades before returned to express their appreciation.

We held all the events of the day at the house on 54th Street Terrace. Pap had worked long hours on the yard, enlisting some grandsons to help spruce up around the house, trim the roses, and weed the garden. It was beautiful and in full bloom as people posed for pictures all over the yard.

In the afternoon, all of us filled the front yard as I conducted a renewal of vows ceremony for Mom and Pap on the front porch. Pap looked dapper in a dark brown suit, still standing sturdy and straight. Mom wore a lovely, light pink dress she had sewn for the occasion. My daughter Judy sang two songs at Pap's request: "Somewhere My Love" and "When Your Hair Has Turned to Silver." Then they joined hands as they renewed their vows, which began, "The years have found you faithful," and concluded, "that all may know that I am still touched by your love."

Quite a journey they had taken together since the day a young buck picked up his girlfriend on her way to work and ran off to Arkansas to get married without her parents' permission. A whole lot of living since the day Pap showed Mom this old house for the first time, an abandoned, dilapidated mess. A different world than the old all white neighborhood, now an all-black neighborhood minus two.

Fred and Mona were present of course, still living across the street, the best of neighbors and friends. After the ceremony, Fred was taking it all in and catching up with all the grandchildren he had watched grow up through the years.

I caught up with him for some conversation, and I remember his words.

"I ain't seen this many white folks around here, maybe ever," he said pointing around the yard and at all the cars parked up and down the street. "You know, Mel, this kind of thing couldn't happen anywhere else."

"What do you mean?" I asked.

"I mean, there's not another neighborhood in the whole city where this kind of thing could happen, not with everybody together, black and white. No chance of that. People just wouldn't come, or there'd be trouble. It just wouldn't happen like this."

"Maybe not," I said. "I know I've never seen anything like it, Fred."

The more I thought about it, I decided he was probably right.

Trying to make sense of this remarkable day, Fred pointed to the couple on the porch. "The only reason it can happen here is right up there—Oscar and Verna. That's why. Those two been a friend and neighbor to all these people. They love all of us, and we all love them right back. Color don't mean nothing. It's a beautiful thing, ain't it, Mel?"

"Yes, it is, Fred. Yes, it is."

***

Family reunions highlighted the summers in the 1970s. The Saturday closest to June 20 had to be the day, the wedding anniversary of Mom and Pap, Joyce and Howard, and Eva and me.

The folks chose a place south of the city in Belton, a public park with a large picnic shelter, ball fields, and a swimming pool across the parking lot. What Pap liked best about the park was the old Frisco locomotive restored and displayed, #1632, a 2-10-0 steam engine, standing proudly on a section of track across the backside of the park, an impressive reminder of our family's railroad heritage. Every year, the next wave of grandchildren and great grandchildren got a personal tour of the old steamer and expert explanation from Pap.

Dan and Bill always flew in from Chicago, and Jack and June drove over from St. Louis with their three kids. Buster's bunch and Joyce's family lived close by in Kansas City, and Eva and I lived in Grandview, just up the road from Belton. The older grandkids came in from all over. Everyone brought abundant food, lots of family recipes heaped on the tables in the shelter house. A late lunch segued into an early dinner—one continuous meal, the kids grazing between dips in the pool. Mom and Pap enjoyed the evening shade under the maples while the little ones napped on quilts.

Invariably, our reunions featured a fair amount of debate about the issues of the day. As you might expect, the Hill family suffered no shortage of strong opinions, whatever the subject. From Mizzou football to the war in Vietnam, from the Watergate scandal to whatever Pap's edition of the Star headlined that weekend, lots of issues found their way into our conversations. Though we all seemed to inherit Pap's strength of conviction, our points of view ranged far and wide. Fortunately, we also inherited Pap's ground rules: make your case, defend your point of view, ask questions, and try to learn something. Nothing personal or mean, or answer to Pap, and no one wanted to do that.

The heart of our annual reunion was the stories, telling the family stories from generation to generation. We all told stories, of course, but none of us ever mastered the art quite like Pap. He was born with stories to tell. As we sat across a picnic table over the meal or gathered around the folks in our lawn chairs, the past came to life in Pap's words. He pulled our family's roots to the surface and exposed them to the light of day, a long life's journey recounted in vivid detail. When Pap's memory gave way to imagination, Mom or one of us would step in and nudge the story back towards reality.

And, yes, at times we tired of hearing a story repeated again and again, year after year. Most of us could tell you about Mom and Pap running off to Arkansas to get married in every detail, or the day that God spoke to Pap on the streetcar, or the Christmas he sold his tools to buy gifts for his kids. We knew the stories by heart, but our kids and their children did not.

For their sake, we tolerated stories that held little suspense for us.

Speaking of the next generation, Pap had a whole second category of stories to tell that had absolutely nothing to do with reality—tall tales, stories to tickle and fascinate the little ones, stories to capture attention and fire imagination in young hearts. Stories that most of the grandchildren grew up believing well into their school years, so convincing was Pap's power with words.

According to his stories, Pap once rode with Buffalo Bill and his Wild West Show. He chased Sitting Bull across the country and finally got his headdress and tomahawk, which he kept up in his attic, and one of these days he'd show them to us. Davy Crockett and Kit Carson crossed Pap's path from time to time. Once he had to help Daniel Boone find his way when he had gotten lost coming across Missouri. Apparently, Santa Claus had a long and complicated friendship with Pap, as did the Easter Bunny. Pecos Bill and Paul Bunyan were also pals of Pap from way back.

Sometimes the weather starred in Pap's tales. So cold was one winter that Pap's goldfish bowl froze solid every night and thawed out during the daytime, but his goldfish were no worse for wear. One time in a tornado, Mom's big cast iron kettle was turned inside out, rolling around with the legs on the inside. His stories stretched the bounds of imagination—stories to savor and share, stories to eventually outgrow but never forget, golden moments of childhood.

Looking back now, we cherish and preserve Pap's stories, his real-life reflections and even his tall tales, knowing that our own stories have their roots in his—the life he lived, the choices he made, the work he completed, the faith he found, the man he became.

***

Old age came to Pap as an unfriendly, unwelcome thief. A lifetime of smoking left him with emphysema that gradually took his breath and robbed him of his strength. The Midwestern winters grew long and isolating, as Pap had to admit he could no longer clear the walks and get Mom to the grocery store.

Joyce and her family picked up the shopping duties, and Buster checked on the folks almost daily.

Remarkably, the walks were always cleared, and the morning paper was brought to the door each day. Trash cans made it to the curb on Thursday mornings. Every week during the summer, the grass was mowed, and in the fall the leaves were raked and bagged. The neighborhood that Mom and Pap had watched over all those years began to watch over them. Pap tried to pay the neighbor kids for doing his chores, but rarely would anyone take his money. Those kids' parents had been schooled in the art of neighboring by Mom and Pap, and their children were taught to return the favor.

Sue and her husband, Jerry, lived in Muscle Shoals, Alabama, and they invited Mom and Pap to winter with them in the milder Southern climate. It began with an extended Christmas visit, and then each subsequent year, Mom and Pap stayed longer, enjoying Sue's five children and being unburdened with the struggles of living on their own.

The dangers of leaving their house back home vacant for several months were very real. Any other house left unoccupied for even a couple of weeks in that neighborhood would have been vandalized, ransacked, or worse. But not Mom and Pap's house. Fred kept an eagle eye on the place, and all the neighbors helped keep the house and yard in good order. Even rowdy teenagers knew that the Hill house was off limits for any mischief.

Eventually, Mom and Pap could no longer make the trip to Alabama or anywhere else. My siblings and I did some work on the house so that the folks wouldn't be required to climb the stairs.

Next came wheelchairs and oxygen tanks, a daily struggle to breathe, just breathe.

Pap went first, leaving Mom to move from their longtime home to a senior care facility.

Less than a year later, she followed her husband, anxious to be reunited.

Their headstone carries three inscriptions. For Pap, *"He lived for others."* For Mom, *"Her faith never wavered."* And finally, under the date of their wedding appeared these words: *"An inspiration to all who knew them."*

Epilogue

A quarter of a century has rolled by since my grandfather's story came to an end. Your storyteller, my father, Melvin Hill, didn't quite make it till the final act, so now it's my turn as the oldest grandchild to wrap things up.

In the spring of 2015, my brother Jerry and I were visiting our sister, Ellen, at her home on Brookside Boulevard in Kansas City. We're all grandparents now and prone to wax nostalgic about the old family stories.

Jerry brought up the old house on 54th Street Terrace, Grandpa and Grandma's home for nearly sixty years. "When was the last time you guys were down there? I haven't seen the house since right after the funeral, when they moved Grandma into the nursing home in Belton."

Ellen struggled to remember. "Me either. I don't remember being there after Grandpa passed."

I didn't have to reach back quite so far. "I went by one day when I was coming in on 63rd Street, probably at least fifteen years ago, but I didn't stop or anything. You know Fred bought the house after Grandma died, and I guess he still lives there. There's a fence around the yard and they screened in the porch. It looks different, and it was sad really. I loved that place, but it wasn't the same without Grandpa's Galaxy in the driveway and his chair on the porch. I decided I wasn't coming back. I'll just remember it like it used be."

Ellen was sympathetic but unsatisfied. "I think we should go now, just drive over there. It's not fifteen minutes from here. Let's just go. If we do this together, it won't be so sad."

Jerry was game for it, but I took some persuading.

"C'mon, Pete. Let's go take a look." My sister does not easily take no for an answer.

When we passed the corner market on Jackson, charred plywood covered the windows and the roof was mostly gone. Chick Elementary still teemed with children streaming out of the old yellow brick building to the field where we used to play in the summertime, as did our aunts and uncles before us. Ellen and I are old enough to remember when this neighborhood gave every evidence of stability, if not prosperity, with tidy streets and well-maintained homes, but those days have long since vanished in poverty and neglect.

Jerry couldn't even imagine the old days.

I steered my car past the house, now surrounded with a tall chain link fence. After turning around in the driveway where the Hendersons used to live, we pulled to the curb across from the Weaver house.

A black family was cooking out in their front yard and a man around thirty years old approached the car.

I rolled down the window and asked, "Hi, can you tell me if Fred still lives in that house?" pointing to my grandparent's house.

The man gave me a stern look and put both hands on my car door. "Who wants to know?" he asked, but I wasn't put off.

"My name's Pete Hill and my grandparents used to—"

"Oscar Hill was your grandpa?" The man broke into a broad smile.

All three of us answered in the affirmative.

The young man stuck his head in the window to see everyone more closely. "You're all Hills? I'm Anthony. I married Fred's granddaughter. Good to meet you all. Yeah, Fred's still going strong, living right there in your grandpa's house. I think he's like ninety-three now. You better go see him. He'll be upset if you don't go in."

I extended my hand. "Nice to meet you, Anthony. Thanks, we'll go to the door. Appreciate it."

Anthony stepped back as he scooped up his little girl in his arms. As I pulled forward, he walked beside the car with an invitation. "When you get done with Fred, you can eat some lunch with us, if you want. We're grilling some burgers. You'd be welcome to stay."

"That's kind of you. Thanks. We've already had lunch, but we'll holler at you before we leave."

Stepping through the gate and seeing that broad front porch flooded all three of us with memories of Grandpa sitting there in his chair, smoking his pipe and spinning stories.

At the front door, the scenario repeated itself. This time a young black man came to the door more than puzzled to see three white people standing there.

I spoke up. "My name is Pete Hill and my grandparents—"

"Oscar Hill was your grandpa? Come on in." He opened the door wide and called inside. "Fred, it's the Hills, some of Oscar and Verna's family."

Fred Sadler, white-headed and thin, rose slowly from his chair by the fireplace and moved to embrace all three visitors. "Well, Pete, look at you. Just look at you. What a blessing. And your sister and your brother....

How wonderful. I should be welcoming you home. This was your family's home for all those years when you was just kids." Tears rolled into his white beard. "I'm so glad to see you all."

Ellen asked if they might look around a bit, see the house.

Fred was pleased to walk them through the startlingly familiar home. Only the light blue paint in the dining room seemed out of place in their memories.

As they walked into the kitchen, Jerry commented softly to his sister, "This is the same floor Grandma had in here."

Fred, still hearing just fine at ninety-three, turned to respond. "You didn't think we were going to mess up Oscar and Verna's house, did you? It was always such a fine home."

Jerry shook his head in disbelief.

Fred led them out the back door, where his grandson had begun replacing the old wood on the porch with new boards. The yard was mowed, but the gardens were overgrown and most of the fruit trees were gone.

"I had to take out the fruit trees." Fred said. "Just too many, I couldn't keep up with them."

I put my hand on the old man's shoulder and smiled. "That's okay, Fred. Grandpa couldn't keep up with them either, even with all of his grandsons helping out."

Back in the house, we settled in the living room and shared stories. I remembered the time when I came for a visit and had traded cars. Fred, living across the street back then and keeping a close eye on Grandpa's place, didn't recognize my new vehicle and came outside with a gun in his hand. They all laughed at the thought of it.

I said, "I remember I put my hands up and said 'It's just me, Fred. Don't shoot.'"

"Good thing I didn't," he said with a chuckle. "Those were rough days around here."

It was a surreal experience for everyone, reminiscing together, half-expecting Grandma to come from the kitchen with a tray and pitcher of lemonade. A faint whiff of Grandpa's Granger Rough Cut pipe tobacco lingered in the air, or was it the power of memory? It seemed real enough. The stairs creaked as they had always creaked, and the pictures hung on the landing had been changed except for one, a picture of Fred and Mona with Grandma and Grandpa on their fiftieth wedding anniversary—like family.

On the drive back home, Jerry reflected on the day. "What struck me was Fred's kids and grandkids. They knew all about Grandpa and Grandma and they weren't even alive back then. They never met them. It's been twenty-five years, and they still know and love Oscar and Verna Hill. Just think of that."

"It's pretty amazing, to be remembered like that, even by the next generation," I added.

Ellen wiped the tears from her eyes and said, "It makes me think of that old poem that Grandpa wrote, the one in the scrapbook he and Grandma gave us. Remember the one about throwing a pebble in the pond and watching the waves go out across the water."

Jerry nodded. "Yeah, and the waves keep coming back all these years later."

For a moment, they weren't driving out of the city; they were sitting on that porch, leaning against the brick column on a summer evening, watching Grandpa tap down his pipe tobacco with his stub finger, listening for his words.

***

I tossed a pebble of kindness
into the pond of life,
And wondered what would happen
in a world so full of strife.

I watched the ripples
as they wider grew,
Saw them touch the lives
of just a few.

Then as I stood on the sands of time,
a ripple washed up that once was mine.

The joy it brought
is too seldom known,
For it told of a seed
of kindness sown.

Oscar Hill

Family Photos

Oscar's father and mother, Melvin and Mae Hill.

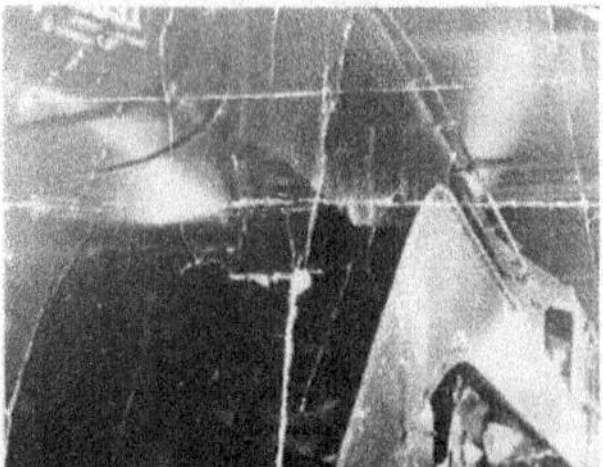

Oscar Hill on the Frisco.

Picture from the front page of the Kansas City Star, 1938: Oscar with Melvin, Joyce, Buster, and Dan.

Oscar and Verna Hill

Front Row: Joyce, Sue, and Verna. Second Row: Melvin, Buster, Jack, Dan, and Oscar, circa 1960.

Oscar and Verna surrounded by their grandchildren.

Oscar and Verna Hill

The copper book, "A Volume of Love."

Oscar Hill on the Frisco.

Four generations at dinner in Maryville, left to right: Melvin, Oscar, Oscar's mother Mae, and the oldest grandchild, Pete.

Oscar Hill, circa 1970.

Book Club Guide

Like any good story, this novel may inspire reflection and conversation on a variety of themes, including faith and family, grace and forgiveness, courage and compromise, bigotry and social justice. The following questions are provided to spark small group discussion.

Prologue

1. Every family has its stories, all kinds of stories, the happy and the heartbreaking, the proud and the shameful. Each new generation is shaped by the stories passed down to them. What stories have shaped your family?

2. What makes a work of fiction ring true? What makes a character like Oscar Hill believable or not?

3. About eighty percent of *Crossing the Tracks* is based on family stories and first-person testimony. Can you guess which parts of the story have been created?

Chapter 1 – Genesis

1. Oscar grew up in two counties notorious for bigotry and lynchings. What influences likely led him to question the racist views all around him?

2. What childhood factors influenced your own understanding of race?

3. After his father's sudden death, Oscar had to grow up fast. What values did shouldering adult responsibilities so early instill in him?

4. How would you interpret Oscar's religious conversion and baptism? Can such experiences be valid and formative in a child's life?

5. What surprised you about Oscar and Verna's courtship and wedding day?

Chapter 2 – Dues to Pay

1. Do you know how your family weathered the Great Depression? What stories do you recall?

2. What does Oscar's experience of hard times say about the expression, "You do what you have to do."

3. How did surviving the hardships of the Depression make Oscar more sensitive to the needs of others?

4. Have you ever bought a "fixer-upper"? Oscar and Verna lived in their home in Kansas City for fifty-four years. In your opinion, what makes a house a home?

~~~

Chapter 3 – Eyes to See

1. What was your impression of Oscar's streetcar experience?

2. Have you ever felt like God was speaking to you through a life experience? How has that experience impacted your life?

3. What do you think motivated Oscar and Verna to practice radical hospitality to strangers?

4. Oscar came from a generation of men who were largely uninvolved with their children's daily lives. Why do you think he chose to invest so much of his limited spare time and energy in his children?

Chapter 4 – Wartime

1. Did you or your family members serve in the military during wartime? What was your family's experience?
~~~

2. What changes and challenges did Oscar and Verna experience during World War II?

3. If our country were attacked today when our culture is so fractured and polarized, do you think we would be capable of a unified, sacrificial response? Why or why not?

4. In our present work environment, few vocations offer apprenticeships like the railroad offered in Oscar's time. What would be the benefit of an apprenticeship in your vocation?

Chapter 5 – All in the Family

1. How do you understand the religious notion of "calling"? What does Melvin's experience and Oscar's response say about a calling from God?

2. Does it surprise you that Oscar, a poorly educated, blue collar working man, was such a romantic? How would you describe Oscar and Verna's marriage?

3. Discuss Oscar and Verna's response to the catastrophe of the flood of 1951. How have you seen communities and individuals respond to such crises?

4. How would you describe Oscar's changing relationship with his children as they grew into adulthood?

~~~

Chapter 6 – Taking a Stand

1. What motivated Oscar's decision to leave Parkway Church and begin attending Garfield? Have you ever attended a church that disappointed or disillusioned you? What causes a church to lose credibility?

2. How did Oscar live out his convictions in his role as a union steward? What would move his union members to elect him as president?
~~~

3. Oscar's strong sense of fairness extended across racial and economic lines. What evidence do you see today of lingering inequities and double standards still present in our country?

4. In the wake of a devastating tornado, Oscar struggled to comprehend the random destruction of homes and families. How did he reconcile the providence of God with the human suffering he witnessed?

Chapter 7 – Opening Doors

1. What do you think are the roots of deep-seeded racism? Why is it so hard to change people's minds about issues of race? What values did Oscar appeal to in trying to sway his fellow union members to integrate?

2. What kinds of opposition did Oscar face as he tried to address the ingrained bigotry in the union? Why do you think he didn't give in to the threats of those who opposed his efforts?

3. As hard-nosed as Oscar could be, he still possessed a good measure of grace for people in trouble. How many times did he offer second chances to friends, neighbors, and family?

4. How did Oscar's persistence and leadership finally move his union to integrate?

Chapter 8 – Homefront

1. Discuss and contrast the different responses in Oscar and Verna's neighborhood when the first black family moved in.

2. How do you define "neighboring"? What are the obligations and the limitations as you understand them? What unwritten rules have you noticed in the neighborhoods where you have lived?

3. What part did the unfolding events of the Civil Rights Movement play in Oscar's attitudes and actions by this point in the story? How do you think he was influenced, motivated or affirmed by the happenings in Greensboro, Birmingham, and Selma?

4. If you had been present the day Oscar told his own story at church, what would have struck you about his life and faith?

Chapter 9 – Fighting Fires

1. Oscar was accused of being unwilling to "leave well enough alone," on the railroad. This was true at church and in his neighborhood as well. What makes some people unwilling to accept things as they are and determined to push for change? Why are so many others perfectly content, defending the status quo?

2. How did Oscar learn to look at life through the eyes of those unlike himself?

3. Discuss Oscar's thoughts and feelings after Sue was attacked at school. How would you respond if your own child was victimized?

4. Why was the decision to move Sue to a new school so difficult for Oscar?

Chapter 10 – Sunset

1. Can you imagine what it must be like to lose one's parents more than fifty years apart? How would you describe Mae Hill's contribution to her son's life?

2. Today, when the majority of people will change jobs and careers repeatedly, Oscar remained a railroad man, a sheet metal worker and pipe fitter, his entire adult life, with strong loyalty to one railroad, the Frisco. How many times have you changed majors, changed jobs, changed careers? What is the price of staying put, positive or negative?

3. Oscar and Verna's six children all considered their parent's marriage to be a healthy model for their own. What positive characteristics did you recognize in their life together?

4. How would you describe Oscar's approach to retirement? How did he invest his retirement years in his family and neighborhood?

Epilogue

1. What is the measure of a person's life? How does one's legacy get passed on to the next generation?

2. Looking back over Oscar's life, what do you find memorable, admirable? What family stories have been passed down to you from previous generations?

3. How would you sum up the contribution of Oscar Hill's life? Had Oscar and Verna never lived, how different would their world have turned out?

Acknowledgements

Writing a novel about a member of my family has been a unique challenge, a blending of biography and fiction, family history and my best efforts to fill in the blanks. I am indebted to my grandfather's two surviving daughters, Joyce Clark and Sue Plaxco, and to my late uncle, Arthur "Jack" Hill, who passed before I could complete the work. All three shared their memories, took countless phone calls, welcomed my visits, and helped me tell their parent's story as true to life as possible. My mother, Eva Hill, was also very helpful. I am grateful to be part of such a family.

About the Author

I grew up in a small town in the Ozarks, playing baseball, riding bikes, mowing yards, and reading comic books, the youngest of eight children. Norman Rockwell could have moved in down the street and felt right at home. These days I live and write in Arlington, Virginia, with my understanding wife and a cat named Truman. Our three kids are grown, and we are begging for grandchildren.

After nearly a lifetime of writing nonfiction – essays and articles, lectures and lessons – I was rescued from my tedium and set free, liberated to explore life and faith in the realm of fiction. Unwittingly, I seem to have acquired an expansive cast of characters along the way, some begging to enter the story, others hiding in the background, hoping to go unnoticed, but I see them all. So many stories to tell.

I am, as Parker J. Palmer put it, "…one who loves to watch life become words and words become life."

For more, please visit Drew Hill online at:
Publisher Website: https://evolvedpub.com/DHill
Facebook: https://www.facebook.com/drew.hill1
LinkedIn:
https://www.linkedin.com/in/drew-hill-24305b24/

What's Next?

Watch for the release of Drew Hill's next novel to release in late 2023.

IT CAME EVEN TO ME

A pastor is torn between grace and truth, clinging to his convictions as he struggles to salvage his family.

Set in small-town Georgia in the present, this story paints a picture of the best and worst in us, of love and forgiveness doing battle with hatred and intolerance.

More from Evolved Publishing

We offer great books across multiple genres, featuring high-quality editing (which we believe is second-to-none) and fantastic covers.

As a hybrid small press, your support as loyal readers is so important to us, and we have strived, with tireless dedication and sheer determination, to deliver on the promise of our motto:
QUALITY IS PRIORITY #1!

Please check out all of our great books, which you can find at this link:
www.EvolvedPub.com/Catalog/

Thank you!

Printed in the USA
CPSIA information can be obtained
at www.ICGtesting.com
LVHW041136071123
763181LV00043B/569

9 798890 250230